JONATHAN L HOWARD

KATYA'S WAR

STRANGE
CheMISTRY

STRANGE CHEMISTRY
An Angry Robot imprint
and a member of the Osprey Group

Lace Market House	Angry Robot/Osprey Publishing
54-56 High Pavement	PO Box 3985
Nottingham	New York
NG1 1HW	NY 10185-3985,
UK	USA

www.strangechemistrybooks.com
Strange Chemistry #21

A Strange Chemistry paperback original 2013
1

Cover art by Lee Gibbons
Set in Sabon by EpubServices

Distributed in the United States by Random House, Inc., New York.

ISBN 978 1 90884 419 4
Ebook ISBN 978 1 90884 420 0

Printed in the United States of America

9 8 7 6 5 4 3 2 1

Dedicated to my fellow Strange Chemists, for their support, kindnesses, and general esprit de corps.

ONE

LUKYAN

The piece of paper looked cheap and disposable and in no way commensurate with the hard work and trouble it was intended to reward.

Katya Kuriakova held up the paper between her index and middle finger and said, "What the hell is this?"

The Federal officer was too busy writing on his pad for several seconds before he could be bothered to answer her. "It's your payment, captain." He glanced up and deigned to look her in the face. "It's a standard Federal compensation form, properly authorised. Payment in full for services rendered."

Even a few years before, the officer might have found it strange to be calling a girl of sixteen "captain," but that was what she was and protocol on such matters was inflexible. That her boat was some battered little utility bug was irrelevant. She stood there in a set of dark red overalls that bore her name and a "Master & Commander" stripe over the left breast pocket, her short blonde hair tousled unattractively by the same lack of sleep that was doubtless responsible for the dark rings under her eyes, glaring at him with aggressive disbelief, and holding up the Federal scrip as if it were a declaration of war or, at least, a grave personal insult.

Still, conceded the officer inwardly, she had a nice nose.

"A scrip? A *scrip*? Two days navigating the Vexations, dodging Yagizban patrols the whole way, pushing test depth for twelve hours at a stretch, and have you *any* idea what the sanitary arrangements on a minisub are like?"

The officer sighed. "Three things, captain. First, the scrip's as good as money. *Second…*" he had to raise his voice slightly to override Katya's furious denial that scrips were damn well nowhere near as good as money, "… I have no leeway on the matter. My orders are to pay captains with compensation forms. I have no money to give you even if my orders permitted it. And third, *there is a war on.*" He hefted his pad under his arm as if it were some marker of rank and walked further down the docking corridor towards another weary-looking captain and probably an identical argument.

Katya watched him go with the muted anger of somebody who knows from bitter experience that you can't fight the system, especially when the system is running in a crisis and has its heels dug in against anything less important than its own survival.

There is a war on.

A single humourless laugh escaped her. *Yes, officer*, she thought, *there is a war on. I helped start it.*

She was glad she had kept that to herself; it really wouldn't have helped matters.

She walked back to the minisub pens, to where her boat sat snugly held in its stall, aft door secure against the stable's open access hatch. Sergei was just finishing draining the cess tank and looking as happy about it as could be expected. His mood was not improved when he saw the scrip in Katya's hand.

"God's teeth!" he muttered with the easy blasphemy of a born atheist. He picked up the toilet paper refill from the deck and held it out to her. "You might as well stick that thing in here. At least we'll have a use for it then."

Katya ignored the proffered box and stepped through the hatch, neatly avoiding catching her foot on the cess drainage tube. Four months previously she had not been so agile and the result had been impressively unpleasant. It was the sort of lesson that only needed learning once.

She sank into the fore starboard passenger's seat and opened the locker beneath it. Inside was a waterproof documents box – "Guaranteed to resist pressures to five hundred metres!" according to the vendor – which she pulled out and unlocked with a four digit key. Inside, amongst all the other hardcopy documentation a properly registered submarine was supposed to carry and keep maintained, was a plastic folder labelled *Magic Money Markers! Collect the set and see the wizerd!* Labelled by Sergei, obviously. Certainly from its tone but not least because he had misspelled "wizard." Within it was a wad of Federal Maritime Authority compensation forms, generically identical to the one that she now added to it. She quickly counted them, summing their worth as she went.

"Fancy going to Atlantis?" she called back to Sergei.

Sergei was just finishing with the cess tank. "Why is it not OK to vent the tank to the sea when it's full, but it's fine to vent it for cleaning after it's been drained?" he asked and, like many of his questions, it was rhetorical. "I mean, like a bit of shit is going to break the ecosystem." He locked down the tank's hatch and cycled water through it from outside the hull. "Fish like shit, anyway. It's got nutrients."

"And deep thoughts like that are why you must never be put into any position of authority, Sergei. Now, pay attention. This is your captain speaking." She waited until he had deactivated the cess tank's cleaning procedure, replaced the deck plate over it, and then slowly swung his hand to his brow to make his usual lackadaisical and mocking salute to her. She took no offence at it; Sergei used to make the same salute to her uncle Lukyan when he had been captain. Lukyan could have punched Sergei clean through a bulkhead if he'd had a mind to, but what was the point? To deny Sergei his minor insubordinations would have been like denying him air.

Things were different now, of course. Lukyan was dead, and Katya was captain and owner of the little submarine, and it wasn't called *Pushkin's Baby* anymore. Also there was a war on. So many changes in so little time. It was good that some things could still be relied upon. Sergei being miserable, for example.

"Aye aye, Captain Kuriakova," he said, his salute a thing of refined slovenliness that hung upon his brow like a dead eel. Belatedly, he realised what she had said and he dropped his arm to his side. "Atlantis? Do we have to?"

She waved the wad of scrips at him before returning them to the folder and stowing it away again. "Only way we'll ever get these things turned into real money."

"I know a man," said Sergei. He had lowered his voice a little and was cautiously looking up and down the corridor alley connecting the pens. "And this fellow, he will buy the scrips off us, no questions asked."

"Oh?" said Katya. "And how much 'commission' will he want?"

Sergei looked at her with astonishment. *He still thinks I'm a little girl*, she thought.

He mumbled something, mumbled it a little louder when she raised her eyebrows, and finally, provoked by her crossing her arms and leaning back in the seat, grudgingly admitted, "Fifty per cent."

She shook her head in disbelief. "Are you serious? Is *he* serious? Six months of hard, dangerous work, and half of it goes to some criminal who–"

"He's not a criminal," muttered Sergei.

"He's buying scrips at half price and then somehow cashing them in for full. That's not legal. So, yes, some criminal who profits from half our work while he sits nice and safe." She spat a descriptive term for the unnamed criminal that hadn't been heard in the boat since Lukyan was alive, and which went a long way to assuring Sergei that, no, Katya was no longer a little girl.

Sergei walked forward and took the seat opposite her. When he spoke, it was in a quieter and more reasonable tone. She began to understand that this wasn't just his habitual pessimism; he was truly concerned.

"Atlantis is dangerous, Katya. I've heard some real horror stories about the Yags attacking anything in the water near there."

"I haven't."

"It's not the kind of thing the Feds are going to advertise, is it? That they can't even defend the volume around the capital?" He leaned forward, almost speaking in a whisper. "Things are going really badly for the Feds. *Really* badly."

Katya looked at Sergei's worried expression, but it did not soften her resolve. The truth, as far as the truth can ever really be defined in wartime, seemed very even-handed. Yes, the Feds were having a bad time of it, but the Yagizban were hardly swimming around without a care in the world. They may have had the technological edge, but they lacked numbers, and – since the FMA had captured one of their advanced war boats at the eve of the war – even that edge had been somewhat blunted. Several of its systems had been reverse-engineered, reproduced and incorporated into serving FMA vessels already. As for the captured boat, it was out there right now, fighting for the Federal cause under its new name, the *Vengeance*.

"The Feds located and destroyed a Yag spy base," she countered. "It was all over the news just before we left."

"Yes, but they *would* say that," countered Sergei, much more inclined to believe the worst in any given situation.

"There were pictures…"

"You only have the Feds' word for it that they were new. Could have been taken months ago."

Katya closed her eyes and rubbed the bridge of her nose. Sergei recognised the gesture and became subdued. It meant she was finding a quiet place in her mind where she could make a decision, a decision that was not long in coming.

"We have to believe in something," she said, tired and morose. "Right now, I have a strong belief that I need a shower and a night where I can sleep in an actual bed. Be ready to leave at oh-nine-hundred tomorrow morning." She climbed to her feet and walked aft to the open hatch. Sergei sighed melodramatically, but did not argue. Like her uncle, there was little point in debating with Katya once her mind was made up. "I'll book the departure with traffic control now," she said as she climbed out. "Good night, Sergei."

"'Night, Katya," he replied, but the hatchway was already empty.

She was in the traffic control office for fifteen minutes, five of which were spent waiting, four logging the departure, and six creating the course. The desk officer was irritated at first when she told him she didn't have a course already plotted and would it be alright to use his console? His uniform denoted him as a major of the

Federal Marines, and his prosthetic right arm was the likely reason he was now piloting a desk and for his generally spiky demeanour. While his comrades were off engaging the hated foe in battle, he was left ratifying civilian travel arrangements and issuing dockets. His irritation was rapidly soothed, however, by the speed and assurance with which she made the necessary calculations and by the time she had finished, he found it within himself to compliment her.

"My uncle used to say I was a prodigy," she said with a wan smile.

"Your uncle? Well, he's…" The officer, a lean man in his early fifties paused, his eyes upon the name of the submarine. "Ah. You're Lukyan's girl…?"

She could only nod. It still hurt even to hear his name.

The officer looked at her with a respect she did not feel she had earned. "He was a fine man, captain. Yes, he mentioned you, more than once." He smiled a little bleakly. "The word *prodigy* was bandied around. Not just family pride as it turns out." The console bleeped and showed a green light by the plotted course, indicating that it was acceptable by marine law and sensible within the complex flows of the Russalkin seas. The officer immediately authorised the plot and entered it into the log.

"My co-pilot is concerned about Yag activity near Atlantis," said Katya. "Anything that we should know about?"

The officer shook his head. "A week ago I would have told you to wait or join a convoy. Nothing's happened out there for days, though. It's likely the patrols have driven the Yag out of the volume, but... be careful all the same."

Katya picked up her identity card and her boat's clock card and stowed them in her coveralls. "I always am. Good evening, major."

Something happened on the way to the hotel. The route she used was a supply corridor that would have been off-limits to foot traffic during the day shift while electric tractors pulled cargo to storage areas and industrial sections. Once the lights dimmed, however, the corridors opened to pedestrians on the understanding that the occasional tractor would still be whirring by, so they should get out of the way when they heard one coming. The submariners were the only people to feel comfortable doing that; most stuck to the main corridors no matter what time it was.

Katya was making her way along the side of the long curved tunnel, when she heard footfalls approaching from the other direction. A moment later, two FMA base security officers – police officers in all but title – walked by her. One ignored her entirely, too busy adjusting the baton in his belt, the other stared straight at Katya as they passed, as if daring her to return the look. Katya did not; she had no desire to get into a battle of wills with them. At the very least they'd demand to see her identity card, and she was too tired for those kinds of status games.

They passed her without slowing and she kept walking, grateful that there was nothing between her, the hotel, and sleep. Nothing, that is, until she turned the corner and found the sobbing man.

He was crouched by the wall, his back to her, crying like a child in a pool of his own blood. Katya stopped sharply enough to make her boots squeal on the concrete. The man gasped with terror and looked furtively over his shoulder at her. She saw his nose was broken, and the white of one eye was bloodshot, the pupil blown.

"Oh, gods," she managed. "What happened? Are you alright?"

The second question was almost as stupid as the first, but she'd had to say *something*. It was as plain that he'd been badly beaten as it was that, no, he wasn't alright at all.

The bloodied eye looked past her, and she realised what he was looking for. "No, it's alright," she said in a quiet, reassuring tone. "They've gone. Why did they do this to you?"

He didn't answer, but she saw the fear grow in him, and the tears mix with the blood and snot from his ruined nose. She saw the defence injures on the back of his hands as he cowered from her, at least two fingers on his right hand seeming broken; she saw his belt lying by his feet on the concrete floor; she saw the smashed teeth and the straight bruises, as wide as a baton's contact area, across his brow.

They remained in tableau for long moments, the only sound the man's miserable soul-deep weeping.

"I'll take you to the medical centre, OK?" she said finally. She crouched by him. "I'll take you to the medical centre. You'll be OK."

She didn't ask again why the FMA officers had done this. It could have been something or nothing. She'd heard it didn't take much to earn a beating these days – a word in the wrong place about rationing, how the war was being handled, how the Feds had their noses into everything – but she'd believed it had been exaggerated in the telling. It seemed she had been the one deluding herself.

The man shook his head, said something like, "I'm fine," rose and walked painfully away from her, back in the direction of the docks. He leaned against the wall as he went, leaving a trail of bloody handprints, each dimmer than the last.

"That's the direction they were going in!" she called after him, but he did not respond.

She called it in. She found a communications point a little further up the corridor and asked specifically for the major in traffic control. When she was put through, she explained what had happened, and that there was a man heading in his direction who desperately needed medical attention.

"I'll alert a response team. Don't worry, captain. He'll be attended to."

"What about the officers?"

The line was silent for a moment. "Did you actually see the assault?"

"No," said Katya, "but there was no one else in the corridor. It had to have been…"

"That's supposition. You're not a witness. It will be dealt with, don't worry."

"But I *am* a witness, aren't I? After the fact, but I'm still a witness. Don't you want a statement or anything?"

Another silence. Katya suddenly wondered if the major was consulting with somebody else.

"That won't be necessary. Base security can take it from here."

Katya wanted to say, "But they won't investigate their own people properly," when she caught herself.

It really didn't take much to earn a beating these days.

"I understand," she said. "I'll leave it with you, major."

"Thank you for calling it in, Captain Kuriakova. Good night."

The line closed before she could reply.

Katya looked back along the corridor. The man's belt was still lying there. She turned and walked away, feeling she'd failed a test.

It wasn't what you'd call a hotel. Many of the larger settlements contained hotels or hostels or similar establishments, but Mologa Station was too small for that. Originally a mining site, its tunnels cut by fusion torches in strange organic curves and meanders to follow mineral seams, Mologa was now primarily a heavy engineering plant producing boats and mobile facilities for the war effort, hence the tight security and strong Federal presence.

Katya's security grade was Beta Plus, a full three grades higher than most civilians and the product of being in the FMA's good books after the events of six months earlier, the very events that had begun the war.

In the same waterproof container that held the boat's papers and her personal documents was a small box made of wood.

Real wood. Real, actual wood, grown as a luxury in one of the larger hydroponics farms. Inside the box was a medal on a little red ribbon, upon which was her name, and the legend, *Hero of Russalka*. There was also a slip of paper, the citation for the medal, which explained why it had been awarded. It used a lot of words like "heroic" and "selfless" when talking about her, and "villainy" and "traitorous" when talking about the Yagizban. It also gave the date on which the honour had been presented to her. That was a little lie, though; the medal had never been presented to her at all. Instead it had been delivered by courier, who'd just had her submit to a retinal scan, handed over a package, and left. The box had been in the package, and the medal had been in the box.

She'd barely looked at the medal. Had read the citation once and experienced trouble finishing it, racked by embarrassment and a faint sense of disgust. It hadn't been like that. It just hadn't. But it was the official version now, and who was she to argue with the Federal Maritime Authority's telling of events? After all, she had only been there, had only lived through it all.

The wooden box, though… the box she liked. Sometimes she would just hold the box, stroking its cover gently with the pad of her thumb, sensing the fine grain against her skin. What must it be like to see trees just… there? Growing where they liked, randomly dotted about?

Still, this was nature, too. Stone was natural, even if
the torches had melted it smooth. She hadn't needed
to follow the signs to the Mologa Hotel – she'd been
there often enough – but lost in her reverie, listening to
her own tired thoughts and the sound of her boots on
the decking grates, it was a surprise when she turned a
corner and there it was. Mologa Hotel, a long, dimly lit
tunnel with staggered rows of hatches set into each wall.
Admittedly, it looked more like a mass morgue, but it
was better than nothing.

She walked along, looking for a green vacancy light.
Unsurprisingly, the ones nearest the tunnel entrance all
showed red "Occupied" flashes with a few amber lights
to show freshly vacated units that still had to be cleaned
before being designated available again. She had little
idea of how often the units were cleaned out. Perhaps
twice a day, she guessed. It didn't matter; she would do
what she always did and walk most of the way along, and
pass most of the two hundred capsule "rooms." That far
along, she was already walking past plentiful numbers of
greens and some ambers. She deduced that whoever was
supposed to clean the capsules perhaps only bothered
with the far end of the tunnel once a day, maybe less.
Once she might have been outraged at such a dereliction
of duty. Right now, however, she just wanted to sleep.

She found a capsule that was identical to all its
neighbours, but that she took a shine to on a whim. Her
boat's docking fee included two capsule rentals, one for
her and one for Sergei, although she suspected he'd sleep
aboard again. Over fifty hours in that confined space

apparently wasn't too much for Sergei Ilyin. Well, good luck to him. She swiped her ID card, waited for the click, and swung the door open.

In the same way that you couldn't really call it a hotel, you couldn't really call it a room. It was no more than a burrow a metre and a half square at the entrance and two and a half metres deep. The walls were covered with a smooth epoxy coating in a "restful" shade of pale blue that was apparently what the sky looked like on Earth, and which the primitive parts of their minds found comforting, or so she was told. The floor of the capsule was covered by a mattress that could be removed and hosed down for cleaning if need be, and there was a clean blanket rolled up to one side. Set into the ceiling above where the occupant would lay their head was a screen on which could be watched a selection of dull programming, available on demand. Beneath the capsule floor was a cubby for putting boots, and Katya sat in the hatchway while she removed them and her thin socks before storing them in there. When she crawled in and closed the hatch behind her, the cubby was covered and kept secure, too.

She struggled out of her clothes, made more of an attempt at folding them than she felt was really necessary, and ended up tossing them into the alcove at the capsule end along with her overnight bag. She pulled the thin blanket over herself, more from habit than necessity as the temperature was maintained at a comfortable level, set the alarm for oh-seven-thirty, and turned off the light.

She couldn't sleep. Tired and listless, she was desperate to, yet her disloyal head kept buzzing and denied her the ease she needed to drift off. She wished she hadn't mentioned her uncle to the major in traffic control, wished he hadn't known Lukyan, hadn't said he was a good man. Yes, her uncle had been a good man, and she missed him so much that it hurt. She felt the tears and did nothing to stop them. It was natural to grieve, even months later. She knew it would be months more before the pain stopped being quite so sharp, when it didn't make her wish she had died along with him.

Each capsule had half a metre of stone between itself and its neighbours, and the doors were designed to be soundproof, but even so this was why she always chose a capsule as far from others as possible, so nobody might hear her cry.

Sergei had cried. In the pause between the threat of the Leviathan killing everyone on the planet being lifted, and the beginning of the civil war that threatened to result in everybody killing one another instead, she had got back home and sought him out immediately. She had to be the one to tell him, it was what Lukyan would have wanted.

She had stood there, willing herself to stay ramrod straight, and told Sergei that his captain, her uncle, his best friend since childhood was dead. Death wasn't so strange on Russalka, after all. The dangerous world killed people all the time for the silliest mistakes and the most fleeting of inattentions. Sergei was made of tough stuff, she had told herself. He'd take it stoically.

But he didn't. He sat down heavily on the floor – on the floor! – and cried like a child. There was no denial, not a single "Are you sure?" She said she'd been there, told him how Lukyan had died, and that was enough. He'd sobbed and looked ridiculous, his face red and snot running out of his nose, and he hadn't cared. Finally she'd sat by him, put her arm around him and cried too. Her tears had been silent, though.

Perhaps Sergei had been wise after all. He had come to terms with his grief quickly and accepted Lukyan was gone forever, his lifelong friend lost for good. She still saw him grow quiet and reflective sometimes, and he might touch the corner of his eye as if dust had got into it, but that was all.

He didn't spend his nights crying himself to sleep in a soundproof cell.

Quarter of an hour later she felt exhausted, puffy-eyed, and again empty of grief and the guilt of the survivor for a while, at least. But, she did not feel sleepy. This seemed very unfair.

Finally she gave up trying to will herself into unconsciousness. Instead she found the gently illuminated controls for the screen and switched it on – perhaps she could bore herself to sleep.

The first feed was an old action drama she was sure she'd seen years before and which hadn't been new even then, made during or just after the war against Earth. It was about an isolated station where a Fed boat has to stop to make repairs and finds itself stuck there with some refugees. Somebody amongst them is a traitor working for the Grubbers and there was a lot of stuff with people accusing one another and then something else happens that means the accused person must be innocent, and so they accuse somebody else.

That the villain turned out to be a Yag – even though he's really a Grubber infiltrator – was probably why they were rerunning such a steaming piece of melodrama about the war in the first place.

The war. Katya realised that nobody had yet got around to coming up with a name for the new conflict. When people said "the war," they always meant the war against Earth, the war that was eleven, almost twelve years ago now. It was a civil war they were currently fighting, but nobody called it that. Nobody called it anything at all.

Katya changed the feed and found herself watching a news channel. There was little new here; the Feds were doughty and honourable warriors while the Yag were dirty, sneaky scum who it turned out had been colluding with the Terrans during the war.

Being caught out as traitors hadn't really been the declaration of independence the Yags had been planning on, but you can't always get what you want, can you?

Katya turned down the sound and dimmed the screen brightness. She lay in the flickering darkness watching earnest newsreaders, pictures of smiling Federal sailors and marines coming back from successful sorties, a few bedraggled and wretched Yagizban prisoners being paraded for the cameras, public information proclamations, some newly decorated hero going back to his old school to give a speech about duty and honour. It was just another man in a dark blue FMA naval uniform until he took his cap off for the cameras and she laughed with delighted surprise.

Suhkalev! From spotty little thug to a "Knight of the Deep" as the caption proclaimed him, and all in only six months. They'd given him a medal and everything, just like they'd given to her.

Look at us now, Suhkalev, she thought. *Look at us with our medals, heroes all. Knights of the Deep.*

She finally passed out soon after that, the screen still flickering images of resistance to the enemy and glorious victory above her face. Her mouth moved, and she may have been saying "Knights of the Deep" as she sank into unconsciousness, then she half laughed, and then she was asleep.

TWO
JARILO

Katya awoke in total darkness. Her first thought was a power failure, but then she realised it couldn't be – every station had back-up generators and slow-bleed capacitors to ensure a total power failure could not happen. After all, a facility without power would be a facility without life before very long. It was more likely to be a local failure, she thought, probably a power bus to the hotel had simply overloaded and was waiting to be reset. Well, if the power had failed, so had her wake up alarm. Sergei was probably down in the pens right now, tutting and muttering as they lost their departure slot.

She checked her chronometer and was nonplussed to discover its face dark. Fumbling with its buttons didn't produce even a flicker of illumination. Now she was becoming worried; a local power failure was one thing, but even personal electronics dying? Probably just a coincidence. Probably. The possibility that the Yagizban had triggered some sort of electro-magnetic pulse weapon and scrambled Mologa's electronics entered her mind and was just as quickly dispatched. Every station's electronics were gauss-hardened against EMP weapons and had been since the war. No, something else was going on here. Well, lying in the dark wasn't going to give her any answers.

She started to reach back to get her clothes when a sudden sharp sound made her freeze – a single loud crack, shockingly close. She froze, her heart suddenly pounding very fast and hard which only served to dull her hearing as the beats sounded through her head. She stayed still for ten, twenty, thirty seconds, but the noise was not repeated.

The silence was less reassuring than she had hoped. Then she realised how absolute the silence was. The tiny yet infinitely comforting sound of the ventilation fan was absent. While she doubted it was possible to suffocate in a capsule room, she didn't care to find out. Besides, the air was growing cloying and hot. She reached for her clothes again, and as she did there was the same awful cracking noise, but this time it continued, and grew. A heavy splintering, a grinding of stone upon stone. The realisation that the stone around her was suffering some sort of structural failure filled her with urgent terror.

She decided she would rather face the humiliation of being on the corridors in her underwear than stay in the capsule a second longer and abandoned her clothes in favour of getting out. As she sat up, however, her forehead banged forcefully into the screen mounted on the capsule ceiling. The screen was probably undamaged, being a flexible polymer laminate sheet, but directly behind it was a single insulation layer and then solid stone. Katya fell back, her head landing on the pillow pad. She blinked away the pain and tried to understand how she could possibly have hit her head on a ceiling that had given her comfortable space to sit up the previous night. Now the ceiling seemed to be lower. How was that possible?

There was another loud crack, the grating of stone against stone, and she finally understood. *The capsule's collapsing,* she realised. *Move! Move! Move!*

She tried to sit up as far as the ceiling would allow, but now it was barely above her face. She started shuffling towards the hatch as fast as she could manage. The hatch's locking handle would be a problem, but perhaps she might be able to disengage it with a kick. She had hardly managed to get five centimetres before the smooth plastic of the screen brushed her face. The ceiling didn't seem to be lurching down at all, but smoothly descending like a hydraulic press.

She tried to move but it was bearing down on her now, pushing her backward into the shallow mattress. She squirmed hopelessly, her face to one side. How had this happened? Had the station been hit by some new and strange weapon of the Yagizban?

The ceiling stopped its descent. Then, with another crack of fracturing stone, it slammed down.

Katya felt her bones break and break again. She felt her skull compress and shatter as millions of tonnes of submarine mountain settled on her. She felt little pain, but only an odd sense of regret as her skeleton splintered, her tongue was crushed, her eyeballs exploded.

And she did not die.

She was smeared, an atom thick, between the rock faces.

And she did not die.

She could feel the mass of the mountain, feel the shift in the drowned continental plate on which it stood, feel the countless billions tonnes of water flow across the planet's surface drawn by an unseen moon beyond the unending clouds.

An atom thick, no, thinner yet, as thin as thought, she enveloped the planet Russalka. Russalka – she'd always thought it a good name, but now she realised it was too small to encompass everything the world was. She could almost reach out and...

The alarm was a relief and a huge frustration. The cubicle lights came up gently along with the slowly increasing volume of the alarm tones, and Katya found herself whole and sweating in the capsule room that showed no signs of wanting to be any smaller than it already was. She reached out reflexively and muted the alarm, looked up at the silent screen where the news was always changing yet reassuringly similar. Fierce battles, broad victories, solitary and inconsequential defeats, proud Feds, subhuman Yags.

Her mind was still echoing with her dream, though. A dream of a united planet. She had felt good, powerful, and another emotion that she equated with confidence yet had been somehow different.

Not such a bad dream, then, although she could have done without the bit about being crushed into liquid. That had been... not so enjoyable.

She struggled into her old clothes, grabbed her overnight bag and left the capsule, its red light snapping over to amber as she swiped her card again and tapped the "Checking Out?" square on the status screen mounted on the outside of the hatch. Now, she decided, before she did anything else that day, she desperately needed a shower.

Twenty minutes later, clean, in fresh clothes, and the last echoes of her dream fading, Katya joined Sergei in the station cafeteria for breakfast. He stirred his scrambled eggs (in reality a 1:3 ratio of Edible Protein Reconstitutes 78 and 80b) onto his slice of toast (Carbohydrate Staple Complex Synthetic – Bread 15, although at least it had seen the inside of a real toaster), and glowered across the table at her. He looked exactly as he always looked. His disreputable coveralls never seemed to get any dirtier, his moustache was never any longer or shorter, his stubble was always one missed shave old.

"What are you so happy about?" he demanded, then shovelled some "egg" into his mouth as if he expected it to be taken from him any moment.

"Had a strange dream," she replied. She was eating kedgeree. The egg was as synthetic as Sergei's, the rice was reconstituted starch pellets, and the spice paste had come out of a laboratory somewhere, but at least the fish was real. "I saw the whole world. I *was* the whole world, sort of. Y'know, Sergei, there's not a problem that can't be solved. I think we're going to be OK."

Sergei's shovelling stopped. "God. If you're going to be like this all day, I'm resigning now."

"Seriously? OK. We both know I can handle the boat alone and the navy's desperate for hands, so just hand in your reserved occupation papers and get yourself into uniform. Oh, and you'll have to keep it clean. They're pretty fussy about that." She smiled sweetly at him.

He looked at her stonily. "I bloody hate you, Kuriakova," he said, and returned his attention to his breakfast.

"'I bloody hate you, *Captain* Kuriakova,'" she corrected him. "I will have discipline within my crew."

She carried on eating, having duly noted Sergei struggling not to smile.

"Wake her up, Sergei."

They were aboard the boat, set to go with a small cargo of assorted parcels, mainly intended for friends and family of Mologa's military staff at Atlantis. That and a few data sticks containing messages in written and video form, both official and personal. Lines of communication were often among the first casualties in wartime. The landlines, never very reliable, had mainly been severed by enemy action, and the surface long wave relays – tethered communication buoys floating above the settlements – were too easy to intercept and jam. That's if some enterprising raider didn't slap them with a couple of torpedoes, of course. With rapid communications difficult, almost everything had to be done by couriers.

Katya had noticed among the parcels some actual letters, forming their own envelopes with a tab of tape to seal them.

"Letters. Imagine that," she'd said, waving one of them at Sergei. "Writing. On paper." Sergei had said nothing, so she'd added, "Amazing!" to emphasise the novelty of it.

"People sent letters on paper in the war," he'd said. It was an extruded fibre weave, but it looked and behaved in much the same fashion as real wood pulp paper, the kind they had on Earth. "Sometimes, y'know, sometimes words on a screen aren't enough. You want something you can carry with you. Sometimes it's all that's left of someone."

Now the bags were stowed, and twenty hours of submarine travel awaited. Twenty hours of brain-freezing tedium, possibly mixed with bouts of bowel-loosening terror should the major in traffic control be wrong about local Yag activity. At least, Katya reflected, the cess tank was empty.

It was the co-pilot's job to run down the pre-launch checklist, and the captain's to oversee it, so Sergei counted off the items and called "check" at each positive, and it was Katya who watched him do it. It was ridiculous, she thought. In her entire maritime career to date, she had done that job once. Once, and only once, she had been co-pilot/navigator. Then she had inherited the boat and become captain. "A battlefield promotion," Uncle Lukyan would have called it.

She snapped herself out of her reverie before it could become maudlin, and listened to Sergei finish the list. "All lights green, captain. All systems go."

Katya opened the communications channel to traffic control. "We're clear to disengage, traffic control. No last minute reports of Yag boats in the vicinity?"

"Nothing new, captain." She recognised the voice of the major. "I can only recommend you stay sharp, and take care. Launch when ready, RRS 15743 Kilo *Lukyan*. Good luck."

"Thank you, major," replied Katya. "Disengaging now. *Lukyan* out."

With a thud as the docking clamps released the boat, and the hum of the impellers taking them out into open water, the voyage was underway.

It had seemed like a good idea at the time, renaming her uncle's boat from *Pushkin's Baby* to the *Lukyan*. It had seemed like a good way to honour him, to remember him. But now every time the boat's name was used, she had to fight the urge to look at the left hand seat to see if he was there. Really, that should have been her seat as captain, but she just couldn't bring herself to take it. She felt a big enough fraud calling herself "captain." Claiming the captain's seat, Lukyan's seat... no. That was too much.

Sergei hadn't wanted it either, but he had seen how she looked at the seat almost superstitiously and decided that he was going to have to be the stoic, pragmatic one. He didn't like it, though, and had spent much of the first couple of months complaining that the seat felt wrong, that no matter how he adjusted it, it just felt *wrong*.

Katya steered until they were clear of Mologa Station's approach volume and then switched on the autopilot. The inertial guidance systems took what data they could from the baseline of Mologa's precise location on the charts and took over, taking them on a slow downward gradient into seabed clutter to try and make them a difficult contact to acquire should a Yagizban boat happen by. In peacetime, echo beacons along the way would have provided route correction, but they had all been closed down now. Anything that might help the enemy was to be denied to them, even if it inconvenienced your own people.

"Arrival at Atlantis docking bays in nineteen hours, forty eight minutes," said the *Lukyan*'s computer voice in the same calm tones that it announced everything from waypoint arrivals to incoming torpedoes.

Katya lifted her hands from the control yoke and watched it move by itself under the autopilot's direction. "I sometimes wonder why boats even have crews anymore."

Sergei was already climbing out of the left hand seat, and was glad to do so. "They used to use drones. Then we got pirates after the war. Drones aren't so great when it comes to out-thinking people who are after your cargo." He sat in the forward port passenger seat and pulled the table down from the ceiling on its central strut that swung down to the vertical and then telescoped out. He pulled up the screen on his side and gestured impatiently at the opposite seat. "Well?"

Katya left the co-pilot's position and climbed into the indicated seat. "What are we playing?" she asked. "Chess?"

Sergei curled a lip and tapped some keys. Katya raised the screen on her side to find a virtual card table already waiting for her.

"Poker," he said. "A proper game, with risk and chance. Just like life."

••••

They played a few hands until Sergei said he was feeling tired again and was going to take a nap. Katya noted that his energy seemed to have a direct correlation to how well he was doing in the game. After a disastrous losing streak that would have cost him his wages for a year had they been playing for real money, he was entirely exhausted and was horizontal across two passenger seats and snoring a minute later.

"Your choice, my friend," said Katya under her breath, logged when he fell asleep and set that as the beginning of his down shift. He would argue about it when he woke up in thirty or forty minutes' time, but it had been one of Lukyan's hard and fast rules. If Sergei had ever thought Katya was going to be a soft touch, he was well on his way to re-education now.

As it was, he actually woke twenty-three minutes later when Katya threw an empty beaker at his head. He struggled upright, swearing copiously until she told him in a harsh whisper to shut up and quiet down. The realisation that the drives were off and they were drifting in the current was enough to calm him instantly. He was up front, headset on, and seat restraints locked inside ten seconds.

"What is it?" he whispered. "Yags?"

"Don't know yet," she replied. "Just caught a glimpse of something on the passive sonar. One-oh-five relative. Might be nothing. Better safe than sorry."

Sergei nodded. "Better safe than dead." He noted the concentration on her face and knew she was listening through the hydrophones, the submarine's "ears," for the sound of engines. Without needing to be told, he pulled up the passive sonar interface on his own multi-function display and started a slow, careful scan, quadrant by quadrant.

Five minutes passed. Ten. At fifteen Katya was about to call it off as a false alert when something showed on the passive sonar at fifty degrees high relative to their heading. She immediately brought the hydrophone array to bear and listened intently.

"A shoal?" asked Sergei with unusual optimism.

Katya shook her head slightly. "I hear a drive. Lock it up at my bearing and give me an analysis."

Sergei told the passive sonar to lock onto the hydrophone bearing and ran the sound through the database. "It's military."

"Yeah. She's no civilian." Military boats carried engines with much higher performance than those of civil transports and carriers. Their turbines ran at greater speed and generated a very distinctive tone that every sensor operator knew. There was still a chance it was a Federal boat combing the Mologa approaches. Not even three hours out and a Yag warboat sniffing around? It seemed... all too likely. The ocean deeps were vast and even a large carrier could shuffle around out there with a whole fleet looking for it and probably stay safe. The station approaches, though... there the game went from looking for a fish in an ocean to looking for a fish in a bath. It was dangerous for the hunters if the station defences picked them up, of course, but war is all about risks.

Another twenty seconds of tracking the unidentified contact passed before the computer decided it had enough information to offer its analysis. "Eighty seven per cent likelihood contact Alpha is a Vodyanoi/2 class hunter-killer submarine of the Yagizba Enclaves," it told them. "It is therefore designated an *enemy*." And to show them what it thought of enemies, the computer changed the contact's symbol on the sonar display from yellow to red.

"A Vodyanoi?" said Sergei hollowly. He had gone very pale, or at least his stubble seemed much more clearly defined. "One of their new boats? The Grubber design? It *would* be." His tone was bitter. "We've never dealt with one of those before."

It wasn't good news. The Yag's Vodyanoi/2 class was a development of a Terran boat called the *Vodyanoi*, the vessel of the notorious pirate Havilland Kane, no less. She had met Kane, and she had been aboard the *Vodyanoi*. It was a highly sophisticated boat, but she knew the Yag copies were not its match; necessary compromises had to be made in their production to keep down costs, and some aspects of the original's technology were beyond Russalkin manufacturing methods. Even so, the Vodyanoi/2s were dangerous predators. If it got a clear lock on them, they were as good as dead.

So, they did the only thing a minisub could do against such a killer; they remained quiet and hoped for the best.

"Do you think they'd hear our ballast tanks vent?" said Katya in a whisper. When you knew people who were keen on the idea of killing you weren't very far away and were actively listening for you, it was difficult not to whisper. "We're about fifty metres above a thermocline. We'd be a bit safer under it."

Sergei shook his head. "I know it's tempting, but it's best not to do a thing, Katya. If they're low on munitions, they might not bother, but if they're flush, they might stick a fish in our direction on a search pattern, and then we'd be pretty screwed."

By "fish," he meant "torpedo." By "pretty screwed," he meant "very thoroughly dead."

Katya knew good advice when she heard it, so she leaned back in her seat and crossed her arms so she wouldn't be tempted to press any buttons just to relieve the tension.

The only thing they could do was watch the sonar screen as the passive return grew stronger. The Yag boat was heading almost directly for them; it would pass by about three hundred metres above them and a little in front. It would be a close call whether they ended up in its baffles – the conical volume astern of a boat in which its own engines blinded its sonar.

Katya had no idea how broad a cone that was. If they were hidden by the Yag's engine noise, they could risk the descent to the thermocline and hide behind the layer of the water where the temperature above was lower than that below, and which could reflect sonar waves. If they weren't, however, the Yag would hear the air venting from their ballast tanks as they gained negative buoyancy, and then the Yag would kill them. Given how nice a boat the *Vodyanoi* was, she reckoned its baffles were small, and that the baffles of her clones might be small too. It wasn't worth the risk.

Katya kept her arms very folded.

Sergei leaned forward. "What the hell is that?" he murmured.

Behind them, a new trace had appeared. If they had been under way the contact would have been lost in their own baffles. Only that they were running silent permitted the sonar receptors to pick up the new contact. Katya quickly brought the hydrophones to bear. Any faint hope that it might be a Federal patrol boat was quickly shattered.

"Ninety per cent likelihood contact Beta is a Jarilo Mark 4 class heavy carrier submarine of the Federal Maritime Authority," the computer told them. "It is therefore designated an *ally*." The contact's symbol flicked from yellow to blue.

"A transporter," whispered Sergei. "It's bound to have an escort!"

On the screen, the Alpha contact slowed and faded. The Yags were coming about for an attack pass. "They'll fire and run," he said. "Those poor bastards..."

Katya's eye fell on the database readout currently displayed on one of her secondary screens. The Jarilo was listed as having a standard crew of twenty. Twenty men and women who would probably die in a few minutes. Then its unseen escort or escorts would engage the Vodyanoi/2 and soon there would be more blood in the water.

"No," she murmured. "I can't let that happen."

THREE
FALSE FLAG

Sergei's eyes were unattractively wide. Fear did that to them.

"Katya, we can't get involved! We're in a minisub, a tiny bug! Even a close detonation will break us open!"

"Then we're just going to have to make sure nothing goes off near us then, aren't we?" Katya was already pulling up the operations screens. "Arm a noisemaker and stand by to dive."

Sergei did neither. "What? No! You'll kill us!"

"Not part of the plan, Sergei. Just do it."

"What plan? We're nothing more than krill compared to the hunter-killers out there! Just stay still and silent and we should weather this out!"

"I am not standing by and letting this happen, Sergei. Noisemaker! Arm one!" But Sergei just looked at her as if she was insane. "I am the captain here, Sergei Illyin! You will obey my orders!"

On the screen the Alpha contact faded away entirely. The Beta contact in contrast grew steadily stronger. It would only be a matter of moments before the Yagizban boat launched torpedoes.

"You can't order me to commit suicide," said Sergei. "*Captain.*"

Katya glared at him, then turned her attention to the controls. In a few quick moves she had frozen Sergei's work station out and taken full control of the *Lukyan*.

"Noisemaker 1 armed," reported the computer. Katya checked the settings she'd given it, and then flipped the cover on a "Commit" button. As a security and safety measure, some functions could not be activated through the touch screens – it was far too easy for accidents to happen that way. These functions, many of which were associated with weapons, had to be confirmed with the actual push of a physical button. Technically, noisemakers were considered weapons in terms of their interface functionality and the fact that they were expendable and expensive supplies. Nobody wanted to launch one accidentally. Katya's fingertip hesitated for half a heartbeat, and then pushed the button with a sense of finality.

A slight click sounded through the hull as the noisemaker's mounting clamp released it. "Noisemaker 1 away," said the computer.

Katya made a point of not looking at Sergei; she knew full well what expression he would be wearing at that moment and it wouldn't be one that bolstered her confidence.

Without pause, she opened the tactical options sheet on a secondary screen and ordered a slow descent below the next thermocline. The computer gauged that they would reach it in about ten seconds, which was encouraging as that was the timing she'd based the noisemaker's programming upon. Now she could only hope that the Yagizban would not open fire in those ten seconds, that her plan – such as it was – would work, and that they didn't get killed in the next few minutes.

Dying would be bad enough, but having Sergei spending their last moments saying "I told you so" would be more than she could bear.

The passive sonar did not report torpedoes in the water, which didn't surprise her at all. She'd seen enough of the military to know that they didn't like jumping in when there was still uncertainty about the situation. In this case, the Yags had almost certainly picked up the sound of air venting from the *Lukyan*'s ballast tanks and were wondering what was out there that they hadn't yet detected. That was enough to take the finger off the firing button.

A moment later the *Lukyan* sank through the thermocline and immediately adjusted its tanks to neutral buoyancy in the shadowed space there, where sonar waves tended to behave unreliably. As they breached the thermal layer where the water temperature changed abruptly, a hundred metres above them, where it had been lazily rising from its release point, the noisemaker burst into life. Essentially a small torpedo with a motor that mimicked the sound of a larger boat, the Noisemaker 1 set off on its maiden and final journey, straight towards the presumed location of the Yagizban Vodyanoi/2 warboat.

Noisemakers were clever devices, but the fact remained that their impersonation could only be reasonably convincing and no more. Inside a minute the Yag boat would have identified inconsistencies in the hydrophone data and the noisemaker would be subsequently ignored. A minute is a long time in a battle, however, and now things started to happen rapidly.

The Jarilo, more than aware that stealth was not its strong suit, anticipated that it was probably already on an enemy's scopes and decided to respond aggressively. A focused cone of sound energy sped out from its bow as it emitted a directional sonar "ping." Suddenly the Yagizban's stealthy manoeuvring was all for nothing as it lit up brilliantly on the sonar screens of the Jarilo, the *Lukyan*, and doubtless the one or more Federal warboats shadowing the transport.

Instantly the situation changed from a stalking game to a straight fight. The Vodyanoi/2 launched one torpedo and changed course dramatically, diving for the thermocline itself. "Oops," said Katya more mildly than this development really deserved; in a moment the Yagizban warboat would be on the same side of the temperature differential as them, and it would be able to see them easily.

Discretion would definitely be the better part of valour, she decided, and opened the throttle to one third ahead. It had turned into a game of judging the angles; she needed the *Lukyan* to get into the Yag's baffles while at the same time not exciting the curiosity of the Jarilo's escort – who, a bleep on the display informed her, had just launched a torpedo themselves – because in the confusion of a submarine battle, the Feds would be sure to fire first and run a sonic profile analysis later. They would probably be very sorrowful about sinking a

Federally registered minisub, but then shrug, say "That's war" and ask what's for dinner.

She made an educated guess where the rapidly fading trace of the Yagizban boat was heading and what its bearing was; drew a line that should be, more or less, its blind spot, and piloted the *Lukyan* into it. Beside her she could hear Sergei breathing heavily, possibly with fear, possibly with anger, most likely both. If she got them out of this alive, there was going to be a monstrous argument afterwards, of that she was sure. For the time being, however, she was entirely focused on the "getting out of this alive" aspect of their immediate situation.

She turned the *Lukyan* to starboard and headed away, hoping for the best. The hydrophones were full of the sound of control surface cavitation, torpedo drives, and noisemakers being shot off in all directions, all of which boded well – the big boys were too busy with one another to worry about a little bug like theirs. There was still the possibility of a torpedo performing a search pattern picking them up, but every second they ran broadened their chances. After ten minutes Katya and Sergei were breathing more easily. After twenty they were as sure as they could be that they'd escaped the battle. Katya slowed to a crawl and "cleared the baffles" to be sure, performing a quiet three hundred and sixty degree circle that allowed the sensors to scan the entire environs. There was nothing out there but the kind of fish that doesn't carry a warhead.

Still Sergei said nothing. In the heavy silence, Katya hand-plotted a change to the logged route that would take them around the battleground and then back on course for Atlantis.

Finally, she'd had enough of it. "Speak up or stop making that faulty valve noise with your nose, Sergei. You've got something to say. Let's hear it."

For several seconds he just stared at her as if he'd never really looked at her before and didn't like what he saw. Then he said, "Why? Why did you do that?"

"The Jarilo didn't stand a chance. We had to do something."

"No," he replied with cold emphasis. "We didn't *have* to do anything. We're just a little boat keeping its head down and out of trouble. We can't change anything. Don't you get it?"

Katya looked at him and some of that sense of revelation came to her, too. Sergei *was* afraid. Sergei had always been afraid. All these years she had seen him just as an adjunct to Uncle Lukyan, or even to the boat, a sidekick to one, an organic module of the other. She had never really looked at him as a person, and what she saw disturbed her and, to her great sorrow, disappointed her. He was just a man with small dreams and small hopes who'd latched onto Lukyan and followed him wherever big, bluff Lukyan wanted to go. All he wanted in life was a steady job and not to be afraid, and not being afraid meant never taking risks.

Once, not so long ago, she would not only have sympathised, she would have agreed with him wholeheartedly. The world had been much simpler then. Now, however... now she'd seen the kind of people who start wars at first hand. The experience had not filled her with confidence that they would be doing everything in their power to bring things to a peaceful conclusion. The FMA was furious with the Yagizban because the Yags had betrayed them not once but twice, first conspiring with the Terrans during the war, and then by preparing for a Terran return that never came. For their part, the Yagizban were sick of the Federals for getting into a war with Earth in the first place, and then using it as an excuse for never-ending martial law. They would fight like zmey over a manta-whale carcass, until one of them was dead, and the manta was torn to pieces.

"No, Sergei. I don't get it. Not anymore." She turned her attention to the controls. "If you want to resign, I'll give you a good reference."

She'd suggested much the same at breakfast, but then it had been in jest. The hard truth was resignation really *did* mean being promptly conscripted into the Federal forces. By the time she realised it was a threat, the chance to withdraw the comment was gone. *Misunderstandings*, she thought. *This is how wars start.*

The following seventeen hours were not the most comfortable either of them had ever spent. Sergei was surlier than usual, and barely spoke. Katya tried to jolly him along for the first couple of hours, but grew tired of his wilful recalcitrance and was soon only speaking to him when she needed to. There was no chance of any more hands of poker and certainly none of a game of chess, so she pulled up a book on a non-luminescent plastic paper screen and read to pass the time. The Russalkin loathing of all things Terran perhaps unsurprisingly did not extend to Earth art in general and literature in particular, so she felt no tremors of spiritual treason in reading a book called *Moby Dick*. It was about a man who had grown obsessed with hunting and killing a sea monster, a great white whale in one of the Terran oceans. Katya doubted it would end well.

It was a relief for both of them when they picked up the Atlantean approach markers, and even when they were interrogated at torpedo point by a patrol boat, because at least it gave them something to focus on outside the toxic levels of animosity inside the *Lukyan*. With the patrol boat captain's suspicions allayed, they were permitted to enter the minisub pens on the western side of the largest pressurised environment on the planet. Some of the Atlanteans went so far as to call it a city, but cities were a grubby Terrestrial conceit, and the term had never really stuck. Its population of a million and a half did make it comfortably larger than any other base or station, however, and it was large enough to support non-vital services.

Katya had heard that Atlantis was the only place on the planet where it was possible to forget that the Yagizban were trying to kill you, at least for a while. There was no chance of that during a three-hour debriefing, however. It was necessary to hand in a journey report to the authorities on arrival. Usually this simply consisted of a copy of the logged course, a plot of the actual course taken, and a brief description of anything that might be of interest to the FMA, although by far the most common style of report was the solitary sentence, "Nothing to report." An actual plot that deviated wildly from the logged course and a description that included the phrases "Vodyanoi/2 warboat," "Jarilo transport," "anticipated ambush," "noisemaker launched," and "torpedoes detected" was never going to go by with a mildly interested nod from the authorities.

By the time they were released, they had been awake for over twenty-four hours with only a few short catnaps, and tiredness made Katya and Sergei even snappier with one another, especially since Sergei appeared to harbour a suspicion that their lengthy debriefing had been all part of a surreal plan of Katya's to make him even more miserable.

They walked down the main southern promenade of the settlement silent and angry, barely exchanging a word.

It was a shame they were so tired and so ill-tempered, because Atlantis was like no other place on Russalka. It had actual shopping "streets," wide concourses with recessed shops and freestanding stalls selling admittedly minor variations of each other's stock. Once, Katya knew, these stalls had also dealt with goods brought in from the other Earth colonies, but that was before the war, when Russalka still had ships capable of reaching their near neighbours. Now there were some odd trinkets, curiosities like bone coral growths and the preserved forms of some of the more unusual fish from the world ocean. One stall was even topped by the massive skull of a zmey – a sea dragon. Neither Katya nor Sergei had time for any of this, though; both wanted sleep and to be out of one another's company; and they wanted these things as soon as possible.

When the Federal officer and two troopers stopped them, it just seemed like another lousy thing to top off another lousy day.

"Captain Kuriakova?" said the officer. Katya had the impression of a tall and efficient woman in the uniform, but what raised her concerns most was the small black insignia at the end of the officer's rank patch on her left breast pocket. She was a captain in Secor, the Federal security organisation. When Secor took an interest in your business, it never boded well. There were grim little rumours about Secor arresting those they found suspicious, spiriting them off to remote secure facilities like the Deeps or R'lyeh, where they would be interrogated, perhaps tortured, and dumped out of an airlock when Secor had squeezed every drop of useful information out of them.

"I... Yes?" said Katya, promptly wishing she hadn't admitted to her identity, and then immediately glad she had. It didn't pay to lie to Secor. That might make them angry with you, and that might make you dead.

"We have some questions for you," said the captain. Her tone was officious and curt. "You will come with us."

"What? But we've just been debriefed once."

"Irrelevant. This is Secor business."

To his credit, Sergei was having none of this. "We haven't slept in over a day, captain," he said, managing to be courteous for once. Speaking to somebody with the power of life and death, with an unpleasant period of "harsh" interrogation between the two, can have that effect. "Can't this wait?"

The Secor captain looked at him as if Sergei was something that might be found in a cess tank. "And you are..?"

Sergei had an awkward habit of saying the wrong thing at the wrong time and getting himself into trouble. Katya stepped in to stop him coming out with anything they might both regret. "He's my co-pilot. Do you need both of us, captain? I'm fine going with you, but my co has business to attend to."

Sergei shot her a "What are you playing at?" expression.

"The cargo still needs to be handed over to the dispersals agent at the dock. Yes, yes," she stopped him interrupting, "I know I said we could leave that until we'd had some rest, but we're overdue as it is. People are waiting for those parcels and letters, Sergei. We should hand them over as soon as possible."

Sergei narrowed his eyes. He knew there was nothing he could say or do that would have any influence on Secor with the possible exception of making them angry, but he didn't want to just leave it at that. Despite the current tension between them, his loyalty was still to her.

"I'll be fine, Sergei. I'll just answer the captain's questions and then we can get on with cashing in the scrips and finding some more work, OK?"

With every sign of not finding it OK in the least, Sergei nodded. "Take care, Katya," he said as he reluctantly took his leave. "I'll see you back at the boat, yes?"

"I'll see you there. Bye for now, Sergei."

He walked back towards the docks slowly, looking over his shoulder now and then.

"He's very protective of you," said the captain.

"Yes," agreed Katya, turning away from Sergei to face her. "He's a family friend."

"How nice, considering you don't have any family left."

Katya blanched. "You're such a bastard, Tasya Morevna. Hard to believe you ever had a family. What did you do, eat them?"

The "Secor captain" smiled slightly. She'd been called much worse in her life, and accused of much worse. Sometimes the charges had even been true. "Lovely to see you again too, Kuriakova," she said. "I was wondering if you'd recognised me. I've even dyed my hair."

"How about I shout the place down, Chertovka?" demanded Katya, exhaustion making her reckless. "How about I point at you and denounce you as a war criminal and a traitor? You won't get out of here alive."

Tasya Morevna, unkindly nicknamed the "Chertovka" or "She-Devil," seemed supremely unimpressed by the threat, even if the two "troopers" with her looked a little worried. "No," she admitted, "we probably wouldn't. Of course, neither would you. And then we'd all be dead, and you wouldn't have found out why we'd gone to all this trouble to speak to you." She smiled icily. "You'd die curious, and I know how much that would irritate you. Walk with me, Kuriakova. We're attracting attention standing here."

Grim and angry, Katya allowed herself to be cajoled into walking alongside Tasya, the two "troopers," whom were certainly Yagizban agents in reality, following up the rear, their maser carbines carried at a "full port" position across their bodies. People avoided looking at the little group; Katya's surly expression, Tasya's smirk, and the two troopers were the popular image of a typical Secor arrest in progress, whether the detainee was guilty or not. Nobody wanted to stare, because that might mean sharing their fate. Even before the conflict against the Yagizba Enclaves had begun, Secor had enjoyed an unsavoury reputation. Now that people's fear of spies and saboteurs – a fear the FMA was happy to encourage – was running wild, Secor did almost anything they liked, as long as it was not considered too overt or damaging to public morale by the ruling council. Impromptu public executions, such as had occurred in the first month of the conflict, had been stamped out. Most Federal citizens assumed they had simply been replaced with impromptu private executions. In this, they were correct.

The advantage of the almost supernatural levels of fear that accompanied Secor agents was that it meant anyone dressed as one was essentially invisible. It was an easy bet that not one of the dozens of people that passed them by would have been able to provide anything but the vaguest of descriptions for anyone in the party.

Tasya led the group to a restricted door into a disused maintenance area, the card she swiped through the lock looking suspiciously like an authentic Secor pass to Katya. She had assumed up to this point that the uniforms had been stolen from a storeroom somewhere, but now she was beginning to have misgivings. Where the Chertovka was involved, it was all too easy to imagine a storeroom with the corpses of a Secor officer and two troopers somewhere, stripped of their uniforms.

The door clanged to and locked behind them, cutting them off from the busy thoroughfare and leaving them in a suddenly very quiet, dank, barely lit access corridor to some part of Atlantis' infrastructure that it probably didn't even use anymore. "There," said Tasya with satisfaction. "This is *much* cosier, isn't it?"

Without waiting for the obvious reply, she moved ahead and Katya – for lack of other options – followed her. The corridor really was an archaeological site, in Russalkin terms at any rate, probably dating back to the foundation of Atlantis over a century before. At some point it had become surplus to requirements and was now just home to a few leaky pipes and some corroded power and control cabling, none of which had carried so much as a joule of energy since before she was born. Tasya clearly knew her way through the narrow corridors of what turned out to be a labyrinthine route. Behind them, the Yagizban "troopers," pleased at no longer having to playact soldiers, slung their carbines over their backs by their straps and held a brief muttered conversation about being glad to be off the thoroughfare as they followed Tasya and Katya.

Katya was both irritated at all the clandestine sneaking around, and slightly smug because she was memorising the route. She might not have many talents, she thought, but trying to trip her up on a matter of navigation was just stupid. She knew they had already re-crossed their path twice, so she was positive Tasya was trying to disorientate her. Well, if crossing the Vexations with an unreliable inertial compass hadn't caused her any great problems, then wandering around a few corridors – each of which was littered with plenty of distinctive features to remember – was insultingly easy. She didn't tell Tasya that, of course; let her think she'd succeeded in baffling poor little Katya.

Then, finally, Tasya reached a door, opened it and waved Katya inside. Katya went with poor grace; she was reasonably sure that if they were going to murder her, they'd had plenty of opportunities up to now and passed on all of them. Thus, she felt fairly safe in giving Tasya the evil eye as she passed her. Then she looked into the room and any thought of such one-upmanship left her.

The poorly lit, dirty little room must have been some sort of supervisor's office once, a long, long time ago. Charts and schematics still hung from the walls, discoloured and watermarked. There was an old desk, a steel thing that had probably been manufactured on Earth, and an old holoconsole of a type that Russalka was currently incapable of making because the technology behind it was of limited use and not vital to survival.

Sitting behind the desk was the most wanted man on the planet.

"Hello, Katya," said Havilland Kane.

FOUR
TOTAL WAR

Katya was literally lost for words for several long seconds. This didn't make any sense. Tasya had worked with Kane when Kane – the "great pirate" and "terror of the world ocean" – had been working for the Yagizban. But then Kane had betrayed the Yagizban, and Tasya – a colonel of the Yagizban military, for crying out loud – had stopped being his friend *very* abruptly. Indeed, there had been some name-calling.

And shooting. There had definitely been shooting.

Yet here they were, the pirate-king and the war criminal, all cosy together. Unless...

Turning to Tasya, she said, "Is Kane your prisoner?"

Tasya looked nonplussed, then she followed Katya's logic and laughed. "No. Havilland is not my prisoner, nor am I his. We're working together again."

"Just like that? I don't believe it." She turned to Kane. "The Yags would never work with you. Not after what you pulled on them."

"Yags, Katya?" He seemed pained. "*Yags*? Really? You sound like one of those FMA scream sheets."

Katya had had enough of this already. She'd had enough of it the very second she saw Kane's face. "Take me back," she said to Tasya. "I've got nothing to say to you, and I've got even less to say to *him*." She indicated Kane with a perfunctory jerk of her head. "Take me back right now and let me get on with my life without having lunatics like you and scum like Kane in it."

Tasya raised an eyebrow. "Her diplomatic skills have simply come on in leaps and bounds, haven't they, Havilland?"

"Katya," said Kane sharply, "stop behaving like a little brat and listen to me. Do you think we took a risk like coming to Atlantis unless there was a very good reason?"

"Of course there's a good reason," said Katya, "but it's a good reason that profits you and the Yags. I'm not helping either of you. That's all there is to it. And if you're not going to take me out of here," she said to Tasya, "I'll find my own way."

Kane grunted with displeasure. He still looked much as she remembered him; in his late thirties, lean, an aesthete in appearance. He always looked as if he should be lecturing in philosophy or literature, not leading a crew of stranded Terrans as his pirate crew around the deep waters of Russalka. He looked a little older now, though. There was grey at his temples that certainly had not been there before. She doubted that was because of the stress of being Federal Enemy No.1; he'd been that for years now and it didn't seem to bother him very much. There was another, darker possibility – that his long-term dependence on the drug "Sin" was finally taking its toll. Sin was no pleasure; it was a method of enslavement. If Kane didn't receive regular doses of it, he would slowly die in agony. Even though he had the formula and a steady supply of the stuff, it was hard to believe that having something so terrible in his system could do anything but harm eventually.

"The Yagizban wanted to win," Kane said. "Me, I just want to stay alive and to keep my people alive."

"Whoopee for you, Kane. You and every family in this…" She stopped as she fully analysed what he had said. "What do you mean, the Yagizban *wanted* to win? I was an unwilling spectator to a shooting match with one of those Vodyanoi copies on our way here. I think its crew were still trying to win. All the torpedoes swimming around, they were a strong hint."

"No," said Tasya, leaning against the doorjamb. "What you saw was the prosecution of a war. That's not the same as trying to win it. That's just not lying down and giving up."

Katya was having problems with the conversation that extended beyond its location and the other speakers. They were talking as if the Yagizban were at least thinking of giving up. It certainly didn't sound as if they had much belly for the fight. Kane was ahead of her.

"Don't think the Yagizba Enclaves are thinking of surrendering. Because they're not."

"We can't," added Tasya with quiet emphasis.

Katya was still near the door with a strong impulse to leave, but she wasn't leaving. She would in a moment, she was sure. Any minute now, she'd be gone. Any moment.

Just as soon as she'd found out what the hell they were talking about.

"What does that mean, 'we can't'?" she said. "It's very easy. You say to the Feds, 'We surrender.' There's no big trick to it."

Kane shook his head. "This war is more complicated than you realise, Katya."

He reached inside the long coat he always insisted on wearing, even in the temperature and humidity controlled submarine environments, the freak. Mind you, he liked the surface, liked standing around on surfaced submarine decks and on the Yagizban floating platforms, even in the howling cold and rain. She'd seen him do it herself, and it still mystified her even if it explained his attachment to his coat.

She decided she needed a stronger word than "freak" to really sum Kane up. Then she remembered that he was Terran by birth; he was already the most extreme form of freak imaginable.

Meanwhile, the freak in question had found what he was looking for. He pulled a waterproof envelope from his inside pocket, unsealed it and produced several sheets of hard copy. "These documents are all top secret," he said offhandedly, as if everybody carried secret papers around with them. "The Yagizba Enclaves have already made diplomatic overtures towards equitable terms for a cessation of hostilities."

He looked at Katya. "That means they're trying to end the war, by the way."

"I know what it means," said Katya, although she hadn't been completely sure.

Unabashed, Kane held up one of the sheets. "This is what they suggested. Immediate ceasefire, normalisation of relations, independence for the Enclaves from Federal authority, and a claim of about an eighth of the planet's surface."

"An eighth?" Katya was astounded and disgusted. That sounded like a lot.

"Yes, an eighth. Bear in mind that the Yagizban represent about a quarter of the planet's human population. An eighth is actually pretty modest. The eighth they want contains no Federal facilities, stations, developed mining sites, or anything else that would need to change hands. It's untouched apart from what the Yagizban already have there."

"What has this got to do with me?"

"As a Federal citizen, it has everything to do with you. Did you know the Yagizban had tried to negotiate? No. Their terms sound better than a war, don't they?"

Katya said nothing. She could see the other sheets Kane had taken from the envelope and scattered on the desk. One of them had the FMA seal in the corner. Kane picked it up.

"This is the Federal response to that olive branch." He saw her frown and added, "Sorry, that's an Earth term that apparently didn't make the trip here. It just means a peaceful overture. Here, read it yourself." He passed her the FMA document.

She took it and skim read it. Unfortunately, it was couched oddly, full of strange legal terms and skimming it did her no good. With the full knowledge that she had four people watching her as she read, she went back to the beginning and went through it more carefully. The first and obvious thing was that the FMA had dismissed the Yagizban peace plan. Most of the rest of the document was a counter-proposal, but even here some of the terms weren't very clear to her. There was something about the Yagizban surrendering unconditionally, something about territories and...

"I don't know this word," she admitted. "I haven't seen it before. What's 'indenturement'?"

Kane didn't reply immediately. He looked at Tasya first. Katya followed his glance, and saw Tasya had gone pale with anger. Abruptly, she stirred from her place in the door and walked out into the corridor.

"It's when you contract to work for someone in return for food, clothes, somewhere to sleep."

Katya was confused. What was a proviso like that doing in a peace negotiation? Now she knew what it meant, she could make sense of the sentences around it. Her eyes widened. They couldn't be serious.

"*All* Yagizban?" she asked Kane. "Mandatory indenturement for a period of thirty years on *all* Yagizban? But, if it's mandatory, if they *have* to do it..."

"Slavery," said Tasya reappearing at the door. "They want to enslave my people. This is what they call a 'peaceful overture.'" Her anger was in danger of boiling over. She took off her Secor cap and threw it in the corner as if it were diseased.

Katya was used to bickering and haggling over terms with traders, and was very familiar with the idea of starting with an outrageous offer. But buying a load of crimson squid fillets and negotiating a ceasefire couldn't work exactly the same, could they? You *couldn't* start by threatening the other party with enslavement or extermination. That was how wars started, not how they ended.

Then she read the last clause. It said in unequivocal terms that this was the FMA's first and only offer. The Yagizba Enclaves must accept it or suffer the consequences.

"I don't understand," Katya said to Kane. "This is a declaration of war for a war that's already being fought. I just..." She looked at the document as if it was dry water or pale black or something else that had no right existing. "What's going on, Kane? What are they doing?"

"Now that is an excellent question," he said, looking at the other documents still on the desktop. "I know what it looks like they're doing." He looked her in the eye. "It looks like they're trying to wipe out the Russalkin."

"You mean the Yagizban."

"I mean what I say." He held up two of the sheets. "More documents I'm not supposed to have. I'll give you the short version and you can read them yourself if you don't believe me. That love letter from the FMA gives the impression that a Federal victory is inevitable. These documents," he waved the two sheets, "are recent loss reports for both sides, and include projected losses. Katya, if the war continues with its current ferocity, in one year's time the global population will be less than a thousand. The only people left will be the ones in the warboats, because they will have destroyed all the settlements."

Katya shook her head. "That's not possible. No conventional war is that destructive."

Kane dropped the papers to the desktop and rubbed his eyes. "Oh, if only that were true. There are two problems with that idea, though. One, it only really applies in places where the planet itself isn't trying to kill you. Russalka isn't a nice place, Katya. We can only live here because we have the technology. We make environments to live in because the Russalkin environment would kill us in hours. Most of it wants to drown us, and the rest of it will kill us with hypothermia. We live in bubbles. All it takes is a big enough pin and any bubble can be burst. And that brings us to point number two."

He slid another sheet towards Katya. From the heading she could see it was a Yagizban intelligence report. "It turns out that the FMA is developing a bigger pin. A fusion device, specifically intended to open underwater bases to the ocean across multiple decks, thus overwhelming compartmentalisation and bulkhead safety measures. Anybody who isn't vaporised, blown up, or drowned in the detonation will just suffocate in the darkness as the life-support fails." He smiled humourlessly. "Even my lot never stooped that low."

"The *Leviathan*," said Katya with pointed emphasis.

Kane winced. "Yes. That's true. The *Leviathan*. But something went wrong with it. It wasn't *supposed* to kill everyone. Just destroy any military capability. What the Feds are planning is genocide. Cold-blooded mass murder. Slavery or extermination. This is your government planning this, Katya. This is happening in your name."

Katya turned to Tasya. "What are you doing about it, your government?"

Tasya pointed at the intelligence report. "We have warning. The Feds may have the numbers, but we've always had the technological edge. We'll have fusion warheads by the time they do. If they attack the Enclaves with these weapons, we will destroy their settlements. If they want total war, they can have it."

Katya shook her head. "This is crazy. This is all crazy. Are you seriously saying this war *has* to end with us all killing one another? I can't... Over a century we've fought the planet just to survive, we fought the Grubbers when they tried to take it away from us, and you're saying it's all as good as over? We were our own worst enemies the whole time? No. No, I can't accept that. We're not that stupid." The others were just looking at her. "We are *not* that stupid!"

She was angry now. Angry with them, angry with all this secret agent rubbish, but most of all she was angry because she had an ugly feeling gnawing away inside her that the Russalkin were more than capable of cutting their own throats rather than back down over a matter of pride.

Of course, all this still left one very large question.

"Why are you telling me this?"

Kane and Tasya exchanged glances. Katya realised that this was not a courtesy visit to tell her all this, or just to say hello and chat.

"We think we have a solution." Katya looked at him suspiciously. Considering he was claiming to have found a way to prevent humans becoming nearly extinct on the planet, he didn't seem very happy about it. "But, you're not going to like it."

"Try me."

So Kane told her.

An hour later Katya was back at the pens. Sergei was relieved to see her, but wisely decided not to say anything when he saw her face. She was clearly furious, fighting furious. Deadly pale and fists clenched, she had shot him a glance that would blister anti-fouling paint and said, "I don't want to talk about it."

Instead she entered the *Lukyan*, and sat down in the left hand seat, the pilot's seat, her uncle's seat. Sergei looked at her back, her shoulders heaving with heavy breaths. "I'll be in the dock cafe, OK?" he said cautiously. She said nothing. With misgivings, Sergei left.

Katya sat at the helm and looked at the darkness of the *Lukyan*'s pen. She was glad of the observation bubble's anti-reflective coating; she had no great desire to see her face there, illuminated by the glow from the screens, appearing to float like a drowned phantom in the water. She especially had no desire to see how she felt – angry, depressed, and terribly, terribly confused. She felt ugly inside her head, and it would just make her day if she looked it, too.

How could this war, this stupid little war, actually be even more dangerous than that against the Terrans? How could some silly homespun conflict fuelled by self-righteousness and point scoring have turned more deadly than a bona fide invasion from space?

The war against Earth had been intense, furious, a new turning point every day, whereas this spat with the Yagizba Enclaves was only slightly more interesting than the fish prices. Specific incidents were barely reported, just the steady drumbeat of "We're at war and we'll win after a while" in the news reports. Either the news was deliberately skipping many stories, or the figures Kane had showed her was a lie. She frowned hard enough to close her eyes. They were all such liars. Who could tell?

The yoke felt reassuring under her hand. Uncle Lukyan had sailed thousands upon thousands of kilometres in that very seat. She wished he was here so badly she could feel her heart clench, her eyes moisten. He'd know what to do. He'd trusted Kane, at least a little, but then he'd died. Was that Kane's fault? Yes, but not directly. Kane hadn't planned it, but then Kane hadn't planned anything. Yes, he had, just a few things, and those had worked. Mostly. But people had died.

Katya wished the smooth, non-reflective bubble was just a little bit closer to the pilot's position. Then she would be able to lean forward, and bang her head repeatedly against it.

So mired in internal debate and self-loathing was she, that it took a minute or two before the shouting filtered through to her consciousness. Glad to be offered some distraction from her troubles, she climbed out of her seat and walked back to the open hatch.

Out on the alley that joined the minisub pens, an argument was going on. No, Katya realised, not an argument. It was far too one-sided for that.

Two pen hatches down from her, a federal officer, a lieutenant, was shouting in the face of a small, plump man, bearded and bald. Katya recognised Filipp Shurygin, a trader who used the same model of boat as hers. Her uncle had known him for years, counted him as a friend, but then Shurygin had shifted his base of operations to take advantage of the trade in high tech items from the Enclaves and they hadn't seen him very often after that. Still, he was a nice man from what she could recall, and Lukyan had often said Shurygin was the most methodical of the sole traders, envious of the little man's reputation for never running awry in the dark waters of the Federal bureaucracy. It seemed odd that the officer was so furious with him over what seemed to be a problem with his papers.

"How could you not know about the packaging directive?" demanded the lieutenant, bellowing in Shurygin's face. "It's been nothing *but* the packaging directive all damn morning! How could you not know? *How could you not know?*"

Packaging directive? Katya had no idea what he was talking about. Behind the lieutenant stood a corporal.

Katya could see that he was possibly more confused than she was.

"I'm sorry, lieutenant," said Shurygin in a small voice. "I hadn't been told. I'll comply immediately, of course."

"All morning!" shouted the lieutenant. Spittle flew from his lips and onto Shurygin. He flinched, which just seemed to make the officer angrier still. "Five times this morning I've been told to enforce this blasted directive and the very first, the *very first* piece of scum I check, hasn't even heard of it. How is that possible?"

The corporal risked speaking. "Sir, I…"

His superior spun on his heel and roared "SHUT UP!" in his face.

"This morning, sir?" said Shurygin. "I've… I've been at sea for the last forty hours. I wouldn't have heard…"

"Been at sea?" The lieutenant said it as if this was very suspicious behaviour for a submarine pilot. He checked his pad. "You're based out of Tartessos, it says here."

Shurygin nodded.

There was something about the officer's stance that bothered Katya. He was leaning forward a little, his shoulders bowed, breathing heavily through his partially open mouth. He looked ill.

"I understand," said the lieutenant. "I understand how you don't know about the packaging directive. I understand now."

"Thank you, sir," said Shurygin. "I'm sorry about the misunderstanding. I'll comply as soon…"

"Tartessos is close to Yagizban waters," the lieutenant said. Then he added as if it were the most reasonable conclusion in the world, "You're a Yag spy."

Shurygin's jaw dropped. It took an effort for Katya to keep her own mouth shut. Even the corporal looked at the lieutenant with unfeigned astonishment.

The lieutenant straightened up and bared his teeth in an expression of pure animalistic hatred and rage. "You're a stinking SPY!" he screamed, drew his sidearm, placed the muzzle between poor Shurygin's eyes, and fired.

Shurygin died much as he had lived; quietly and without fuss.

Katya cried out involuntarily and the lieutenant looked wildly at her, ignoring the body of the man he had just murdered. He seemed to become aware that, apart from Katya, there were other submariners standing there in shock, staring at him.

"Spy," he said in a high cracked voice. "He was a spy. A Yag. A spy. Spies and saboteurs. Can't you see them?" His voice rose to a scream. "CAN'T YOU SEE THEM?"

He raised his maser pistol again, the barrel twitching as he trembled. He fired a second time, and Katya heard a cry behind her, further down the alley. Then his gaze settled upon her. "I can see them," he said in a dry whisper, and he levelled his maser at her.

Katya heard the "crack" very distinctly, even five metres away, and watched as the lieutenant fell headlong to lie prone on the deck. The corporal stood over him, his baton raised for a second blow if the first hadn't done the job properly, but the lieutenant lay motionless. Quickly putting his baton back in his belt, the corporal drew his handcuffs, and placing one knee in the small of the downed man's back, quickly cuffed his superior officer. Only then did he check for a pulse.

The corporal looked up at Katya. "He'd gone insane! You saw that, didn't you? I had no choice!" His expression was one of profound horror, perhaps even a kind of grief. He'd overridden a lot of training and service discipline to strike a superior, and Katya could see the panic in his eyes.

"You had no choice," she assured him. "You saved my life. Maybe his, too." She looked back down the corridor. A submariner was sitting on the floor, cradling his forearm while his shipmates fussed over him. "You'd better call in a medical emergency," she said to the corporal.

As he went to a wall communicator and called for help, Katya knelt by Filipp Shurygin. He was lying on his back, looking at the ceiling with an expression of wide-eyed optimism. The deep, dark burn between his eyes that penetrated skin, skull, and brain indicated that such optimism had been uncalled for.

Knowing full well that in a few minutes she would be a trembling wreck herself as the realisation of how close she'd been to death set in, she made the most of the calmness of denial, those precious few moments before you have to accept that something awful and terrifying just happened. She put out her hand to his face and gently closed his eyes.

Poor Shurygin, she thought. *What will they put on his post mortem report? Killed while being helpful?*

FIVE
PLUMBING SUPPLIES

Katya had her second encounter with Secor in one day, although this time they were the real thing. She thought it odd that they should have taken an interest in what seemed to be simply somebody cracking under the stress of war. It was tragic, of course, but it happened.

Katya was expecting the station police to deal with it, but they just took her statement while Secor sat in on the interview, occasionally throwing in questions of their own. Katya had heard that the "packaging directive" that the lieutenant – it transpired his name was "Loktev" – had been so obsessed by had indeed been announced that morning, but was only coming into effect in ten days' time. All that the directive demanded was that cargo packaging be kept unlocked to speed up security checks. That was all, and for this a man had died.

Secor seemed very uninterested in that. They just wanted to correlate her story against that of the other witnesses, confirm that it was highly unlikely that Shurygin was actually an enemy spy – Katya undiplomatically snorted in derision at such an assertion – and only seemed to grow interested in their jobs when they got around to threatening her with dire consequences should she speak to *anyone* about the event. She'd agreed, neglecting to mention that she fully intended to tell Shurygin's family what had happened the very next time she got over to Tartessos, if only to assure them that he hadn't suffered.

Then after she had been dismissed and was getting up to leave, she had paused. The slightly routine way the men from Secor had demanded her silence had rankled at first, but now it made her suspicious "Have there been other incidents like this?" she asked.

"The interview is over, citizen," said the senior agent, and that had been that.

There was one small piece of good news awaiting her return to the *Lukyan*, however: Sergei had secured a cargo.

"Plumbing parts?" said Katya, reading the manifest.

Like most Russalkin, Katya didn't actually like water very much. She had the mandatory basic swimming standard that all Russalkin were required to attain, but hadn't been near a swimming pool since. She would drink water happily enough, and shower in it, but quantities much larger than a sinkful of the stuff made her nervous. It felt like an enemy within, a little brother of its vast sibling waiting just beyond the next airlock or on the other side of the submarine hull. Waiting to rush in and crush, drown, drain the life heat from your very body. The Russalkin respected the sea, because the Russalkin feared it.

Plumbing just seemed like a good way to aggravate it.

Sergei shrugged. He tolerated drinking water, but regarded showers as agents of the great elemental enemy and usually made do with a wet sponge and no shame. Why anybody would want to shift a consignment of pipes, heaters, and shower heads around was one of the intractable mysteries of the universe as far as he was concerned. That they would get paid for it, however, was something he could understand. The plumbing supplies themselves he would leave to the dangerous intellectuals who had uses for such things.

The supplies were delivered sharply on schedule the following morning and loaded carefully. On an impulse, Katya made sure the boxes were unlocked. The directive was still days away from becoming mandatory, but it couldn't do any harm to get into the habit ahead of time.

When she was returning from picking up some fresh food for the journey, she walked past a law enforcement agent talking to one of the pen managers by the hatch to Shurygin's boat, the *Lastochka*. From what she overheard, they were discussing what they were going to do with it.

"Well, the family can't get anyone here, and it's not as if we can spare anyone," said the manager.

She stepped through the *Lukyan*'s hatch and sealed it. She sidled forward past the pallet loaded with plumbing supplies, saying, "They don't know what to do with Shurygin's boat."

"It'll just end up being used in the war effort," said Sergei, running through the pre-launch checks. "Everything gets used in the war effort, one way or another."

"Sergei," said Katya. She waited until he looked back at her before continuing. "Mind if I take that seat?"

He raised an eyebrow, surprised. "She's your boat, Katya. You sit where you like, but…"

"I just thought, you know… Just… Well, I don't think Lukyan would be very happy with me being pilot and not…" She shook her head. "And not behaving like it. Responsibilities. He was always very keen on people accepting responsibilities."

"He was." Sergei nodded, and smiled. "I'll be glad to be out of this seat, to tell the truth." He unlocked his harness and climbed into the co-pilot's seat with a blissful sigh. "I'm a right-hand seat kind of feller. Never felt comfortable over there. Too *much* responsibility."

Katya took the pilot's seat, adjusted it, locked her harness and put on her headset. "Sergei. That business on the way here…"

Sergei interrupted her. "Nobody died."

"What? How can you know that?"

"While you were in here doing all that mad brooding after Secor had finished with you, I went to the cafe, remember? Next table, the weapons officers of the two – count 'em – *two* warboats that were shadowing the Jarilo, arguing over what happened. They can't have heard about your report, yet. Anyway, gist of the discussion, lots of torpedoes, lots of confusion, no hits. Not even the Jarilo got tabbed."

Katya sighed deeply. "I was lucky."

Sergei made a dismissive sound. "We make our luck."

••••

Atlantis Traffic Control ran them quickly through the departure protocols and bid them the traditional wish for a safe journey as the *Lukyan* slipped out of her lock and into the open sea. Within her, the atmosphere was a great deal more relaxed than when she'd docked. Sergei was a pragmatist at the core, even if he hid it beneath a deep crust of cynical pessimism. Rationally, he was satisfied that Katya's actions had been reasonable after all, even if they hadn't seemed that way at the time. Emotionally, he had no desire to stay angry at her for long. Katya might not have been blood family, but he felt like an honorary uncle to her, always had done, and now Lukyan was gone he took that role all the more seriously. An hour out of Atlantis he expressed his desire to put the past behind them in the manner time-honoured within the little submarine.

"Would you like a game of chess?" he said with an unconvincing attempt at casualness.

Katya looked over at him and grinned. *Only an hour*, she thought. *He's mellowing.*

"I'd love a game, sure. Let me just get us to the first deep waypoint and I'll hand over to the autopilot." She had plotted a tortuous route to Dunwich Down, a small fish farming, protein processing, and hydroponics food facility built into a former mining site. The facility was in a cleft in the ocean bed, and there were few submarine mountains or even hills near it. This meant there was little cover on the approaches and unwary submarines could potentially be detected from kilometres away. In peacetime that was unimportant; Dunwich was not the sort of high value target that attracted pirates, and so civilian boats had travelled there and back without fear of attack. All the rules changed in war, however. Food was vital to the Federal war effort. A single Vodyanoi class warboat could target every transporter in the volume around Dunwich from a safe distance, and be away before the first torpedoes were even detected. This was hunters' territory now, and the transport captains were justifiably fearful to go there.

Stretched tight, the FMA could only afford to have a single obsolete Sadko class patrol boat circle the site, its drives adjusted to give the impression to listening enemies that it was something larger and more dangerous. If the Yagizban had any sort of intelligence network in place, this was a wasted effort, as everybody knew about the hapless Sadko and its fake acoustic signature. Indeed, it was joked about in every base in Federal waters.

Given the high likelihood that the Yagizban knew all about Dunwich's paper tiger, this meant that civilian pilots remained very cautious approaching and leaving the facility. In Katya's case, she had plotted a complex route that took advantage of every rockfall, mound, and isotherm she could find in the newest navigational charts. The *Lukyan* was programmed to creep, dash, and scuttle its way from cover to cover like a nervous parack, a form of five-legged crustacean native to Russalka that would never be a byword for bravery. To have steered the route manually would have been painfully wearing on anyone's nerves. Katya, grown as pragmatic as Sergei in her experiences, was content to leave it to the computer.

She still had her pride, however; she would steer to the first waypoint on the evasive pattern close to the sea bed before handing over.

As they descended in a long gentle arc into the depths, Katya experimentally waggled the control yoke, listening to the whine of the manoeuvre impellers through the hull as she did. Frowning, she took her hands from the controls and looked at the yoke, which did nothing at all in response.

"Sergei, is the feedback broken on this side?"

Sergei looked over at the motionless control yoke and sniffed haughtily. "No. I just turned it off. I don't like feeling it move in my hand. Why?" He looked suspiciously at the co-pilot's yoke before him. "Have you turned on the feedback for this one?"

"Don't worry, it's not going to jump at your throat. I returned it to your settings when I handed it over. If you had feedback turned off in those, then it's off now." She opened the system controls screen on her main multifunction display and selected the yoke options. "I'm just used to having some feedback. Feels weird and dead without it. Here we go."

She checked the box against "Yoke Feedback" and confirmed her choice. Immediately the control yoke started to shake. With mild surprise, they both looked at it juddering a centimetre or so from true. "Well, that's not right," said Katya finally.

"The feedback relays must be buggered," said Sergei knowledgeably. "I'll have a look at them when we get to Dunwich."

Katya was still frowning. She pointed at the co-pilot yoke. "Turn your feedback on, just for a minute."

Sergei nodded; it was a sensible suggestion. In a few moments he had his position's controls screen active and selected the feedback option. The instant he confirmed, his yolk began to shake too. He watched it for a few seconds before deactivating it. "Not the relays, then," he said.

Katya swore. It was a particularly harsh term she had never used before, which combined disrespect for the subject's mother with an unambiguous accusation of incest.

Sergei raised his eyebrows. Katya looked at him, her anger slightly tempered by embarrassment at her outburst. "Not you, Sergei. It's that... that..." She could feel the bile of her anger rising again. "There's nothing wrong with the damn controls." She slowly throttled back the *Lukyan*'s main impellers, bringing them to a gentle halt. As they did so, the shuddering in the yoke became less violent before fading away altogether.

Sergei began to suspect he should be worried. "What's going on, Katya?"

For her answer, she twisted the yaw controls, making the boat turn on the spot until it was facing directly back in the direction they had come. Then she lit the powerful light array mounted around the large semi-spherical cockpit portal before them. The water was slightly murky, and the lights could penetrate only some twenty metres before the gloom grew too strong for them, but that was enough to show the submarine prow before them.

"Nothing wrong with the controls," repeated Katya. "We were caught in that thing's bow wave."

Sergei was staring wide-eyed at the shadowy shape before them. "That's no Fed boat," he said in a horrified undertone. "That's a Yag."

"No," replied Katya. She was grim, her anger simmering beneath the surface. "It's not a Yag. It's a pirate."

This news failed to calm Sergei. As they watched, the pirate's bow split along three seams and yawned wide like the maw of some horror of the deep. As they watched – Sergei wide-eyed, Katya with her arms crossed and a scowl upon her face – the pirate moved forward in a slow creep, the open jaws moving closer and closer. Sergei reached for the controls, but Katya said, "No!" sharply, and his hands fell away from the yoke.

"We can't outrun them, and if we try and manoeuvre while those jaws are closing, they might breach us by accident."

"By *accident*?" said Sergei. "If they're pirates, why would they care one way or…?"

"I know that boat. I've been on it before."

Sergei's jaw dropped. "It's the *Vodyanoi*? Killer Kane's boat?"

Katya snorted. "Killer? Him? Ha."

The *Vodyanoi* came on until the *Lukyan* was entirely engulfed within the salvage maw, and then slowly and carefully closed its jaws.

Once the maw had been pumped empty, the hatchway into the main forward compartment opened. On the dry side stood two of the *Vodyanoi*'s crew accompanying

Tasya Morevna, now looking far more comfortable in Yagizban fatigues with a colonel's flash on her epaulettes than she ever had in her stolen Secor uniform. On the wet side stood a silently fuming Katya Kuriakova and Sergei, who kept swallowing nervously. When he saw Tasya, he blurted out, "You're that Secor officer!"

"And you must be Sergei?" she replied sweetly. "How do you do? I'm Tasya Morevna." He blanched as he recognised the name, and she smiled a true killer's smile as she watched the fear grow in him. "You probably know me better as the Chertovka, yes?"

"Leave him alone, Morevna," snapped Katya. "What's this all about?"

"Another one of Kane's little schemes, I'm afraid, Katya," said Tasya, entirely unaffected by the waves of hostility emanating from Katya. "I told him he was wasting his time, but he's got this idea from somewhere that you're more than just a stupid little girl."

Katya scowled. "You're trying to provoke me."

"Ah," said Tasya lightly. "Not so stupid after all."

"It won't work because I'm already as provoked as all hell. I told you *No*, and I meant it."

"I'm not the one you have to convince. I'm just a passenger myself. You'll have to talk to the captain." She stepped to one side and bowed mockingly as she indicated the direction of the *Vodyanoi*'s bridge. "This way."

Katya ground her teeth for a second, mastering her rage. "Fine," she said, walking past Tasya. "Fine. I'll see Kane, tell him what he can do with his plan, and then we're leaving. We've got a cargo to deliver."

Tasya let her walk precisely three paces before saying casually, "Yes. Plumbing supplies, isn't it?"

Katya stopped so abruptly that Sergei, who was looking over his shoulder at Tasya, bumped into her. Katya stepped around him and narrowed her eyes. "How did you know that?"

Tasya smiled pleasantly and shrugged. "Lucky guess."

Katya glared at her for a long moment during which Tasya's smile never wavered. Only a small, sensible voice at the back of her mind, telling Katya that Tasya was a highly trained soldier who could likely kill Katya a dozen different ways with one hand tied behind her back, stopped her running at Tasya with her fists flying. Instead, she turned on her heel and strode off, Sergei close behind her.

She led the way directly to the bridge and made an unannounced entry that silenced the place. "What are you, Kane?" she demanded of the somewhat bewildered captain in his command chair. "Stupid? Don't you understand 'No' means 'No'?"

One of the bridge crew smirked at this, which was a mistake. Katya was by him, glaring into his face in a second. "Shut up," she said. "You *child*." The smirk melted away instantly.

Katya turned back to Kane as Tasya arrived, having dispensed with her escort en route. She looked at the scene and said, "That's alright, Kuriakova. Make yourself at home."

"Sorry about... this, Katya," said Kane, seemingly sincere. "It's just... well... There is so much at stake."

Katya wasn't interested. "Our cargo, Kane. The plumbing stuff. You placed it, didn't you?" Sergei glanced at her with puzzlement, and then realisation dawned.

"So you'd know where we were going," he said, half to himself.

"Yes," admitted Kane. "Sorry about that, too. A small deceit." He was wearing dark grey trousers, a pale cream shirt and, over it, some sort of buttoned sleeveless top similar to an armoured vest except with a V at the front and made out of normal looking cloth in a shade of brown. It didn't seem very functional to Katya's eye, undoubtedly some fatuous item of Terran clothing. From one of the small pockets on the garment protruded a clumsily folded envelope, and this Kane took and held out to her.

"This is twice the agreed transport fee, in Federal notes. Please, take it for putting up with the imposition." He smiled, a little weakly. "You can keep the supplies, too. If you like. You should be able to get something for them."

"I don't want your money, Kane."

"Yes, she does," said Sergei quickly. He stepped forward and took the money. As he returned to Katya, he said quietly. "Money, Katya! Actual money! Don't let your pride get in the way of eating."

"OK," conceded Katya with poor grace. "We'll take your money, and now we're done. Let us go."

"Sorry. Again," said Kane. "I can't do that. Not after going to all this trouble."

Katya glanced around, trying and failing to formulate an escape plan.

"You could try screaming and seeing if help comes," said Tasya, with mock concern.

Kane shot Tasya an impatient look that she accepted with a bored nod of her head. Kane turned to Katya. "Katya, you once said that the worst thing I do... that I've done... is not to tell people what's going on until... well, sometimes, when it's too late to help."

"I remember. I also remember saying that I never wanted to see you again."

Kane bridled at that, and some of the steel Katya knew lurked beneath the scatter-brained persona he wore like a shield glinted for a second. "I don't need some truculent schoolgirl lecturing me. I need you... this whole *world* needs you... to help steer it away from Armageddon."

"I don't know what that word means."

"I doubt any Russalkin has ever even heard it before. It's nothing good, believe me. I just need a couple of days of your time to show you what is happening. Then you can make your own mind up. And you can help us, or you can go. I won't stop you." He glanced at Tasya. "*We* won't stop you."

Katya wasn't so angry that she couldn't see that a fait accompli had been dumped in her lap. She could spend the next ten minutes shouting at Kane, but she knew it would be ten minutes opposed by his particularly impenetrable brand of apologetic stonewalling, and with an accompaniment of languid sarcasm from Tasya. It was not, she bitterly admitted to herself, a winning proposition. The best she could hope for was to hang onto a few shreds of dignity.

"Two days, then. And you'd better have something worthwhile to show us at the end of it. Oh, and twice the transport fee isn't going to come close to paying for the trouble we're going to have with the Feds when they find out we apparently went off in a random direction instead of going to Dunwich – you're going to have to up that sweetener." Without waiting for a reply – Kane's startled expression showed her response had hit home – she said, "C'mon, Sergei. Let's get our stuff from the *Lukyan*. Then they can show us our cabins."

She walked out of the bridge with Sergei, his nervousness evident, following in her wake. As soon as they were a couple of metres through the exit into the corridor, she gestured for Sergei to hold his tongue and stepped silently back to stand in the shadow of the bulkhead by the hatch. She listened intently, trying to make out specific voices over the usual hum and report chatter of an active bridge.

"We're spending a lot of time and effort to convince Kuriakova," she heard Tasya say. "I still don't think we need her. There are other ways of getting in."

Kane didn't answer at once. When he did, he sounded worried and unsettled, a man who had bet everything on very long odds. "All your ways involve killing people, Tasya. I don't want to try to end the bloodshed by spilling more."

"Not all my plans involve killing, Havilland. I did table a stealth infiltration, too." She sounded very slightly offended.

"Yes, that's true, you did. But even you agreed that it would almost certainly be detected before the job was done. Then there would be shooting. No, Katya's our best chance to get this done silently and without the Feds realising what's going on until it's far too late."

"You overestimate her."

The bulkhead safety override timed out and the door to the bridge slid shut, cutting off Kane's reply. Katya snorted with irritation. She walked past Sergei without looking at him. He glanced nervously at the closed hatch, and followed her.

SIX

ARMOURED MERPEOPLE

It was strange being aboard the *Vodyanoi* again. Katya could never quite get past the feeling that this was not just a hostile boat, but that a strange air of otherness hung around the cabins and corridors. She knew why, too – this boat was alien. The *Vodyanoi* had been borne to Russalka in the belly of a Terran invasion ship, and that sense of enmity could never be purged. Her design philosophies were a little different too; she felt sleeker and more confident, almost smug, in her lines both inside and out. Equipment was stowed a little more efficiently than aboard a Russalkin boat; a hundred little gimmicks and gadgets made life aboard just that pleasurable shade of convenience better.

It had taken her a while to understand that Russalka had never really won the war against the invaders from Earth – it had just weathered it longer than the Terrans were prepared to fight. Presumably the decision makers of Earth had looked at their spreadsheets and decided Russalka was worth no further effort. The initial invasion force had proved insufficient, and even the dreadful *Leviathan* had failed to crush all resistance. That was all they were prepared to waste, and so they abandoned the attempt, the machines, and even the men and women of the assault forces. These had done the best they could, throwing in their lot with the Yagizban.

The crew of the *Vodyanoi* was entirely Terran, she knew. It disturbed her that she found them perfectly human, even likeable in some cases. Part of her hated them for what they were, what they had come to Russalka to do, but it was a small part. In the flesh, they were just people who were doing their jobs. For all that, however, she didn't speak to them much. Casual conversation would sooner or later touch upon the invasion, and that was not something she wanted to talk about to people who may have been personally responsible for her father's death.

Sergei had watched her easy familiarity with the *Vodyanoi*'s layout with something like superstitious fear, as if knowing where the head was required witchcraft. Yes, he knew she had travelled in the *Vodyanoi* before, but the proof of that tale still came as a shock to him. Katya had the uncomfortable feeling that the simple fact that she knew her way around was somehow treasonous in his eyes.

Sergei and she ate together in one or other of their cabins – never with the crew. She'd wandered around the boat for a while after she'd slept the first night, but the atmosphere in the corridors was unwelcoming.

Last time she'd been here, the crew had been open and friendly. She had been a hero then, after all. She'd saved the day, and all the days after it. Now, however, the battle lines had resolidified. She was no longer a hero who happened to live under Federal rule. Now she was a Federal citizen who was once a hero, and the Federal Maritime Authority wanted the Vodyanois dead.

Life was tough even for Knights of the Deep, she told herself.

At least things were just as unpleasant for Tasya. The Chertovka rarely left her cabin either, from what Katya had observed, and when she did the Vodyanois treated her with the same coolness. Perhaps they had discovered that in her role as a Yagizban colonel, Tasya had once given orders for the *Vodyanoi* to be hunted down and sunk without mercy. If not, Katya would be delighted to tell them.

Sergei, on the other hand, wandered the corridors with impunity. Given his lifestyle, he had long since become immune to any discourtesy short of a slap in the face, and if the crew were distant with him, he didn't notice. Instead, he walked around the ship like a man who'd found himself in the belly of a manta whale and didn't want to miss any of the experience.

It was after one of these wide-eyed walks that he turned up knocking urgently on Katya's cabin door early on the second day. Katya, bleary with disturbed sleep, opened up to find him frantic on the threshold, looking up and down the corridor as if he was being pursued. He pushed past her and wordlessly pantomimed that she should shut the door again quickly.

"Come in, Sergei," she said with heavy irony. Sergei, being Sergei, didn't notice.

"I was just on the bridge…" he began.

Katya sucked in a breath sharply. Sergei had never been formally trained in submarine operations, and had never been aboard anything bigger than a passenger shuttle or a transporter piloted by one of his cronies in his whole life. It occurred to Katya that perhaps she should have told him that bridges were routinely off-limits to non-crew. Just wandering in like that would not have made him popular. Yes, she'd marched in herself the other day, but she'd been angry *and* expected, so it wasn't quite the same thing. Belatedly, she realised she'd probably set a bad example.

"They kicked you out?"

"No, I left myself. They didn't seem to mind me being there."

Katya doubted that, but let him continue.

"The thing is, I caught a glimpse of the navigator's screen. Katya," he lowered his voice to a horrified whisper, "they've taken us into Red Water!"

If he was expecting Katya to throw up her hands and faint dead away, he was to be disappointed.

"They're pirates, Sergei. I don't think Red Water bothers them very much one way or the other."

"But we're in interdicted waters! If a Federal boat finds us here, they'll kill us!"

Katya sighed. She could almost feel her snug little bunk getting colder behind her. "This is a pirate boat, Sergei. What's the FMA going to do if they find us? Sink us more than once?"

She sat on her bunk and thought wistfully of coffee. Real coffee, the expensive stuff from the hydroponics farms. If only the delivery job to Dunwich had been for real. She bet they grew coffee there. But, there was no coffee here and now. Only Sergei, panicking. Not really the same thing at all.

"But they'll know we're here now! The FMA's going to have picket sensors all around Red Water, they're bound to! There'll be boats coming for us right now!"

"Calm down, Sergei. Just quieten down a bit. No, there won't be any boats. Think about it. There's a war on. Red Water's just to warn off civilian traffic. Military boats on both sides will simply ignore it. There'll just be undetonated weapons or a sunken boat here they're planning to salvage or something boring like that."

"Picket sensors..." said Sergei again, refusing to be fobbed off with common sense quite so quickly.

"Those things aren't cheap. In their boots, where would you place them? Around some volume of water nobody much cares about or on guard around military facilities? Don't worry. There are no pickets. The Feds will probably only ever find out if a civilian boat's been in Red Water either because they have the lousy luck to run into a FMA boat while they're in there, or because it shows up in their navigational data if customs bother to check."

That, finally, reassured him on the subject of Red Water, although only by giving him something else to worry about. "The *Baby*... I mean, the *Lukyan*'s nav data! How are we supposed to explain this side trip?"

"We won't have to. There's a tech on the *Vodyanoi* who can fake the data anyway you like. We'll come up with some story about the drive going boggy on us for a while and slowing us down, and the nav data will back up every word."

"You're sure?"

"Positive. They've done it before. The Feds went through the *Lukyan*'s memory – back when she was still *Pushkin's Baby* – the last time she went for a ride in this boat. They didn't find a thing out of place." She stretched. "Well, I'm awake now. Might as well get a shower and some food. Kane's got this big whatever-the-hell-it-is to show us today that's supposed to change everything. I'd hate to be awe-inspired on an empty stomach."

While the concept of a shower evaded Sergei, food was a much easier idea to grasp.

The summons came at just before midday, Standard Russalka Time. That almost the whole planetary population lived underwater and even the Yagizban in their floating towns never saw the sun above the dense cloud cover had made the question of time zones moot; midday was midday the world over.

Katya was called to the bridge by name and Sergei was not, so she took him along anyway just to irritate Kane. She found the bridge subdued, the usual interplay between the crew positions muted and serious.

"Range to station locks, three and a half klicks and closing," called the navigator.

"Thank you," said Kane. "Is that drone ready yet, Mr Quinn?"

"Reconnaissance drone prepped and ready for launch, sir."

"Good. Stand by to launch at one kilometre."

On the bridge's main screen was displayed their current location. It clearly showed them in the heart of the FMA-declared Red Water, which raised an obvious question.

"What station?" asked Katya. "There shouldn't be anything out here."

"Shouldn't there?" said Kane. "Depends on what you think Red Water really is."

Katya looked at him curiously. "It's a danger zone. Everybody knows that."

"Ah," said Kane, and Katya knew from infuriating experience that he was about to say something obscure. Nor did he disappoint. "But a danger to who?"

"Are you going to explain that?"

"I won't have to, soon enough."

Katya decided not to give him the pleasure of rising to the bait, and instead turned back to the screen with an expression of serene indifference. Inwardly, however, she was counting slowly to ten to avoid screaming at him.

The *Vodyanoi* crept closer and closer to its destination on one third engine power. Finally, Kane ordered the drives be cut and they drifted to a range of one thousand metres on the boat's dwindling inertia. "Launch the drone, Mr Quinn," said Kane.

Quinn lifted the safety cover from the Number Three fire control and pressed the button beneath. The pattern of lights above it changed. "Drone away, captain. Closing tube door."

"Good. Sensors, do we have telemetry?"

"Telemetry is online, sir," called the sensors officer. "Signal is strong. Manoeuvring in to five hundred metres before I begin the survey."

Katya didn't want to give Kane any further opportunities to be mysterious with her, but her curiosity was devouring her. As nonchalantly as she could, she wandered over to stand by the captain's chair.

"Surveying what?" she said, trying to give the impression it was something of the mildest possible interest to her. "What are you looking for?"

Kane's eyes never left the main screen. On it was displayed the *Vodyanoi*'s current position, the rocky hillside they were investigating labelled *NoDa3*, and a tiny pulsing dot representing the reconnaissance drone as it moved smoothly from the former to the latter. "A way in. If there's one left."

"Pulse imaging on," said the sensors officer.

"Main screen, if you please."

The tactical display was replaced by a sonar image generated by the drone emitting a complex sequence of active pings across a spectrum of frequencies in a sixty degree cone. The returns were instantly processed and presented as a startlingly precise virtual model on screen. It was like looking at the actual structure in clear air, albeit painted in shades of red, yellow, and blue to represent differing materials. The rock of the hillside was blue, the concrete emplacement in its side red, and the metal of the docking positions yellow. But what should have been clean, hard lines of the construction were crumbled and askew.

"They're ruined," said Katya under her breath.

"Have you heard the news recently, Katya?" said Kane in so casual a voice that she didn't realise he was talking to her for a moment. She shook herself from her reverie.

"When I can. It's hard to avoid."

"Then you know of the Federal Maritime Authority's recent great victory over the craven, sneaking scum of the Yagizba Enclaves?"

She thought back to the story she had mentioned to Sergei when they'd been at Mologa. "The spy base? That's it?" She looked more keenly at the sonar image. To cause that sort of damage, it must have come under sustained attack with some very heavy weapons.

"That's it. Thank heavens the FMA were able to find it and save you all from such a nest of assassins and saboteurs." Kane spoke tonelessly, as if reciting a news story in his sleep. His eyes never once left the image of the ruin.

"It's a real mess, sir," said the sensors officer. "I'm filtering out returns from tumbled concrete fragments and there's a lot of wreck contamination in the water."

"We can't dock, captain," added the first officer. She entered some data on her station and an overlay appeared on the main screen showing a wireframe representation of what the docking area should have looked like superimposed upon the sonar image. The two images had little in common. "Only Dock Two isn't covered in debris, but the outer door is buckled. Probably the inner one too."

Katya swallowed hard as fear fluttered through her. No submariner likes to hear of a hull breach.

Kane breathed slowly out through his nostrils as he regarded the scene. "Forget the frontal approach, then. Plan B. Sensors, take the drone around to the secondary lock. Helm, take us around wide and clear. Don't crowd the drone."

The drone set off on a trip around the drowned hill. On the main display, the sonar image returned to the tactical map view and Katya could see the drone was making for a location on the far side of the feature marked *Aux. Lock*. The *Vodyanoi* followed slowly, crabbing around the waters above the hillside on its lateral impellers. The drone reached *Aux.Lock* long before the submarine did, and was already building a sonar model of the location by the time the *Vodyanoi* was in position five hundred metres behind it.

In contrast to the image of the main locks, this one was clean and well-defined. "No damage, sir," said the sensors officer, stating the obvious. "The Feds never found this."

"But," said Kane, "it's only an auxiliary lock. Too small for us." He glanced at Katya and seemed to read her thoughts. "Yes, a minisub like the *Lukyan* could make it, but there's no power on the lock doors. Is she fitted with an external bus arm at the moment?"

Minisubs were the multirole vessels of Russalka's seas, capable of most jobs, but only if they were fitted for them.

"No," said Katya. "It's all been cargo work recently. She has the lighting array and one small manipulator arm on her at the moment, mainly because there's nowhere else to store the array, and the arm's a bastard to remove. No power gear, though."

"Don't suppose we've got one in stores, have we, Number One?" Kane asked his first officer.

She took a moment to pull up a list of inventory, but from the way her head started shaking before she was halfway through searching, she was already sure of the answer. "No, sir. I don't think we've ever carried one compatible with a minisub. We have a man-portable unit, but it won't have any of the automatic locking mechanisms a sub's would. It wouldn't work, even mounted on a manipulator."

"Right," said Kane. Apparently the answer came as no surprise to him, and he had already moved onto a new plan. "Nothing for it. Prep four ADS units, please."

"With MMUs, sir?"

"Gods, yes. I wasn't planning on walking. And break that power unit out of stores. I don't fancy manually pumping the airlock dry, either."

"Understood. Who's going, captain?"

"Me, obviously, because I love risking my life. Ms Kuriakova here, also obviously, as she's the one this is all being done for."

"What? Me?" Katya looked at him as if he'd just ordered her shot.

"Well, yes, you. Why do you…"

"No. I mean, an ADS? Me? You want me to go outside?"

"Yes. You in an ADS. You could try swimming over there in your underwear, I suppose, but I wouldn't rate your chances of making it."

Katya was not in the mood for jokes; as far as she could see, sending her out in an atmospheric diving suit – an ADS – was tantamount to a death sentence anyway. "I... I can't," she stammered. "I'm not rated. No training. I'm not certified."

Kane frowned. "Russalkin hydrophobia rears its ugly head again. I have to say, Katya, I'm surprised. After the things you've done, I really didn't expect a drop of water to bother you unduly."

"A drop... A *drop* of water? It's Russalka, Kane! It's the whole planet! The whole thing wants to kill us every day! Every single day! And you want to go for a stroll out there?"

"Heavens, no. That's why I've asked for manned-manoeuvre units to be prepared, too. We're going over there in style, like merpeople. Big, scary, jet-propelled armoured merpeople." A thought occurred to him, and he smiled suddenly, "Like real Russalki and Vodyanois!" He noted this did not modify her attitude in the slightest, and the smile wavered. "Little cultural reference there. Thought you might have appreciated it, but never mind."

"Ms Kuriakova." The First Officer, Ocello, had risen from her chair and joined them. "You don't need to operate your MMU. We can control it remotely from here. You saw how good Mr Sahlberg is with a drone – you would be in very safe hands."

Sahlberg turned at the mention of his name, and managed a nod that was both modest and reassuring.

In truth, Katya *was* beginning to feel reassured about the whole endeavour. She would be placing her life in the hands of the *Vodyanoi*'s crew, but they were very probably the best and most experienced crew on Russalka. They'd fought for Terra against Russalka, and then spent the next ten years successfully running and hiding from a concerted Federal hunt. Yes, they'd had Yagizban help, but that was still a very long way short of invulnerability when a pack of FMA shipping protection vessels were hot on your trail.

Katya took a deep breath. "OK. OK. Just... don't get me killed."

"There," said Kane encouragingly. "That's the can-do, two-fisted, afraid-of-nothing Katya I know. Very nearly."

Katya ignored the snipe, however well meant it was, and said, "Who's going in the other two suits?"

"Me," said Tasya.

"No," said Kane. "Not you."

"What do you mean, Kane?" she said, her tone dangerously calm. "That is a Yagizban facility. I have more right than anyone else on this boat to go there."

"That is as maybe, Tasya. I'm just... Forgive me, Tasya, but I'm worried that you may lose your temper when you're actually in there, when you see what's over there. You're dangerous enough when you're calm. I don't want to have to deal with you if you lose control."

Katya noticed that even Tasya's lips had paled. Her anger was almost palpable, warded behind walls of iron self-control though it was. "I lose control when and only when I want to lose control," she said. "When and only when I believe it would be tactically wise."

Kane looked up at her from the captain's seat. He regarded her in silence for a moment, as if weighing her words carefully. "Very well, Tasya, I'll take your word on that. If you let me down, if you put us into even the shadow of danger because you let your temper slip, I shall kill you."

They locked eyes for a few seconds, and it was Tasya who broke contact first with a careless nod of acceptance. Apparently death threats were an everyday occurrence for the She-Devil.

"As for the fourth member of our merry band, Mr…" he nodded to Sergei. "I'm sorry, I've entirely forgotten your name."

"I'm not going," said Sergei without hesitation.

"An ADS is just like a mini-minisub," said Katya, who was beginning to look forward to the experience despite her earlier misgivings. "You'll be fine."

"It's not safe," said Sergei, and Katya noticed he looked at Tasya when he said it. So that was it. Katya tried to look for an argument that might sway him into going on an expedition mounted by pirates and featuring a feared war criminal, but couldn't think of anything at all.

"It's OK, Sergei. You don't have to go if you don't want to."

"I'm not scared. I just don't see the point."

But he was scared. *Poor Sergei*, she thought. *If it was my choice, you wouldn't be in this situation at all.* "You're right. There's no point us both going."

Kane had watched the conversation between them and the look in his eye when he momentarily caught hers told her he understood exactly what was going on. "Ms Ocello, please assign Mr Giroux to the fourth suit. We may have need of his muscle."

As Ocello returned to her seat, Kane said to Katya, "ADS EVAs are fun." He saw her blink and added, "EVA, extra-vehicular activity. Sorry, that's more space jargon than anything. From my brief time as a cosmonaut." His half smile became bleak. "Make the most of the EVA. What we find at the other end won't be fun at all."

SEVEN
RED WATER

As a child Katya had been fascinated by a drama series
in which secret Federal agents had special atmospheric
diving suits that also amplified their strength, carried
weapons, and – in one episode – flew just long enough to
save the day. She and her friends had run up and down
the corridors in the residential section, imitating the
sound of sonar pings and launching "minitorps" at one
another. Andrei Ivanovich always said his imaginary ADS
was the one that could fly and, furthermore, it was the
only one that could fly, and he defended its uniqueness
with cuffs and shoves to any who would attempt flight
in theirs. But then, Andrei Ivanovich was a bully and a
bastard.

The reality was scarier than Andrei Ivanovich could
ever have aspired to.

The best place from which they might be deployed was
undeniably the *Vodyanoi*'s salvage maw; it was relatively
spacious and when the jaws were open wide they would
give plenty of clearance for the suits to reach the water.

The minor problem of the maw currently being occupied by the *Lukyan* was easily solved – Sergei would pilot it out, the maw would be closed and emptied, and the suits taken in ready for the expedition members. Sergei was very happy at this part of the plan, at least until Kane put a Vodyanoi aboard the *Lukyan* "just so I have another pair of eyes on the site." Perhaps he was telling the truth, but Sergei clearly understood the gesture to mean Kane wanted a "pair of eyes" specifically upon Sergei.

Fifteen minutes after the *Lukyan* had left the boat, Katya was called to the salvage maw. The floor and walls were still wet from the recent departure, but her attention was entirely focused upon the four looming forms that now stood there in a T formation, the crossbar closest to the aft bulkhead, to provide each with as much space around as possible in the maw's tapering beak.

Each atmospheric diving suit was, as Katya had told Sergei, essentially a submarine in itself. Unlike a normal diving suit, these were rigid, machine-like forms that maintained a normal atmosphere for their operator. There would be no need for specialised breathing mixtures, compression and decompression schedules, or hyperbaric chambers with these. The foreboding robotic appearance of the suits, their arms extended as if about to clutch at anyone who walked in front of them, was intensified by the MMU units that swathed them from the waist downwards. These Manned Manoeuvring Units locked entirely around the suits' legs, making them look like half statues of robot gods rising from metal plinths. Each suit had a small stepladder by it, and a dedicated technician who stood silently by like an acolyte to the metal divinities.

Kane, Katya, Tasya, and Giroux were met by the ship's doctor who gave each one of them a quick check-up as they waited in coveralls.

"Nothing to worry about, Ms Kuriakova," said the doctor as he checked her pulse. "Your heart rate is a little elevated. Would you like a mild sedative? Just something to calm your nerves?"

Katya shook her head. "Thanks, but no. I'd like to stay a bit nervous."

As the doctor worked down the line, the technicians were up on the stepladders, opening the suits. The heavy helmets fell forward as the suit backs were unlocked and lifted, giving the impression that the suits had suddenly fallen asleep. Most of the diagnostics had been completed before the expedition members had even arrived, and the techs quickly ran through the remainder. Katya caught a glimpse of the pad the technician for her suit was carrying, and was relieved at the sight of an orderly list of green ticks down the checklist.

Finally, all was ready, and Katya and the others stepped forward.

Kane almost scampered up his suit's ladder. "I love this part," he said as he grabbed the handles at the top of the entry port in the suit's back, lifted his legs and slid in. "It makes me think of knights from the olden days, armouring up before a battle."

Katya was less enthusiastic about the experience, but nevertheless found getting into the suit far easier than she'd expected. Her suit's technician had measured her height and the lengths of her arms and legs earlier and adjusted the suit's internal braces so that they would receive her comfortably. He certainly seemed to know his job; the suit fitted her like a glove. She allowed her arms to slide into the suit's arms as the small of her back rode over the lower edge of the access port and, by the time she was fully in and upright, her hands were inside the suit's gauntlets.

A Knight of the Deep, she thought. *Well, at least now I look the part.*

"How's it feel?" asked her technician as he checked her cap, a close-fitting cloth skullcap that had her communications microphone and earphones attached. Unlike a simple headset it could not accidentally fall off, an important point inside a helmet.

"Snug," said Katya.

"Snug *tight*, or snug *comfortable*?"

"Comfortable, thanks."

"Good to hear. OK, the next stage is the helmet. Then I'll seal the suit and you'll be on your own oxygen from thereon. Understand?"

Katya tried to give a thumbs up, but the gesture was barely noticeable when translated into a small twitch of the heavy articulated gauntlet. She nodded a little instead and said, "Understood."

The technician reached forward and pulled the helmet back into its upright position, locking it against the head support. As he did, it encased Katya's head, the sound of the locking mechanism engaging seeming very final.

It was as if Katya was suddenly severed from the real world. Outside sounds became distant and muffled, and her breathing became very loud in the confines of the helmet. She swallowed and concentrated on not panicking, about just living in the moment and not thinking about what all this foreshadowed, that soon the technicians and the doctor would leave, that the hatches would seal.

That the sea would enter.

Katya swallowed again.

Then, she heard the technician speaking to her through the still-open back of the suit. His voice was shockingly close given the sense of isolation the helmet had created, close and warm, humanly intimate. "Everybody feels a bit strange their first time in a suit," he murmured. "Just remember, the type you're wearing is the top of the line. Its test depth is twice what you'll be experiencing. This will be nothing to it. You'll be out there with three others who have all done this kind of thing before, you've got the best drone pilot in the water steering you, and you have two boats watching your every move." He let that sink in for a moment. "How are you feeling, Ms Kuriakova?"

Katya closed her eyes, steadied herself, and when she re-opened them the panic had been put away somewhere inside where it could do her no harm. "Call me Katya," she said. "And I'm fine. Thank you."

"My pleasure. I'm Mike. I'll close the suit now, carry out the last checks, and then you're off on your daytrip. See you when you get back, Katya."

Katya smiled despite herself. "See you, Mike."

She felt the suit cover slam shut, heard the locks click, and yet she kept the sense of isolation, of abandonment away this time. There were eight other people in the maw, she told herself, three of them experiencing exactly what she was experiencing. All these people watching out for her, and with the experience and equipment to step in immediately if anything went wrong. But nothing was going to go wrong, because these experienced people knew what they were doing. She visualised her suit's checklist again, saw the happy column of smiling, encouraging green check marks. All systems go. She nodded slightly. The trip was going to be easy.

And, typically for her, as the spectre of the short journey through the ocean abated, she began to think about what they might find at the other end.

She'd seen dead bodies before, but never bodies that had been in the water for any length of time. She heard the stories, of course; corpses floating in water cloudy with their own putrefaction, bloated, grotesque, the eyes gone. She admitted to herself that it was a frightening prospect, but it did not fill her with the irrational fear the suit had at first. Rather, it was a muted revulsion, something she knew she would hate, but that must be endured.

OK, Kane, she said to herself, *I'll face your horror show, and I will loathe you for making me face it. And afterwards, my answer will still be "No."*

The checks on the suit seals were rapid, yet thorough. One by one, the technicians rapped on the helmets of their divers to indicate that they were ready to go. Mike made a point of standing in Katya's eye line and giving her a double thumbs up. She made the effort to bring both arms up slightly and waggled the thumbs enough to be noticeable. Mike saw them, laughed, nodded to her, and slapped her suit on the arm as he walked by to pick up the step ladder and his gear. A few moments later, she heard the bulkhead door slam, and the four of them were left alone in the salvage maw.

"Comms check," said a voice in her headset. Katya recognised Ocello. "Captain, are you reading me?"

"Loud and clear, thank you." Kane sounded blithe, as if he was about to do nothing more enterprising than read a book.

"Ms Kuriakova? Do you read me?"

"Very clear. Please, call me Katya. It's quicker."

"As you wish, Katya. Colonel?"

"Loud and clear," said Tasya. She sounded impatient. She only seemed to have two modes, though, thought Katya. Impatient tending towards violent, and languid tending towards pleasant (with occasional outbreaks of violence). Once Katya had heard Kane refer to Tasya as having a "feline temperament," but Katya had no idea what that meant. She'd remembered the word and looked it up later, but it had been of little help – "Belonging to the cat family or pertaining to cats, catlike." A "cat" was some sort of Earth animal. She tried to imagine what one might look like from the description; quadruped, clawed, furred. Every animal she'd ever seen had been be-finned, be-tentacled, be-pincered or, on one memorable creature, all three. Her imagination couldn't manage "fur," never mind the other aspects.

While she'd been distracting herself thinking about the fauna of Earth, Giroux had also completed his communications check, and the bridge stood by to commence the EVA, as Kane had called it.

The water did not burst in upon them, but rose smoothly and rapidly as the salvage maw was flooded. She could just see the base of Kane's MMU, a tapering angular column covered in inlets and impeller nozzles, all painted in a pale anti-fouling green paint unlike the yellow and black of the suits themselves. The *Lukyan* was painted in yellow and black, too, she realised, and it somehow made the suits seem a lot friendlier.

The water level climbed up to the grating on which they stood, and then further, rising up the sides of Kane's MMU. Katya knew that it must be doing the same on hers, but she was completely unaware of it. There was no sense of pressure or coldness. Intellectually, she had appreciated that the description of the rigidly armoured suits with their wedge ring segmented joints as "personal submarines" was about right, but part of her had still feared the water being so close. That she couldn't feel a thing through the suit made the idea concrete though, allowing her to screw down the lid on her anxiety so much tighter. She no longer just felt calm about it; now she began to feel confident.

The water rose and rose. Even when it burbled up past her helmet's visor, she felt relaxed. She'd been in the *Lukyan* when it had been in a dry dock, just prior to being refloated. She'd watched the water rise past the canopy then with pleasure simply to be watching such a novelty. She felt just the same now.

"Maw's fully flooded," said Ocello. "Adjust for neutral buoyancy. Sahlberg will do that for you, Katya."

The MMU's flotation tanks had been fully filled by the technicians to prevent the suits bobbing around like so much flotsam when the maw was flooded. Now the tanks were partially emptied with compressed air until the average density of the MMUs, the suits, and the suits' contents equalled that of the sea water.

"Neutral," called Giroux, closely followed by the others.

"Looking good across all units," confirmed Ocello. "Opening the jaws now."

Katya looked up and saw the two seams running along the ceiling slowly start to widen. As they separated, she could see nothing beyond but darkness. That was the sea, the naked, angry sea of Russalka. She would not be frightened, she swore to herself. She would not let herself down. She imagined Lukyan watching her, and she determined to make him proud.

The *Vodyanoi*'s jaws reached their furthest extreme, leaving the four suits floating in the void between them.

"Right," said Kane. "Here we go. Single file. Follow me."

The murk illuminated in her suit's lights suddenly stirred violently as Kane triggered his manoeuvre unit's impellers and then he was moving smoothly away from her. On her helmet's head-up display, a small navigational caret glowed, showing her their destination.

"This is Sahlberg. Here we go, Katya." She felt the vibration of her own MMU's impellers coming to life and, almost instantly, she was moving steadily forward through the water. She watched the jaws taper away over her head before they vanished altogether from view. She was clear of the maw, now. In the open sea. And she felt... She barely had to examine her feelings.

She felt great. The fear had been for nothing. She felt safe, she felt protected, she felt excited for the adventure of it all. She was surrounded by the world ocean on every side, no part of her skin more than a few centimetres from the great deadly, terrifying, wonderful waters, and she felt suddenly so ecstatically good she could almost have wept for joy.

She had always loved her world, but it had been a love for the Russalkin civilisation, its spirit, and its courage, even its more human flaws. Now, though... now she felt love for the world itself, the great glorious grey orb floating in space, the majesty of the waters, the elemental fury of its skies somewhere far above them.

"It's beautiful," she said under her breath.

"It is," replied Kane, startling her. The microphone pick-ups were much more acute than she'd expected.

"What are you talking about?" said Tasya, somewhere behind them. "You can't see anything but plankton."

"Even plankton has its charms," said Kane mildly. It was a comment designed to shut Tasya up, which it did. Katya smiled and said nothing more. She knew what she had meant, and she knew Kane did too.

The column travelled onwards in silence for a few minutes. When Katya and her friends had been playing at being ADS-equipped super agents, they'd run around with their heads down, mimicking the torpedo-like movement of the agents' suits in the drama. This was very different. They travelled almost upright, but for a very slight forward lean. They were presenting a lot of surface area, and the drag was terrific, but if they had been travelling head first, they wouldn't have been able to see a thing through the opaque helmet tops. As in so many things, fiction was more exciting that the sensible reality.

"I can see the lock," said Kane suddenly. He slowed and, a moment later, Katya felt Sahlberg gently slacking off her own manoeuvre unit's motors too. She had considered asking for a minute of two of manual operation, just to see what steering the suit was like. The time didn't seem right, however. Perhaps she'd ask on the way back.

Out of the gloom, detail started to build around the navigation lights on Kane's suit as Katya grew closer. "Sahlberg, use Katya's suit as a drone and relay pictures of the lock. Let's see what we're dealing with here. Sorry, Katya. Needs must."

"That's OK," she replied. "I want to see the lock anyway." Sahlberg took her in past where Kane hung almost motionless, and switched up her lights to full intensity. Out of the darkness, she could make out an artificially exact and level overhang, the top edge of the airlock's surround. She descended slightly as she advanced, slowly gliding beneath it.

"I see it," she said. "Looks untouched."

"Good," said Kane. "Anything you can add to that, sensors?"

"I'm looking at an enhanced image here, captain," reported Sahlberg. "And it seems fine here too. You should be able to get in once the lock's powered up."

"Understood. Move Katya out to the side, please, but keep her lights on the access panel. Giroux, you're on."

The impellers hummed and Katya was carried gracefully backwards to halt a couple of metres away from the lock, her lights focused exactly on the panel beside the auxiliary airlock. She had to admit, Sahlberg had an extraordinarily sure touch on the controls. Every move he made with the suit felt as natural as walking.

Giroux was just as competent at his job. He swept by her, decelerating as he approached the panel and coming to a full stop by grabbing the panel cover. The cover, intended to prevent marine life taking up residence in the power sockets and manual crank mechanism rather than keeping water out, opened easily. Giroux unclipped the power unit from the side of his MMU and mounted it on the hook provided by the socket for exactly that reason. He unrolled half a metre of cable, pushed the plug home and twisted it. In that one simple move, the water was expelled from within the hermetic seal between plug and socket, and the power unit was activated. They all saw the panel's lights glow, but Giroux reported "Power unit placed and active" all the same. "Cycling the airlock now."

As they watched the lock's outer doors slide open, Katya found her mind wandering onto what was on the other side of the airlock. She knew it wouldn't be pretty, but that was war. Precious little glory, but plenty of hardship, and fear, and horror. The Yags had placed a spy base close by Federal shipping lanes, hidden in Red Water. The Feds had detected it and wrecked the place, probably killing everybody inside. She couldn't blame the Yags for building the place, she couldn't blame the Feds for destroying it. It was an ugly incident, but wartime is made up of ugly incidents. Once again, she wondered what Kane hoped to gain by bringing her here.

"The lock was already flooded," said Kane. "Interesting."

Katya understood him to mean that whoever had last used the lock had been exiting the base. Had somebody escaped?

The interior of the lock was large enough to accept a minisub, so they had no trouble manoeuvring in and setting down on the concrete floor, Giroux starting the pump cycle before joining them. As Katya watched the water level drop past the front of her visor, she realised that she was feeling tense again. She didn't want to leave her suit in this strange, forbidding place, but she had no choice; out of the water and even with the MMUs detached, the suits were too heavy to walk around in for long. From a symbol of a potentially dangerous journey through the waters, her suit had become one of security. She was very sorry to see the water level reach floor level, and to hear Kane order them to emerge from their armour.

In her case, she had no idea how to open the ADS from within and had to wait for Giroux to help her. With the back panel open and the helmet forward, she was just wondering how to climb out when she felt his hands under her armpits and she was effortlessly lifted out. As he put her down, she could see Tasya managing it for herself, drawing her arms from the sleeves, gripping the shoulders and pulling herself up to sit on the lower edge of the open back of the suit. It was just as well that the MMUs were so heavy, anchoring the suit upright while their occupants wriggled out.

The lock stank of sea water, and the pump gullies were still awash with it as the last few dozen litres were drained. Katya's feet came down with a splash in a puddle left on the concrete. She looked at the closed outer doors and noticed a small trickle of water running down between them. "That seal's not perfect."

"It's an auxiliary lock. Was probably only checked once a month at best," said Tasya. "Or maybe a pressure wave from the Federal attack damaged it. We can expect much worse inside." She had recovered her watertight equipment bag from its stowage within the MMU and was clipping on a webbing harness. Katya noticed it came with a holstered maser.

"Is that necessary?" she asked as she shrugged into her own harness, switching on the shoulder mounted light.

Tasya drew the maser, checked it and returned it to its holster. "I don't know. Let's find out." She went to the inner door controls and pressed the "open" button.

EIGHT
DEAD WATER

The inner doors opened inwards into the body of the airlock, a common trait in locks that were expected to be used with less frequency. If the outer door were to leak water in, the mounting pressure would just close the inner doors all the more firmly. The logic for them was plain enough, but watching the two heavy steel doors swing inwards towards them made a small shudder travel across her shoulders. Katya didn't believe in ghosts, a stupid Earth superstition if ever she'd heard one.

At least, she didn't *usually* believe in ghosts.

But this was a place of the dead, and the doors gliding open like those of a crypt from a Grubber story did not help her nerves.

Katya drew a slow breath through her nose, half expecting to smell rotting flesh, but there was nothing, nothing but the scent of the sea and damp concrete. Irrationally, she started to wish she was armed, too. She had noticed that, like Tasya, Giroux was carrying a sidearm. Predictably, Kane was not.

Kane fished in his equipment bag and produced a translucent ball perhaps fifteen centimetres in diameter. "Here's a pretty gadget from Earth," he said, held the ball out in one hand and clicked a small device he had mounted on his harness with the other. Instantly the ball started to glow fiercely, rose from his hand and travelled forward three or four metres just above head height. It flew through the open doorway and hovered there, as if waiting for them to catch up.

"Not even military issue on Earth," he said. "I picked it up from a camping supplies vendor." Without pausing to explain what "camping" was, he walked forward, and the orb flew ahead, always maintaining the same distance from him and lighting the way. The others fell in behind him. Tasya was right behind Kane; she looked as cool and calm as she always did, but Katya noticed her unconsciously slip her holster's retention band off the maser's frame, freeing it for a fast draw. That a killer like Tasya found the facility unnerving did little for Katya's state of mind.

They made their way slowly up a slight slope in the broad, dark corridor. The construction was of the lowest practical finish, and the speed with which the place had been built was evident in every economy. The corridor was wide and the walls were concave, caused by two overlapping fusion bores being used to cut it through the rock of the mountain. The floor had been levelled, filled with some black synthetic, but the walls and ceiling were bare stone. Over their heads cables ran in bundles, crudely stapled to the rock at frequent intervals by large steel "U" pins. Equally crude was the corridor lighting, consisting of utility lamps not even attached to the rock but simply hung from the underside of each staple and wired into a power cable in the bundle. With the base's power off, the lamps hung dark and useless.

Ahead of them the corridor was blocked by a bulkhead that filled the six metre wide corridor, secured around its edge by more of the black synthetic used for the floor. In the middle of the bulkhead was a metre wide manual door, looking strange and out of proportion in the middle of the large bulkhead. It stood open, swung towards them on its hinges.

Katya coughed and everybody looked at her, startled. Kane noticed Tasya's hand had fallen onto her pistol, and said. "I think we all need to take a moment. This facility is dead. We have no reason to think anyone but us is alive here. Not a nice thought, but nor is it a threatening one in the most realistic sense. Let us not have any... accidents, hmm?" Out of the corner of her eye, Katya saw Tasya thumb the retention band back into position and drop her hand away from the weapon. Katya thought this was probably the closest that the Chertovka would ever come to expressing shame.

Kane played around with the light globe's control until he induced it to fly through the open hatch. It was fascinating to watch the device, which flew easily and quickly yet never let itself get closer than twenty or thirty centimetres to any surface. It clearly contained a contragravitic drive, but anything so small was unknown on Russalka. That it wasn't even new technology to the Terrans was unsettling.

They followed Kane through the hatch and found themselves on a level section of corridor. It seemed likely that the previous section had been intended as a safety buffer between the auxiliary lock and the main body of the base, as subsidiary corridors were now visible branching off the main one.

"Mr Giroux," said Kane. "Scout on ahead, will you, please? Find the next main bulkhead, but don't go beyond it. Call in when you get there, yes?"

"Yes, captain," said Giroux and went ahead in a dogtrot.

Katya had glanced at her own communications unit when Kane had mentioned Giroux calling in and noticed the display had changed. "Kane. I've got a problem with my gear. I'm not picking up the *Vodyanoi*'s channel anymore."

"Really? Let me see."

"None of us are," said Tasya. "Not this side of the airlock, I'd say. This facility must be EM secure. It *was* supposed to be hidden, after all."

"Ah," said Kane. "That is a nuisance."

"EM?" said Katya. "Electromagnetic?"

"The whole base is effectively inside a giant Faraday cage," explained Kane. "No electromagnetic radiation gets in or out. It's to hide the place from sensors. There'll be a comms relay outside the cage that's hardwired to the command centre by cable. We don't have that luxury."

"So... there's no way we can talk to the *Vodyanoi* or the *Lukyan*?"

"None." He brightened. "Still, we shouldn't need to. We'll just see what we need to see, and then leave."

"And what exactly is that? Why can't you just tell me?"

"You wouldn't believe me." Katya started to say something snide, but he stopped her. "And... even if you did, it's not enough that you believe me. It's not enough. You have to *know*. Know it first-hand. Know it for yourself so there's no denial." He looked around, searching. "No denial," he repeated to himself. Then, "This way."

"Why?" asked Katya, curious despite her desire to stay cold to Kane and his plans. "What's this way?"

"I don't know. But, whatever it is, it will probably be as good as anywhere else." He walked on, unaware of the look Katya was giving him.

"That doesn't work," said Tasya, amused. "Believe me, if looks could kill, Kane would have been fish bait years ago."

They followed him down one of the spur corridors, the glow of the light orb turning him into a walking shadow ahead of them. Katya kept looking around, trying to glimpse just what was so astounding that she had to see it with her own eyes. It was hard to believe it was the spy base itself; it was competently built for all the obvious haste, but otherwise entirely unremarkable. She had once been in an abandoned mining site and it had looked a little like this. The one thing that seemed odd was that it was so large. The phrase "spy base" had put images in her mind of some small stealthy facility tucked into a cleft in a mountainside, just large enough to serve a small sub crew in their work of sneaking around and monitoring Federal transmissions, and watching traffic from the edge of the Red Water. This place was an altogether larger proposition. They hadn't even seen the living quarters yet, just a medical section and… She looked up at a sign stencilled onto the rock and stopped.

"Hold on," she said. "We're walking in a circle. This is the way to the medical section, but that was on the other side of the main corridor."

Kane came to a halt. "Perhaps there is more than one medical section." His voice was neutral and the flying globe kept him limned with light, reducing him to a silhouette, yet Katya caught something hidden in the comment.

"Why would a spy base have more than one medical section?" she demanded. "Hell, why does it even have one? All they'd need would be a sick bay. What were they doing here, Kane?"

But Kane wasn't listening. He had moved to the wall and was examining it. Even in the oblique light cast by the orb, Katya could see there were windows set into the wall and, a little beyond, a door. For the first time she realised that every doorframe she'd seen had been sealed into its surround, every door had been waterproof.

Usually doors within the areas between bulkheads were conventional, both for reasons of economy and convenience. If something terrible happened and a section flooded, the bulkheads would contain the water within that section, but the doors of the rooms in the section would not stop the water for a second.

Yet this place was heavily compartmentalised. Why the paranoia?

Kane had unclipped his personal torch from his harness and was angling it, trying to look through the window. As Katya and Tasya approached, he suddenly stepped back from the glass as if startled.

"This is a mistake," he said quickly, the words tumbling over one another. "I made a mistake bringing you here. I... I... There'll be somewhere else here. Somewhere else for you to see. Not here, though. I never anticipated... We must go back."

"What have you found?" said Tasya.

"It's flooded in there. You can't see anything. We'll go back to the main corridor."

"You're a miserable liar, Havilland," said Tasya. She sounded like somebody getting ready to lose her temper. "What's in there?"

"Please, Tasya, I'm begging you. Don't look."

And he *was* begging her. Not on his knees, but plucking miserably at her arm as she strode past him to squint at the thick armour glass. There was condensation on it and she rubbed angrily at it with her sleeve, before putting her face close to the glass. After a moment, she copied Kane's action in unclipping her torch and shining it close to the surface away from her face to cut down reflection.

Katya looked at Kane, but he barely acknowledged her, backing away from the windows in distress and horror.

"Oh, gods," said Tasya, quietly. She stood, rooted to the spot by what she could see. Then she extinguished her torch and walked to one side. "They knew," she said to Kane. "How could they not know?" She was calm now, an icy calm that scared Katya in ways that a towering rage could never have done. "The operation's cancelled, Kane. Forget it."

"Tasya…"

"Forget it, Kane. It's war. It's just war. Until we're all dead. Just war." Without a second glance, she clipped the torch back on her harness, switched it on, and walked back the way they had come.

"Tasya!" Kane shouted after her. "Think what you're saying! Please! You can't go back to your superiors and tell them to scrub this!" Tasya didn't slow her walk at all, and Kane became angry. "I told you what would happen if you lost your temper! What would happen if you threatened the operation! I warned you!"

She didn't stop. "That you'd kill me? Then perhaps you should have come out with a gun."

His bluff called, Kane was reduced to running after her, calling at her to stop, to think, to talk.

And Katya was left alone, watching the bobbing light of the orb disappear down the corridor.

She looked across the corridor, at the dark windows. She could see the reflection of her own torch in the one directly opposite to her, but nothing else. There couldn't simply be bodies on the other side, she thought. Kane had seen enough death, Tasya had *caused* enough death that it would take much more to make them react like that.

Katya looked down the corridor again. Kane's light had vanished altogether.

She was very aware that she had a decision to make, and that once made it would be irrevocable. If she didn't look through the window, they would soon leave here, probably forever, and she would never again have the opportunity to do so. But, if she *did* look, whatever she saw could never be unseen.

Kane said she needed to know something, something she would find here. If she looked, would it be simple curiosity, or because of a true need to know? It hardly mattered; what had happened here was as much her business as anyone else's. Ignorance might be blissful, but bliss was not something she could look for when lives were being lost all around her.

With an ugly feeling that it wasn't curiosity but rather some awful spiritual masochism that drew her towards the glass, an unsuspected and unwelcome taste for martyrdom, she walked slowly forward, unclipping her torch as she did so.

She hesitated then, a small beat of the passing present when she argued with herself one last time against looking, and lost. She pressed the torch against the glass as she had seen Kane and Tasya do, and looked into the flooded room.

At first she could make out nothing at all, the plankton and debris in the water close to the glass being the first thing she focused upon. With an effort, she looked beyond it, trying to make out what was so terrible in the room. It had been shocking enough to make Tasya blanch, which had led Katya to expect something obviously horrifying, but she could make out very little.

The room was painted in white, or at least some pale colour, and she could just see another door in the far wall. Unlike the door to her right, this one hung open. Having so many waterproof doors probably proved counterproductive, she thought. All that whirling the locking wheel one way, heaving the door open, climbing through, slamming it shut, whirling the wheel to relock the door into its frame – people were just people and that sort of irritating routine was exactly the first kind of thing that people got sloppy about. Before long they'd be leaving doors open because "I'll be going back in a minute" and that would become "I'll be going back in ten minutes" or an hour and, before long, people were forgetting to close them at all. When the Feds attacked and the base was inundated with water, probably half the doors were standing open.

There didn't seem to be any obvious clues what the room was for, however. There were a few boxes or metal frames of some sort lying around, maybe as many as twenty. There was a lot of debris floating in the small trapped pockets of air that still existed in the deep ridges that some builder had cut with a fusion torch while squaring the curved sides of the room off in an attempt to make it more room-like, but whatever it was floating up there was hard to make out. Some sheets of material mixed in, perhaps, but the rest was just irregular forms. No bodies, she was relieved to see, or at least none within visible range.

And yet... part of her was telling her to move away, to rejoin the others. That small voice telling her to go, a voice cracking with horror, as if she was looking but not seeing, as if she was refusing to comprehend.

She wished for a long time afterwards that she had obeyed the small voice rather than concentrating harder on what lay beyond the glass. She wished that she had obeyed her instinct and not focused her intellect.

Katya angled her torch's beam down to illuminate directly under the window, where several of the boxes she had noticed had been swept into an untidy pile by the flood water. The most mundane everyday object can be rendered exotic and unusual by placing it in a different context. The boxes, or crates, or frames or whatever they were seemed dull and inconsequential precisely because she had recognised them as soon as she had seen them, and the feeling associated with that stimulus was disinterest. Now she looked at them again, however, she consciously recognised them, and then the ramifications of their presence, and the identity of the room.

Her mouth fell open. She wanted to cry out, but pure horror froze the sound in her throat. She stepped back away from the glass, her mind filling in every element of what had occurred here in ruthless detail, her imagination acting it all out in sadistic clarity. She thought of the dark shapes floating in the air pockets in the ceiling and knew exactly what they were. It even explained why this room of all the rooms had windows facing out into a dead end corridor. The objects on the floor, twenty or so of them, were not simply boxes, or crates, or steel frames. They were cots.

Katya was looking into a flooded nursery.

••••

She found Kane and Tasya close by the junction with the main corridor. Tasya was standing with crossed arms listening while Kane spoke quietly to her, his nervous hands speaking more loudly than his voice. He turned as Katya approached, took one look at her pallid complexion, and said, "You looked."

"What were children... *babies* doing here, Kane?" she demanded. "Why?" She could feel a sob forming in her throat and choked it down. "*Why?*"

"The obvious reason," answered Tasya. She sounded tired and depressed. "To escape the war."

"This isn't a spy base, Katya," said Kane. "That's a Federal lie. Yet another Federal lie. This was an evacuation site. There was nobody here but those too old, too young, or too injured to fight, and the staff needed to look after them. This facility is... was militarily unimportant."

"The FMA couldn't have known," said Katya. "They *couldn't* have known. They must have found the place and just attacked first."

"Oh, Katya," said Kane sadly. "Even in the middle of an atrocity, you're still looking for some get out, some way of saying this was down to stupidity or incompetence."

Tasya waved her over. "I found this when I came back this way." She walked to the next spur corridor and shone her torch down it. The beam first picked out the wall. There was a ragged row of spots where the rock had melted momentarily, just enough to mark it. Half way along the row was a break and beneath the break – Tasya lowered the beam to light the corridor floor –

lay a corpse. Katya recognised a medic's insignia on the body's sleeve.

"They came in?" said Katya. "They came in? But... they'd have seen..."

"And they did it all the same." Kane was standing in the corridor entrance, his light globe bringing the scene of the murder into full relief. "There was no mistake here, Katya. They destroyed the main entrance and sent troops in through the auxiliary lock to clean up. There is no possible way they thought this was a military facility."

Katya took an unsteady step towards the body. Perhaps – distant, hopeless, vain hope – perhaps they weren't dead. Perhaps some small victory could be wrested from the clinging horror of the place. Tasya gripped her shoulder, stopping her in her tracks. "No!" she snapped. Then more gently, "The body's booby-trapped. There's a thermobaric grenade under it with the pin out." She drew Katya into a crouch to show her. "If you moved the body, the arming spoon would release. I guarantee the fuse has been set to zero seconds."

Katya straightened and backed away. The Feds couldn't even leave the dead in peace. The Feds. *Her* side.

"I don't understand," she said. "I don't understand how this happened. When did we become the bad guys?" The Grubbers, the loathed and loathsome Grubbers had fought a hard war against Russalka, but it had always been to cripple her military. The Grubbers only ever killed non-combatants by accident, as "collateral damage" in the phrase of the news reports. Her side, the great and heroic Federal Maritime Authority, protector of Russalka, champions of her independence, they were the ones who murdered infants, they were the ones who shot unarmed medics in cold blood and then planted traps on the corpses.

Her pride was gone, trampled in blood. She didn't know what she was anymore.

"This was all more... traumatic than I expected, Katya," said Kane. "I'm truly sorry. Even I had no idea the FMA would go so far. We should leave. I think we're done here."

"I'll do what you want," said Katya. Her voice was small, defeated.

Tasya looked away, seeing what they had done to Katya, and felt ashamed once more.

Kane clasped his hands together, and said, "You'll be a traitor, Katya. Once they realise what you've done, they'll hunt you down. They'll probably shoot you on sight."

"A traitor?" Katya laughed, a humourless coughing sound. "They betrayed me first. They betrayed all of us."

"More than you know," said Tasya. She said it as an aside, but Katya was on it in a second.

"What? What do you mean more than I know?"

Kane winced. With a reproving sideways glance at Tasya, he said, "It's... it can wait."

"Don't lie to me, Kane. I am sick of lies. I want to know what she meant."

The ping of an incoming signal from Kane's radio provided an unexpected distraction that he gratefully leapt at. "That'll be Giroux," he said unnecessarily before opening the channel. "Hello, Mr Giroux. We were just wondering what had become of you."

"My torch failed, captain. I'm using a cold light stick, but the illumination's not so good. I've found the next main bulkhead."

"Never mind. From what we've seen, the other side is flooded anyway. We're heading back to the entry lock. How long do you think it will take you to get back?"

"Captain, there are signs of a fire fight up here. I can make out maser hits on the bulkhead and the walls."

"Yes, we've seen them too. How long until you can get back?"

"There's a body here, captain. Civilian clothes. It looks like…"

Kane drew breath to warn Giroux, but never had the chance to utter it. They sensed the detonation through the rock before they heard it, a wave of sensation through their boots as if the mountain itself had felt its flesh creep.

Tasya looked in the direction that Giroux had gone. "That's no grenade…"

Then the shockwave reached them.

NINE
FALLEN ANGELS

There was no sense of intervening time. Katya was standing near Tasya and Kane when Giroux called in. Then she was lying on the ground, Tasya leaning over her and shaking her roughly. "Get up, Kuriakova! Wake up, damn you!"

Katya blinked at her, trying to patch events together and failing. Tasya's harness torch was playing its beam directly in her face, and she only had the vaguest impression of Tasya being behind it. The voice, tone, and the violence of the shaking was all the evidence Katya needed for a positive identification, however.

"What happened?" said Katya, trying to sit up and regretting it as nausea wracked her. "Where's Kane? Giroux?"

"Oh, you found her!" she heard Kane say, answering the first question. Tasya turned as he arrived. Kane held up a handful of pieces of smashed plastic. "The orb didn't ride the blast wave very well," he said ruefully. "I don't suppose the supplier does mail order deliveries at interstellar distances, so no chance of a replacement. Perhaps I can repair it." So saying, he placed the fragments in a belt pouch with the guileless optimism of a young child who believes anything can be fixed.

"Where's Giroux?"

Kane looked surprised. "Oh, you must have taken a knock, Katya. Your short term memory…"

"Giroux's dead," said Tasya bluntly. "He found a body and, like an idiot, searched it. It was booby trapped."

"I remember a body with a grenade under it…" Katya's memories were beginning to sort themselves out although she would never remember the few seconds before the explosion. She remembered the body, the maser marks, and then she remembered the flooded room. She felt cold and finally realised that there was a thin sheen of water on the floor, flowing past them in the direction of the auxiliary lock.

"The one Giroux disturbed must have been a detonator. That explosion sounded more like emplaced charges. The upper bulkhead's been compromised. The sea's getting in." Tasya stood and held out her hand. Katya took it and allowed herself to be drawn to her feet. "We're just lucky those Fed bastards aren't as good at setting charges as they are at killing babies or we'd be sucking water now."

A deep vibration thrummed through the structure, making them all look into the darkness in the direction of the damaged bulkhead. "It's giving way," said Tasya. "*Run!*"

The ingrained Russalkin fear of water was with them in that moment. They turned and ran for the auxiliary lock as they had never run before, Tasya pulling quickly ahead with long, loping strides, Katya following in a hard sprint, and Kane at the rear in an untidy kinetic mass of flailing arms and pumping legs.

They reached the first bulkhead at the head of the slope leading down to the auxiliary lock and stumbled through the small door in the large wall. The water level was already well over the door's lower lintel and beginning to surge as a much greater volume of water entered the flooding section behind them. As soon as Kane was through, Tasya threw herself at the door to try and close it, but the water was on the side the builder's had reasonably concluded was the less likely to be a threat. Now the pressure of water was forcing the door open, not shut, and that pressure was rising.

"Go, go, go!" she shouted at Katya and Kane. "I'll hold it as closed as I can."

Katya hesitated for a moment, but Kane grabbed her arm and pulled her away. They ran down the incline, the water sluicing past their legs. Ahead of them in the dancing beams of their torches, Katya could see the auxiliary lock's doors open before them, fifty metres away, but she could also see the water climbing over the lintel and starting to flood the interior of the airlock. The realisation that simply reaching the lock might not be enough to save their lives chilled her for the moment it took for it to crystallise in her mind. Then she put it aside; there lay panic, and panic would kill them.

She reached the door ten strides ahead of Kane and jumped through. She was on her communicator the second her feet splashed down in the shin-deep water. "Tasya! We're in – come on!"

"Close the doors."

Katya frowned; she had misheard. She must have misheard. "Say again?"

"Close the airlock doors, Kuriakova."

Katya looked uncomprehendingly at Kane. He gave her what was presumably intended as a reassuring nod, and said, "Understood. Closing doors now." Before Katya could stop him, he had reached out and twisted the door controls. With a hum of power, they began to swing shut.

"Kane! What are you doing?"

He smiled a little nervously. "I'm trusting her. You have to remember one thing about Tasya." He turned on the lock's internal lights, then joined Katya where she stood. He pointed through the narrowing gap up the slope of the corridor. "She's a survivor."

Into the glow of the lights, the steady sheen of water abruptly became a wave, a surge that could only mean Tasya had abandoned the door and let the rising water through. And in the middle of that surge, she rode down. Almost standing, almost lying, leaning back into the wave with her legs together and her arms steering her, she shot down the corridor towards the closing doors.

At the very last, she folded her arms across her chest, straightened her legs and made an arrow of her body, an arrow that shot into the airlock, brushing both her shoulders against the steel doors. They slammed shut behind her, a single sardonic clap of applause for the latest exploit of the legendary Chertovka.

"You truly have the luck of the Devil," said Kane casually, as if it was a dull day that only featured one death-defying escape. He set the lock controls to drain away the water that was lapping around their thighs. Katya just gawped.

"I'm soaked," said Tasya, as she rose from the waters. "These coveralls are going to ride up in the ADS, there's nothing more certain. Nothing's ever comfortable in this world."

Kane was leaning into the back of his diving suit and fiddling with the more powerful communications unit in it. "Still no signal. We're going to have to get into the water before we can talk to the boat. Right, Katya first, I think."

The airlock's floor was now only wet, not flooded, and Kane helped her doff her gear and stow it away in the MMU. Then with help from Tasya, he lifted Katya up she could get into the suit once more. As they locked her in, Tasya said, "What about Giroux's suit?"

Katya heard Kane's bitter sigh. "Poor Bruno. Despite all we've seen in this world, he was probably the only Vodyanoi who wouldn't have believed somebody could stoop so low as to booby trap a corpse. We'll seal up his suit and Sahlberg can bring it in under drone control once he's brought in Katya."

"I was looking at the controls on the way in," offered Katya. "I think I could pilot it. Well enough to get back to the *Vodyanoi* anyway."

"It would save some time," said Tasya, with a tone of approval that Katya was slightly embarrassed to realise she enjoyed. Now she cared about the opinion of war criminals, she thought. How much further could she fall? But she was only a war criminal because the Federal authorities said she was; the same people who had planned, sanctioned, and carried out the extermination of a civilian evacuation centre.

At least you knew where you were with the Chertovka. Usually in deep trouble.

They finished sealing Katya into her suit and turned their attention to other matters. While Tasya stored her and Kane's gear – she found the pouch with the fragments of the light orb in and shook her head like a long-suffering mother emptying the pockets of her son's clothes – Kane closed Giroux's suit and assigned its MMU a drone control channel. Then he went to his own suit and tried gamely to clamber in, an action which, without a stepladder, proved challenging to him. Still showing a long-suffering expression, Tasya gave him a boost which he gratefully accepted. As Tasya closed his suit he asked, "How will you get into your suit, Tasya?"

"By being competent," she answered, and Kane shut up after that.

"Pride comes before a fall" was proving to be an idiom with which Tasya had little if any experience. She got into her suit with ridiculous ease, and had it sealed and secure by herself faster than either Katya or Kane had managed with help. She had even had the foresight to "walk" her suit on the corners of the MMU's base so she could reach the airlock controls once she was in it.

"Flooding airlock," she called before pressing the valve controls.

As the water rose, Katya's thoughts were very different to when she had last stood in a filling lock. Now she didn't care about the trip, even if she was going to be piloting her suit this time. She was finding it hard to care about anything at all. Everything seemed to be becoming detached and inconsequential. She had lived her entire life as a citizen under Federal law, and Federal protection. The Federal administration was there to serve the people, to keep them safe, and to maintain services. They were the angels, the guardians, the heroes in advanced AD suits that could fly for a little while, damn them.

Damn them. Damn them.

But, no. They were just little people with too much power who did what little people always do when they have too much power. They abused it, and said it was for the greater good. Perhaps they even believed it. Perhaps when they entered the evacuation site and saw beyond any doubt that it offered no threat to them, they ordered the survivors massacred and traps placed because they honestly thought it was a necessary evil.

But, doesn't every evil seem necessary at the time?

Katya didn't want to think anymore. She just wanted to sleep for the rest of her life, or at least until some morning came that was like the mornings before the war, before the chaos. Before Kane.

"Opening the lock." Tasya's voice coming through her cap's earpieces startled Katya momentarily. The outer doors moved ponderously aside and, as they did so, their communication units re-established contact with the *Vodyanoi*.

Katya looked at the channel acquisition alert projected on her helmet's head-up display with confusion. The channel allocated to the *Lukyan* showed blank.

"Captain!" Ocello's relieved voice sounded through all their suits. "I was just putting together a search party to go after you."

"Hello, Genevra," said Kane, blithely using her first name and breaking the *Vodyanoi*'s paramilitary disciplinary protocols at the same time, a privilege of rank. "No, the communications blackout was simply because the facility is shielded."

"We were concerned…"

"I know, I know. It hasn't all been clear sailing, though. I regret to say we've lost Bruno."

There was a beat of silence. "How?" said Ocello, her previous excitement gone.

"The Federals mined the place. I'll brief you when we get back. Please tell Mr Sahlberg to bring in Bruno's suit on drone channel Epsilon. Ms Kuriakova will pilot herself back."

"Kane?" said Katya.

Kane continued to speak to the *Vodyanoi*, but his next question showed he knew exactly what was on Katya's mind. "Speaking of Ms Kuriakova, I suspect she's feeling a little anxious that we're not picking up her boat's comms channel. What's the *Lukyan*'s status, please?"

"Sir," said Ocello, "I regret to say that we've lost contact with the *Lukyan*. We picked up some noise on the comms channel, sounded like shouting. Then she went silent, and headed away at best speed."

"Didn't you go after her?" demanded Katya, her impatience making her cut in.

"We couldn't, Ms Kuriakova. Our orders were to stay on station in case you needed us."

"Don't worry," said Kane. He seemed to be reaching for a sympathetic and encouraging tone, but he just sounded tired. "It will just be something silly. We'll get back to the boat and then we'll look for the *Lukyan*. *Vodyanoi*, we're coming over now. Let us get clear and then bring in Mr Giroux's suit last, please."

"Going to neutral buoyancy," reported Tasya. Katya put her worries about Sergei and the *Lukyan* to one side for a moment, and adjusted her suit's buoyancy. The controls were simple and unambiguous, the MMU's computer doing all the physics for her. She simply set the suit's desired buoyancy level, and the MMU emptied its ballast tanks to exactly the right level to comply.

Tasya was first out of the lock, heading off into the gloom directly for the glowing marker on her HUD that told her the location and orientation of the *Vodyanoi's* waiting salvage maw. Katya found the MMU controls mounted high on the "podium" front of the MMU at stomach height. The left control was a simple throttle, the right a twistable force stick. She had piloted utility pods to get her crew licence, and a pod's simple controls were almost identical to this.

"It's pretty straightforward, Katya," said Kane. "The right hand control…"

Without answering, Katya gently opened the throttle, directed the manoeuvre jets with the force stick, and lifted her suit from the airlock floor. She moved out into the ocean with as much grace and assurance as Tasya had before her, and set course for the *Vodyanoi*.

"Oh," said Kane, doing a poor job of hiding his surprise. "Well... I'm sure you'll pick it up... as you go along." A few seconds later, he announced that he, too, was seaborne.

"This is sensors," called Sahlberg. "I'm bringing in the fourth suit now."

Not "Giroux's suit," Katya noticed. There would be quiet commemorations for Bruno Giroux among the Vodyanois soon enough, but right now his fate was not something they could focus upon.

In silence, three survivors and a dead man's suit were coming home.

The recording didn't tell them anything at all. There was an incoherent shout which didn't sound like Sergei, then a cry that might have been him, some tumbled ambient sound of a microphone being buffeted and then the transmission cut off. Since their return, Katya had listened to it through headphones five times, her eyes shut, trying to imagine what had occurred aboard the *Lukyan*. Nothing would form in her imagination that might explain it.

It *sounded* like a fight, but Sergei wasn't the kind of man who looked for fights. Yes, he was surly, sarcastic, and opinionated, but on the occasions he had pushed someone too far, he'd backed down and apologised before it came to blows. At first she'd thought he did that just because he didn't see the point of taking some bruises for the sake of a smart comment. More recently, however, now she was spending more time with him, with Uncle Lukyan dead and the war colouring every aspect of life, she'd realised Sergei didn't just want to avoid unnecessary violence; he wanted to avoid it always, in any form, for any reason. Only an idiot went looking for trouble, but a refusal to deal with it in kind when the only alternative was to let trouble have its way? There was a word for that, and it was an ugly one.

Katya liked Sergei for all his faults, even that one, but it did make her fear for what might have happened to him. An indiscrete comment about pirates, raised tempers, an apology that was too little or too late – that would be all it would take.

"The man you put aboard the *Lukyan*," demanded Katya of Kane, "who is he?"

Kane seemed nonplussed, and looked at Ocello questioningly.

"Vetsch," said Ocello, pulling up a personnel file on the console in the *Vodyanoi's* officers' mess. "Laurent Vetsch, engineer, second class."

"Vetsch?" Kane frowned. "But... he's the most inoffensive man on the boat. Katya, I can't believe Laurent Vetsch would start a fight, no matter how much Sergei pushed him."

"Sergei's not the fighting sort either."

She was slightly distracted by noticing how much livelier Kane seemed since they'd got back. Of course, she realised, he hadn't been tired at all. His Sin addiction had been making itself felt. He must have gone straight to his cabin to dose himself as soon as he was out of his suit. It was a terrible burden he would carry until he died, and Katya always felt ashamed by how she had reacted when she first found out about it.

She had been educated at school to believe that all drug addicts were victims of their own selfish weakness. That a totally addictive drug with fatal withdrawal effects had been developed purely as a method of enslavement was part of a further education she would rather have lived without. That Kane had deliberately addicted himself to it in a vain attempt to prevent an apocalypse – an apocalypse that almost came anyway – only served to impress upon her that life has too many random factors for comfort.

"Well, something happened." Kane ran the sound file again. A shout of anger? Rage? Pain? Followed by Sergei – probably Sergei – crying out. "That doesn't sound very friendly." He leaned back in his chair. "It's only been just over an hour. They can't have got far. Set a pursuit course, Number One. Fifty percent faster than the *Lukyan*'s rated top speed, and broad passive scan in progress."

"Aye, captain. We'll pay special attention to the sea bed. There's a lot of clutter that a little bug like that could hide amongst." Ocello rose and left.

"That wasn't very kind, calling your boat a 'bug,'" said Kane when Ocello was safely out of earshot.

"I've heard her called worse," said Katya.

She looked at the console display that Ocello had been examining and quickly skim read Vetsch's profile before Kane could object. He didn't, but just watched. Vetsch seemed exemplary. Apart for a couple of trifling offences that anyone would pick up out of sheer bad luck over a long period, he was entirely clean. Ocello had noted that it was unfortunate that, since the *Vodyanoi*'s crew had barely changed in the last ten years, there had been no opportunity to promote Vetsch. In the usual run of things, he would have made Chief years ago. That he was stuck as a second engineer was no reflection on his abilities or attitude. Words like "patient," "tenacious," "gregarious" did little to suggest Vetsch might suddenly turn into a raging...

"Have you noticed any... odd behaviour?" said Katya suddenly.

"What, with Vetsch?"

"With anyone. Not just in your crew. Just, you know... generally?"

"It's a war, Katya. It's all about odd behaviour."

"I mean... crazy."

"My last comment still applies." He frowned. "What are you thinking?"

"I saw a Federal officer shoot an innocent, unarmed man dead in cold blood for no reason at all. He'd have carried on killing everyone in sight if he hadn't been brought down."

"It may seem a horrible thing to say, but my last comment *still* applies. War puts pressures on people. Psychotic breaks happen. People go crazy."

"I've heard about other times it's happened. The FMA tries to keep it quiet, but there's gossip. People talk." She saw Kane seemed unconvinced. "Secor interviewed me about it."

That made Kane sit up. "They *what?*"

"They asked me a load of questions, and I really got a strong feeling they had asked those same questions before for other cases. When I asked if it had happened before, they were so keen not to say anything that they all but admitted it. It made me think. There has been that gossip, all that scuttlebutt between captains, but I didn't give it much attention. I'm starting to wonder, now."

"That's strange. That's really very strange. I'll ask Tasya to see if the Yagizban are noticing a marked increase in psychosis amongst their people. More than is to be expected, anyway." He leaned forward towards her. "Are you saying you think either Vetsch or Sergei may have suffered one of these... incidents?"

"Sergei would not go off station without a good reason. I can't imagine him turning and running like that." *At least*, she admitted to herself, *unless he felt threatened*. There had been nothing to threaten him, however, which left only one possibility. "I think Vetsch has done something to him. He cracked up and attacked Sergei."

"Not the other way around?"

"Sergei wouldn't."

"That's a coincidence, because I've got a lengthy personnel record here along with my personal experience of the man that says that Vetsch wouldn't either." He closed the file, revealing a navigation chart, showing the *Vodyanoi*'s current position, speed, depth, and heading.

"We're heading deeper into the Red Water," Katya commented. Kane didn't answer, but just stared at the screen. There was a subtle change in his manner, as if she was watching his mood change in degrees, right before her eyes. She watched him in silence for some seconds, then asked, "Why is this Red Water still here anyway?"

"The Peklo Volume," said Kane, watching the symbol representing his boat slowly moving across the map.

"This is the Peklo? I didn't know. Uncle told me a bit about it, but not much. Who was Peklo?"

"Not a who. A *what*. It's a word borrowed from a neighbour of your ancestors. It's another word for 'Hell,' as if humanity hadn't made enough hells for itself already."

"Uncle told me that there was a sunken Terran vessel there, full of unstable weapons. They were too dangerous to disarm, so they just left them down there and interdicted the volume."

Kane closed his eyes as if thinking, or remembering. When he opened them, he was looking directly at Katya. "Is that what he said? Well, he was largely correct. There is a sunken Terran vessel down there, and its contents are very dangerous. We're heading in that direction, anyway," he added, talking half to himself. He opened a line to the bridge. "Number One, any sign of the *Lukyan*?"

"Not yet, captain. If she was trying to get away from us, she's bound to have changed her heading by now. I'd be running quiet and deep."

"That's what I thought. OK, let's try something different. We'll try a search grid. One thing, please make the first waypoint at the grave of the *Zarya*."

There was a distinct pause.

"The *Zarya*, sir?"

"Yes. I'm of a mind to show Ms Kuriakova just what her world was up against when Earth first invaded."

Another pause.

When Ocello spoke again, it was in a quiet and very serious voice. "Captain. You will appreciate why I have to ask twice. Are you sure you want us to go to the *Zarya*?"

Kane looked as if he wasn't sure at all. It seemed to take an effort of will for him to say, "Quite sure, Genevra."

As soon as he closed the link Katya said, "But what about the weapons? We'll be right over them!"

"The weapons aren't what you think at all, Katya." He got up to go. At the doorway, he said, "I've already apologised for what we saw in the evacuation site. I had no idea that would be the first thing we would discover. What I will show you at the grave of the *Zarya*, however, I make no apologies for. You said I kept too many secrets from you. If you're not already wishing that you could unlearn some of those secrets, you soon shall."

TEN

ZARYA

The hull groaned. Beyond it, Russalka was trying her very best to crush the *Vodyanoi* into a tattered wreck and drop her to crash beside the *Zarya* in the lightless deep.

"We're two hundred metres past test depth. Continuing to descend."

Kane was back in the captain's chair, behaving a little too manically for Katya's comfort. "I like the sound of a groaning hull. Don't you, Katya?" he asked. "Makes you feel alive, when you think of all those millions of tonnes of water just out there, and how narrow a rope we walk in this life. Just one silly, inconsequential thing – *seemingly*," he corrected himself, "*seemingly* inconsequential thing could kill us all in a tenth of the time it takes to think, 'Well, gosh, that's a lot of water.'"

Katya didn't care for his fatalism, but she noticed that the bridge crew took no notice of him at all. She guessed that in the ten years they'd been stalking the depths, they'd seen their captain make far more outrageous little speeches than this.

Now and then Tasya would wander in, frown with impatience, and walk out again. It was easy to understand why; the plan Katya had flatly refused to help with at Atlantis and then agreed to at the evacuation site was complicated and desperate as it was without further difficulties being introduced. The plan depended on Katya being above suspicion, and that meant everything being normal. If she turned up back at Atlantis without her boat, even the slowest Fed might doubt that she'd swum there. They should have been looking for the *Lukyan* and yet, although this was formally the beginning of the search for the minisub, it was an odd place to start.

Odder still was that Tasya expressed her impatience with only a frown. This from a woman who had reputedly once shot someone dead for being ten minutes late. Katya had asked about that earlier, cagily approaching the subject sideways in case Tasya didn't wish to be reminded.

"Did I kill someone for being ten minutes late to the beginning of an operation? No, that's nonsense," Tasya had said. "No, he was late *during* a mission. I just shot him in the foot at the end after exfiltration so he was taken off active duty and would never screw up anything important again." She'd laughed at Katya's silly little misunderstanding. "As if I'd kill somebody for being a little tardy."

Whereas, it seemed, masering a hole through somebody's foot for it was perfectly reasonable.

Yet here she was, clearly angry at the delay but saying nothing about it, never mind resorting to gunplay. Kane received a unique degree of tolerance from her. Some of

Katya's old school friends would have been quick to assign thwarted romantic feelings to Tasya, but that didn't seem quite right to Katya. It was more like the protectiveness of an older sister to a slightly stupid younger brother. Havilland was actually the elder by a little way, but his eccentricities often made him seem very immature for his years.

"We're here, captain," reported the helm, "directly over the wreck of the *Zarya*. Continuing to descend."

The news seemed to sober Kane. Indeed, the atmosphere on the bridge became sombre. Katya was not surprised; the Vodyanois were Terrans, and the *Zarya* must have contained hundreds of their compatriots.

"Take us down to fifty metres above the wreck, please. Mr Sahlberg, Mr Quinn, prepare a drone if you would."

Every few seconds, the hull creaked again under the increasing pressure, but never as sharply or, at least, never as unexpectedly as the first time. It was an impossible sound to enjoy, but at least it became bearable in the knowledge that they would not be exceeding the *Vodyanoi's* design depth, never mind its more problematical crush depth.

The drone was launched before the submarine reached its prescribed depth, travelling down ahead of its mothership. The water was relatively clear, and when the *Vodyanoi* activated the searchlights in its visual array, the great bulk of the stricken Terran starship immediately leapt into view.

Despite herself, Katya gasped. The array was scanning a directional sonar search over the *Zarya* assisted by the drone's pulse emitter and superimposing the results over the camera image along with range and scale information. "It's vast," she said out loud.

"She's big," agreed Kane. "I remember being shocked when I saw her in the flesh for the first time."

Katya looked at the smooth, wide lines of the drowned ship, and felt some small recollection nagging at her. Something from when she was just a kid. "Have you been here many times?"

"Yes. Once a year ever since I arrived on Russalka. But this isn't how I remember her. The first time I saw her she was in space, in Earth's orbit. I had gone up the orbital elevator from Libreville to the high port. She was just hanging there. In space, it can be difficult to get a sense of scale sometimes, but then I saw the shuttles going back and forth. I knew how big those were, and they were dwarfed by the *Zarya*." Katya glanced sideways at him, and saw he was lost in the memory. "I watched her depart geostationary orbit, watched her until she was no bigger than the stars. Then, soon enough, she was gone. It was a hard thing, to watch her go, and to have to stay behind."

Katya looked at him, confused. This did not match well with what she knew. "You were supposed to be aboard her?" He nodded absently, still looking at the image. "But, you weren't in the military, were you? I don't understand. Why were you supposed to be aboard an invasion ship?"

"There are invasions, and there are invasions. Look at her, Katya. Tell me what you see."

Katya turned back to the main screen, her confusion not at all diminished. "She's big. I suppose that's not a surprise; she was carrying a whole invasion force. Very wide in the beam. Long, but not as long as the *Leviathan*. And..." It suddenly struck her that she wasn't seeing something that should very definitely have been there. "Kane... where are her weapons?" The old memory from her school days nagged at her again and she could almost recall where she'd seen something very like the *Zarya* before.

Kane smiled a little sadly, like a teacher with a slow pupil who had finally understood a simple point. "There aren't any."

That didn't make sense, except it did, but Katya didn't want to think about that, because that way led something awful that she shied away from. So instead she scoffed and said, "It must have weapons. It's an invasion ship."

"The ships that came a year later, the ships that came in response to the *Zarya*'s last distress signal, that came to avenge her, *they* were armed. But that was a real invasion. The *Zarya* came to re-establish links with the lost colony of Russalka, to continue what had begun a century before." He pointed at the screen. "Five thousand colonists. Mr Sahlberg's sister, brother-in-law and two nephews. Ms Ocello's sister, sister-in-law, nephew and niece. Two of Mr Lowe's cousins." He paused and swallowed, and said very quietly, "My wife and daughter."

Katya remembered the toy Kane had once given her: a "yo-yo," all the way from Earth. "I bought it for my daughter," he'd told her. She had never asked why he still had it. She looked at the image on the screen. Somewhere in that wreck...

No. It couldn't be so. It *could not be so*. The Grubbers started the war. Everybody knew that. The Grubbers turned up in a ship bristling with weapons and demanded obedience. They fired first. The FMA destroyed the invasion ship in a desperate and bravely fought battle. She'd seen dramas of it. She'd read about it in class. She'd heard war stories from veterans. It couldn't all be lies.

"You're lying. I don't know what that ship is, but it can't be the *Zarya*."

Even as she said it, she knew she was wrong. The memory from school strengthened. It was a history lesson. The class was watching a recreation of the original colonisation. The broad, smooth lines of the colony ships...

"There are invasions, and there are invasions, Katya. The Terran government are not nice people, by and large. They monitor the population, curtail freedoms. Believe me when I say that the people who volunteer to be colonists are glad to leave the place. They came to Russalka expecting to find a well-established colony here. Or, just possibly, everybody dead, in which case they'd have to start again. Earth had tried to communicate with the place, but received no reply. So they assumed the FTL communications relay satellites had failed. Or, as I say, everybody was dead and there was no one to answer. It didn't matter. The *Zarya* was supposed to be the second wave of the colonisation effort. A century late, but there'd been the small matter of a world war on Earth that turned hot. You don't get over things like that quickly."

"That's not true. The FTL satellites were in place. We were using them to communicate with the other colonies. The Grubbers destroyed those satellites in orbit when they arrived."

"Yes, they did. There was nothing wrong with them up to that point. You're missing the obvious – Earth received no reply from Russalka because the FMA decided *not* to reply. They didn't say a thing until the *Zarya* was in orbit. Then they told her they'd had satellite problems, were very glad to see them, and could they set down just *here*." He pointed at the screen. "It was an ambush. She never stood a chance."

Katya couldn't find anything to say. Kane continued, quietly crushing almost everything she had ever believed. "What happened at that Yagizban evacuation site wasn't an aberration, Katya. The Federal government hasn't suffered some sort of personality change overnight. They have been doing things like this for years. Somewhere in that long century when Russalka was on its own, your ancestors gave the bureaucrats too much power. They became very comfortable with that power and very protective of it. So they sold you a lie: of things always being on a knife edge; of disaster being just around the corner. How you must all pull together or perish.

"The *Zarya* represented a huge threat to them. All those new faces, new minds that hadn't been indoctrinated with generations of the lie, that would ask questions and have direct contact with Earth to discuss matters. The government could see the good times coming to an end. So, they just made the lie a bigger one still, but in a way that would appeal to the populace. Now you were the innocent victims of a warmongering colonial power. It was a beautifully convincing lie. The Russalkin bled and died for it in their thousands. The only risk the government could see was that they might lose the war, but I'm sure they had contingency plans in place for that.

"The one thing they didn't anticipate was the Yagizban actually believing what the Terrans told them. When the war fizzled out and Earth didn't send reinforcements, the Feds believed it was business as usual. You can see how well that worked out. Ten years of growing Yagizban resentment and a lovely new war that the Federal government thinks is worth fighting to the last drop of somebody else's blood."

Katya felt empty, exhausted, sickened. She wanted to cling to the reality she had grown up in, but now everywhere she touched it with her mind, it crumbled and rotted away.

She kept thinking of little things that she had always simply accepted, but that now made a new and terrible sense. The existence of Secor boats, and how it was always just expected that they would be part of flotillas and wolf packs. How many times had decent people fired on innocent targets using data and "pirate" identifications provided by the Secor command boats? The Russalkin had suffered, been called "heroes," and regarded those who complained as verging on traitors. All the time they thought they had been proud warriors, they had been nothing but patsies for the biggest confidence game in the galaxy.

"You're wasting your time searching a grid," she said. "If Sergei is still at the controls, he'll run for the nearest station where he feels safe. That will be Dunwich. Find him and the *Lukyan*, Kane. We can't do this without them." She left the bridge without another word.

They picked up the *Lukyan* twenty kilometres from Dunwich's sensor line. Kane wasn't in the mood for subtlety – the *Vodyanoi* swooped quickly on the minisub, approaching in her baffles so it wasn't detected until it was too late. The salvage maw gaped wide and swallowed the *Lukyan* in a perfectly performed manoeuvre that hinted at how many times the crew had practised it in the past.

Tasya wanted to go into the maw with two others, all armed, but Katya wouldn't hear of it. Sergei was her friend, her employee and her crew, the *Lukyan* her vessel, and every Russalkin knew better than to get between a captain and her boat. She climbed through the hatch into the maw as soon as it was drained, Tasya – armed of course – at her heels.

Katya cast an eye already rendered professional by a few months of ownership over the *Lukyan*, noting the damage caused by its violent capture. Scuffed paintwork, punctured air tank, snapped strut on the lighting rig – four to six hours to repair if she and Sergei worked on it together.

She walked around the front to look in through the forward observation bubble, but the internal lights were out. The light from the maw's own illumination strips seemed to show a dark bundle on the floor next to the crate of plumbing supplies which Sergei had insisted on keeping aboard.

Katya walked back to the minisub's aft hatch where Tasya was waiting. "I can see something on the floor in there. It might be a body."

"Only one?"

"Why guess?" said Katya, and operated the hatch control.

A strange organic smell rolled out of the open door, and it took Katya a moment to identify the mixed scent of blood and urine. Tasya didn't wait that moment; she stepped inside, drawing and aiming her maser at the shape as she did so. She kicked it, and it whimpered.

"On your feet," she ordered.

The shape clambered painfully up, and Katya saw it was Sergei. Her joy at seeing him alive was immediately dissipated by the state he was in. He had a deep cut down the left side of his brow, and the blood had splashed all the way down his habitual green coveralls to the waist. But there was blood, too, on his sleeve cuffs.

"We need a medic," Katya called back to the open maw hatch where Kane and a couple of the crew stood watching. Sergei cried out, making her turn quickly back.

Tasya had him held against the wall of the minisub by his throat with one hand while the other held her gun unwaveringly between his eyes. The last time Katya had seen a gun held to someone like that, a second later Filipp Shurygin was dead. "Tasya? What the hell are you doing?"

"*Where's Vetsch?*" demanded Tasya, her voice cold with suppressed violence.

"Katya!" croaked Sergei through Tasya's firm grip on his windpipe. "Help!"

"Tasya, let him go! He can hardly breathe!"

Tasya released his throat, but kept the maser's muzzle aiming steadily between his eyes. "Don't make me wait for my answer, Ilyin," she said.

Sergei shot her a terrified glance, although somebody unexpectedly knowing his surname was probably enough to do that. "He attacked me. Look!" He pointed at the cut.

"Sergei," said Katya gently in an attempt to calm him, "please, tell us what exactly happened."

"He was as nice as anything to start with. I thought he was OK for a pirate." Belatedly realising what he had said, he started to stumble out some apologies, but Tasya just waved the barrel of her gun impatiently. This served to concentrate his mind wonderfully.

"Then he said the boat was his."

"The *Vodyanoi*?" asked Kane, stepping into the maw. He noticed Tasya bristle, and added, "Never mind me. Just an interested party. Carry on. You were saying?"

"No," said Sergei. "The *Lukyan*. Katya's boat. He said he was in the captain's seat so that made him the captain. I'd taken the co-pilot's seat. I'm happier there."

"He is," said Katya to no one in particular.

"So I gave him the pilot's seat. Then he says the *Lukyan* belongs to him, because he's the captain. I thought he was joking, but then he gave me a bad look, a real bad look, and I thought *He's stealing her because Kane told him to, because they're pirates.*"

"Word of honour, for whatever that's worth," said Kane. "I told him to do no such thing."

"And I said she belongs to Captain Kuriakova, and he said, no, she belongs to him because... because he was sitting in the captain's seat, and that meant he owned her now. He meant it, too."

"What happened then?" demanded Tasya.

"I laughed. I sort of thought he might still be joking. And... he went crazy. He grabbed the extinguisher and smacked me in the side of the head with it. I unstrapped and got into the back, trying to get away from him. He came after me. He was crazy. He was shouting about how I was trespassing aboard his command and he would kill me before giving her up." He was looking pleadingly at Katya. "I sort of danced around that crate full of plumbing gear, just trying to keep away from him. He was getting angrier and angrier. I've never seen anyone go like that before. His face was all scrunched up but he was dead white. Then he tried to dodge past the crate and hit me and he fell over." He fell silent, his eyes on the maser and Tasya's face.

"What then?" she said.

"I... hit him. He'd dropped the extinguisher when he fell over, and I grabbed it and I hit him." He gulped, the sweat showing on his face. "I hit him a lot of times. I didn't want him to get up again."

"Did you kill him?"

Sergei nodded miserably. "I think so."

"And then what? You dumped the body out of the dorsal lock?"

If Sergei had been reluctant to admit that he had killed Vetsch, even in self-defence, it was nothing compared to now. His gaze flickered from face to face, cornered and desperate.

"What did you do with him, Sergei?" said Katya gently, then far less gently, "Lower your gun, Tasya, for crying out loud!"

Tasya kept it aimed at Sergei's forehead for another three seconds and then slowly, very slowly, lowered it, leaving them all in no doubt she could still put a maser bolt between his eyes in an instant if he tried anything.

As the gun lowered, Sergei's fear ebbed just a little. "I didn't throw him out. He... climbed out himself."

Katya frowned; she must have misunderstood something. "So, you didn't kill him after all. Obviously."

"I couldn't find a pulse. I... I felt his skull break when I hit him the last time. That's why I stopped. I didn't want to kill him. Just knock him out. But I'd hit him too hard. So I checked for a pulse, and there wasn't one. I even used the monitor from the medical kit. It said he was dead, too. I thought the pirates would kill me. So I ran. I'm sorry, Katya. You know them, I thought you'd be OK. But they don't know me. I'm so sorry."

Katya couldn't find it in herself to be angry with him. There he was, injured, bloodied, terrified, and so scared of pain and death. Of course he had run. "It's OK, Sergei. I understand."

Tasya had no interest in forgiveness. "He was either dead or he wasn't. What did you do with the body?"

"I was in my seat, trying to get away. I had the hydrophones turned up, listening for if you were chasing

me. I didn't hear him at all until the inner hatch closed
and the controls showed the airlock was cycling. I
thought he'd gone mad… *more* mad, or the head wound
had made him confused. I tried to stop him! I swear! I
tried to stop the cycle, but by the time I put in an abort
command, the outer hatch was open. It was too late.
Katya, tell them! Tell them how quickly the lock can
fill!"

Katya shrugged helplessly. "I've never had any reason
to use it," she said to the others. "I've never seen it filled.
But it *isn't* very big. You can just about get one average
person in a flexible diving suit into it. It must fill pretty
quickly, especially if there's someone in there."

"Stow the pistol, please, Tasya," said Kane. "Mr
Ilyin's story is easy enough to confirm or refute using
the available evidence." He waved the two Vodyanois
behind him in and said, "Take Mr Ilyin to a secure cabin
and keep an eye on him. Kid gloves, please; he's a friend
of a friend. I also want pictures of his injuries before the
medic gets to work on him."

Sergei was led away, subdued and silent. As he was
taken past her, Katya said, "Don't worry. We'll get this
all sorted out. Just rest, OK?" He looked sideways at her,
but his expression seemed resentful rather than hopeful
or grateful. Katya had a bad feeling in her gut that their
relationship would be forever changed by this incident,
and not for the better.

ELEVEN
PSYCHOTIC BREAK

The *Vodyanoi* couldn't provide much in the way of forensic equipment, but it didn't need much to prove that what evidence there was of the fight aboard the *Lukyan* entirely corroborated Sergei's account. The small handheld extinguisher that had been used as a weapon was from the bracket to the left of the pilot's position, out of reach for anyone in the co-pilot's seat. The pilot's communications set had been adjusted for Vetsch, the co-pilot for Sergei. All steering data apart from some random inputs at the time of the fight was from the co-pilot's seat, the interface configured in Sergei's own idiosyncratic pattern. While the medic couldn't gene type the blood found, he could at least test it for antigens, and so was able to differentiate between Sergei's and Vetsch's. Both types were found on the buckled edge of the extinguisher, Sergei's in a spray across the co-pilot side, Vetsch's pooled by the crate in the passenger section. The blood on the medical kit's monitor handle and touch screen was Sergei's; that on its sensor pad Vetsch's.

There was a *lot* of Vetsch's blood found beneath the floor grill. Watson, the medic, thought it likely that anybody losing that much would at least suffer shock. Thus, she was at a loss to explain more of Vetsch's blood smeared on the hatch release, leaving an easily identified set of fingerprints. The clinching evidence was that the *Lukyan*'s activity log had recorded a manual cycling of the dorsal airlock from within the airlock itself.

"Could the log have been faked?" asked Kane, when he, Ocello, Katya, and Tasya were considering the gathered evidence.

"Of course," said Vymann, the *Vodyanoi*'s senior technician who had also helped in the investigation. "But not quickly, and you'd have to know exactly what you were doing and be using specialised equipment to do it undetectably."

Kane sighed loudly and pushed the medical hard copies away from him. "Ilyin's telling the truth, then."

"No," said Tasya stubbornly. "His story fits the facts. That's not the same thing."

"He's not lying," said Katya. "I know him. I know how he lies. He just keeps denying things and hopes people will believe him. But he won't come up with a story more complicated than 'It wasn't me.' He can't."

"He isn't very intelligent."

"He isn't very *imaginative*," replied Katya sharply.

"Finished, Tasya?" asked Kane. "Yes? Good. So, Ilyin's telling the truth, then. Y'know, I honestly wish he wasn't. I wish he'd killed Vetsch, got the body into the dorsal lock somehow and spat him out into the ocean. Then we could just interrogate him to find out why. Instead we've got a sudden breakdown in one of the nicest people you could hope to meet, resulting in delusions, paranoia, psychosis and then, just when it can't get any stranger, he rises from the dead long enough to commit suicide. No offence, Katya, but you can see why this would all be a lot easier if Sergei *were* the prime mover behind the incident."

He drew the papers back towards him and flipped through them in a desultory way, only half examining them as he tried to understand the affair. "It's all a bit mysterious, and I can't say I'm very fond of mysteries."

He seemed glad of the distraction when Quinn appeared in the doorway, although that gladness diminished somewhat when he saw Quinn's expression. "What's wrong, Mr Quinn?" he asked, already rising to his feet.

"It's Giroux," said Quinn. "We just picked up his communicator signal. He got out somehow, captain."

"Impossible," said Tasya, now on her feet too.

"He doesn't have a suit," said Kane, utterly astonished. "Never mind how he survived the explosion, he doesn't have a suit."

They were on the bridge seconds later. "It's faint, but the signal's good enough to detect the encryption assigned to Giroux's channel," reported Sahlberg.

"Where is he?"

"Back at the evacuation site, sir."

"We were not far from there when we came back from the *Zarya*. Why didn't we hear him then?"

Sahlberg shook his head. "I can't tell you, captain. Maybe he found the facility's communications room and is using its relay to get a message outside the Faraday cage."

"Oh, gods. Poor Bruno." Kane was horror-struck. "Set course. Best speed. We have to do what we can."

The course had already been set in anticipation of the command, and the lean shape of the *Vodyanoi*, the fastest boat in all the seas of Russalka, surged forward. It was only when Kane took the captain's seat that he realised he was still holding the evidence reports from the Vetsch investigation. He looked from them to the main display – currently showing the boat's course and an area of likelihood where Giroux's signal probably lay – back to the reports and finally at Katya who was standing to his right.

"This has been a very odd day," said Kane.

It was to become odder still. While the *Vodyanoi* had been on station outside the evacuation facility waiting for contact to be re-established with the expedition, it had continued its survey of the mountain within which the facility lay. One of the elements it had positively identified was the disguised communications relay by which the facility kept in touch with the Yagizba Enclaves. As they grew closer to the mountain, and the probable location of Giroux's transmission was refined into a smaller and smaller area, it became obvious that the two did not match up at all.

"That puts him physically outside the base," said Sahlberg. "How did he manage that?"

Kane said nothing, but watched as the search area shrank steadily as they grew closer. Suddenly he leaned forward. "Mr Sahlberg, that area seems to be on the move. Is that an effect of varying signal strength, or…"

"No, sir," said Sahlberg, studying the figures on his console. "He's moving. Just a moment, we should be just about… There!"

On the main display, the search area resolved into a single point. "He's descending the mountainside," said Sahlberg, astonished. "What does he think he's doing?"

"Is he falling?"

"I don't think so, captain. His path is following a ridge line. No, look! He's following the escarpment downwards. He's not falling, sir. He's climbing down."

"Do we have any sort of inventory for the evacuation site? Would they have AD suits?"

"Unlikely, sir. Just soft suits for maintenance."

Katya knew why Kane was asking. Giroux was descending too fast. In a soft suit, he would be breathing a mixture of gases that included helium rather than nitrogen, and he should be taking rests to allow his body to acclimatise.

"He's approaching a cliff, captain. He'll have to stop."

The bridge fell silent but for Ocello trying to raise Giroux on the radio. They watched as the sharp contact point moved closer to the edge of a great cliff that stood above a gorge.

They watched as he reached it.

They watched as he jumped.

"Range, damn it! How far away are we?" shouted Kane.

"Three kilometres, sir. We'll never get there in time."

They could only watch as Giroux plunged into the abyss, deeper than their test depth, then deeper than their design depth, and then the contact went dark.

"There's a Soup lake down there," said Ocello quietly. "He's gone in."

However Giroux had survived the explosion, however he had had escaped the site, they would never know. The Soup was a dense emulsion of heavy metals in particle form, created in a natural process that had baffled Russalkin scientists ever since it was discovered in the early seabed surveys. No submarine dared enter it; no diver could hope to return from the crushing pressures within the toxic lakes.

"He must have been dead long before he reached it," she said. "The pressure change was too rapid. Nobody could have survived it."

"Nobody could have survived that explosion," said Kane to himself, but Katya caught his muttered words. Abruptly he stood. "I shall be in my cabin. You have the bridge, Ms Ocello." Without waiting for confirmation, Kane left the bridge in deep thought, the reports still clenched in his hand.

Katya went to see Sergei. The Vodyanoi who had been left to keep an eye on him was visibly relieved when she came in, and she could understand why; being in a confined space with a despondent Sergei would depress anyone. She had years of experience and had developed a resistance to it, but she could imagine what a drag it would be on the soul of somebody exposed to such accomplished passive-aggressive semi-professional martyrdom for the first time.

"Just wanted to tell you what's happening, Sergei. I can't tell you what the final conclusion will be for sure, but the evidence corroborated your story, so…"

"It wasn't a story," he said sullenly. "It's the way it happened."

"Don't, Sergei. I have enough to deal with without you being miserable about good news. The captain believes your account, and even Tasya's come around to it. Considering she was all for shooting you at first, that's got be good, hasn't it?"

Sergei managed a small reluctant nod, as if being found innocent and being allowed to live was only fractionally better than a maser bolt in the brain and an undignified burial at sea through a torpedo tube.

Satisfied that this was going to be the biggest outpouring of emotion she could expect from him, Katya turned to leave, but Sergei stopped her.

"Katya, what's all this about? Why do they need you so much?"

It suddenly struck her that he would know nothing about what had happened in the evacuation site, no idea of what they had found there, what they had seen. Nor had he seen the wreck of the *Zarya*. To him the Feds were still just a bunch of snotty official types who ran things because they always had. "They want me to do something. Something scary. It will be dangerous, too. I don't want you to go with me, Sergei. I'll drop you off at Dunwich."

The Vodyanoi crew man coughed and said, "I'll just wait outside. I'll be right outside if you need me." He stepped through the doorway, sliding the door shut behind him.

When he had gone, Sergei said, "I don't have any family left, Katya. Not blood family."

"I know."

"You're the closest thing I have left. I'll go with you."

"Sergei, it's not just going to be dangerous at the time, it's going to be dangerous afterwards, too." She closed her eyes and tried to marshal her thoughts. It was inevitable that she would have to tell him exactly what Kane and Tasya had asked of her sooner or later. It might as well be now.

She opened her eyes, looked Sergei in the face and said, "It's treason. They want me to commit treason. If the Feds catch me, they'll kill me. I doubt there'd even be a trial."

Sergei's mouth dropped open. He was a typical Federal citizen in so many ways – he would complain and whine and resent "those Fed bastards" every day, but they were still *his* bastards. His loyalties had lain with them so long, any ability to see them as anything but part of the natural scheme of Russalkin life had withered years ago. Treason was insane, beyond his capacity to understand.

Katya smiled wanly. "Exactly, and that's why you're not going. I can't ask you to help me. I *won't* ask you to help me. Just... when it happens, if I succeed... don't think too badly of me. While you were gone, I saw... Everything has changed, Sergei. Russalka is dying, *will* die. It will take something... major to stop what's happening here."

"Katya. What do they want you to do?"

She shook her head. "It's much, much better you don't know. If you know, it makes you an accomplice." She prepared to go, conscious she may already have said too much. "I'll speak to Kane. Get you released."

"Katya, please, whatever they've asked you to do, don't do it. I'm begging you..."

It was more than she could bear. Sergei represented ever Federal citizen who would turn their backs on her, every friend she had, almost every face she knew. "No. You didn't see..." The images flashed through her mind. Dark glass, shadowed forms, the murdered innocent. "Oh, Sergei. What they've done. What they've done in our names..." A deep grave, five thousand souls, blood in the Red Water. "It has to stop. It has to stop."

She wrenched the door open and staggered out into the corridor, her eyes tearing up. She walked quickly past the astonished guard, forcing her emotions back inside until she could reach her cabin. There she sat on her bunk, refusing to sob while the tears ran down her cheeks.

She was dead, she knew it. Everything she had been had burnt in the truth of what she now knew. She was hollow, destroyed, nothing more than a walking bomb to end the world within which she had grown up. She would destroy it all in the slim hope that not doing so was worse.

She knew about fanatics, how they would push themselves to the utmost and willingly die for their ideals and their beliefs. But she wasn't a fanatic. She didn't feel a righteous, irresistible need to do anything. The FMA or, at least, the little group at the top of the FMA who made the decisions, they had betrayed her and every Federal citizen they represented. She wished she could feel vengeful, feel some passion for what she was going to do.

She wished she could feel anything at all. She only felt numb, detached, inhuman.

Then she felt something else, something that seeped from the numbness, a sense of order and methodical action, of doing what had to be done. She might be emotionally distanced from what was coming, but perhaps emotion, passion and commitment weren't necessary. She could see the future mapped out as a series of events, like waypoints on a boat's course.

She didn't awaken, because she wasn't really asleep, but the sense of regaining consciousness was still there. She could feel where her tears had dried. The sensation of them irritated her and she washed her face quickly in the cabin's little basin. She checked her chronometer and discovered she had been sitting there for half an hour. That was OK, though, because now her mind was settled.

Whereas before, the future had been chaos and fear, now it was bright points on a good chart. Even the point that represented the moment she would be identified as a traitor and probably killed seemed of no more concern than any other. She wondered vaguely if this was how fanatics felt. She had expected more fire, not this cold indifference. She preferred it this way, though. She preferred to feel nothing.

At Kane's door, she took his vague grunt at her knock to be assent, and entered. He was at his desk, running through what looked like crew timesheets. Beside him were the investigation reports, badly creased from being in his fist but showing signs he had tried to flatten them out.

"Kane," began Katya, "Sergei's been under watch for almost a day, now. You said yourself that..."

"He's innocent," said Kane, not looking up. "Obviously he's innocent. Well, of Vetsch's murder anyway. I can't speak for what he gets up to in his own time."

"So... he can be let out?"

Kane looked at her with a baffled expression. "Haven't I already let him go? No?" He touched a button on his desk console. "Hello? Genevra? Katya's friend..." He paused, tried to remember, failed, and looked at Katya.

"Sergei Ilyin," she said patiently.

"Katya's friend Sergei Ilyin didn't kill Vetsch. Please release him. Thank you." He terminated the link without waiting for a reply and went back to studying his screen.

"Yes. Well, anyway," said Katya, trying to sound nonchalant, "when do you want me to do it? The..." she gestured vaguely, "the treason thing."

"In a minute," said Kane, comparing what was on the screen to the reports. He stopped abruptly and looked at her. "I mean to say, we'll talk about that in a minute. Not that you'll do it in a minute. You have to be in Atlantis to do it, as you know." Finally realising he was making a fool of himself, he pointed at the screen. "This is interesting."

Katya knew from past experience that when Kane was in one of these moods, it was best to indulge him. She looked at the display. "Timesheets. Capitalisation reports. I learned about them when I was studying for my crew card, but I've never actually used them. The *Lukyan's* too small a concern to need that kind of detail."

"Good for discipline on a boat like this," said Kane. "Good to know who's been doing what, who's pushing themselves too hard, and who's swinging the lead. That's an old Terran term, you know? Very old. Anyway, recent history has cost me two good men, and I am not very happy about that. I am especially not happy about not knowing exactly what happened to them. If it can happen twice, it can happen a third, fourth, however many times."

"You're looking for clues in the timesheets?"

"It tells me what they were doing in half their waking hours, so it's a start. Now, look here. Vetsch never had the opportunity to enter his time aboard your boat onto his sheet, but look at the last thing he did."

Katya followed Kane's pointing finger and read off, "Intake maintenance. So?"

"Now, look at Giroux's. He was on munitions inventory, but that didn't take his whole shift. The last hour or so…"

"'Miscellaneous,'" Katya read, and then Giroux's additional note, "'Helped out in starboard drive room.' Where was Vetsch working?"

"Ah, you're seeing it, aren't you? Vetsch was clearing the intake filters in the starboard drive room. He was the only one sheeted as working in there, so that's who Giroux was helping."

Katya leaned against the cabin wall and crossed her arms as she considered this. "With respect, Kane, the *Vodyanoi*'s no *Novgorod*. She's not huge. People cross paths all the time aboard her."

"Oh, I know, I know," said Kane. He leaned back in his chair and crossed his arms too, unconsciously mimicking Katya. "It could well be a coincidence. Probably *is* a coincidence. I'm just trying to find a pattern where there may be none. Still, I'm going to have a look in the starboard drive room later just to see if…" He shook his head and sighed. "Sounds a bit desperate when I say it out loud; looking for clues. I can't imagine what a clue that helps explain all this would even look like."

"Perhaps they were just talking and said something that set one another off. Yes, I know – like what? I have no idea, Kane."

"This planet of yours, Katya. No other world amongst the colonies is a water world. Well, there's Novus Hellespont, I suppose, but they've got an archipelago they built on there, and it doesn't storm all the time either. Perhaps extended submarine living drives people crazy after a while."

"These cases are recent, Kane. We've been fine up to now."

"Ah, but the war. And now another war. A combination of factors, resulting in psychosis. Vetsch, possibly Giroux, the Fed you saw, the other cases they seem to be covering up." He grunted a semi-laugh. "Even the *Leviathan* went mad." He suddenly fell silent. When he looked at Katya again, his expression was serious. "Even the *Leviathan* went mad," he repeated. He unfolded his arms and started sifting through files on the console. "There's a pattern. There's something going on here. And," he concluded, "it's not going to be among the timesheets."

He switched off the display and turned to her. "You said you'd take the mission, but you said it when you were shocked. You've had a chance to think about it now."

In her mind, waypoints glittered, charting her path through the next few days. It was all she had. "I'll do it."

TWELVE
LAST REQUEST

The *Lukyan* was directed to dock at lock fifteen at Atlantis. This was the same dock where the *Lastochka*, Shurygin's boat, had been when he was murdered. When she stepped out of the hatch, her foot came down on the exact spot where he had died. Like many Russalkin, Katya professed a disbelief in omens and portents, yet noted them all the same. This didn't seem like a very good one.

Not that it mattered; she expected to be dead within the next twenty hours. Completing the mission was all that mattered. She remembered heroes going off to face certain death in the dramas. "My life isn't important," they'd say while the romantic interest wept messily over them. Then they'd go off and somehow survive anyway.

Katya couldn't see it working out that way for her. If she didn't manage to escape Atlantis and reach her rendezvous with the *Vodyanoi*, she would either be shot, or captured, interrogated, and then shot. They'd throw her to Secor, and there was no escape from them. When they finally put a gun to her head, it would come as a mercy after a Secor interrogation.

The official checking her permits was frowning. "Where's your co-pilot, Ms Kuriakova?" He examined the documents. "Mr Ilyin. Where is he?"

"Sergei fell ill when we were at Dunwich."

"Anything serious?"

"Not really, but not the kind of thing you'd enjoy sharing a minisub with. Put it this way – we were transporting plumbing supplies there. Sergei must be pretty pleased their bathroom facilities are up to spec at the moment."

The officer winced sympathetically. "Will he be coming here when he's better, or are you going back?"

"The plan is to find a cargo for Dunwich and I'll go back and pick him up. Things are so tight, every trip has to pay its way."

Katya felt she was standing outside herself, watching as she chatted with the officer, so calm and *normal*. If he asked to check her shoulder bag as he was perfectly entitled to do, he would find a strangely bland piece of equipment, an aluminium box twenty centimetres by thirty centimetres by four centimetres, with a couple of metre lengths of cable, tightly coiled and tied, plugged into one end, and a covered switch at the other.

It clearly wasn't a standard piece of equipment. If asked, she was to say it was a custom unit she had designed to filter hydrophone data to help in the war effort, but disappointingly the device didn't work as well as she'd hoped. Any technician who opened the box would see this was a lie. Katya knew the cover story was thin, and that her best chance of succeeding in her mission was for no Federal officer, agent, or technician to even see the box until after it had done its job.

"Well, good luck finding a cargo for Dunwich," said the officer, signing off her papers. "We don't get much traffic heading for there. It's pretty much self-sufficient."

Katya nodded as she accepted her papers and crew card back. "I sometimes get lucky with personal mail and packages."

The officer cast a cautious look around. "Secor's tightening up on that sort of cargo," he said quietly. "It's getting so they have to read every letter and open every parcel."

"Yes. True. That packing directive was Secor, then?"

The customs officer wrinkled his nose as if even the word "Secor" smelled bad. "Yes, but don't tell anyone that. They ran it through our channels, so now we have to pretend it was our idea."

"I won't tell a soul," said Katya, smiling. She waved the officer goodbye, and went off into the halls of Atlantis to commit high treason.

Katya liked coffee, real coffee, but it was an expensive and rare treat. She went into the most elegant drinks salon she could find, and ordered a pot. It was a terrible extravagance, but as she was going to be dead soon, she wanted to have at least one thing happen in her last hours that she could wholeheartedly enjoy.

"Elegant" did not say a great deal on Russalka, but the place was clean and quiet and convivial, and the staff took justifiable pride in how they prepared the coffee. Her coveralls did not earn her cold looks as they might on other worlds; here almost everyone wore them at some time of the day. The salon staff wore white shirts and dark red trousers, which alone made it the fanciest place she had ever been. Everyone wore uniforms, she knew, but the novel thought of a world where it was not expected occurred to her now as she drank the first cup from the pot.

There was so much that she had never really considered. So many things about her life that she had always accepted because that's the way things were. Everybody had this view of the Federal government as an amorphous brain constructed from pure bureaucracy. It did what it did, and there was no point in arguing because nobody was really responsible for policy. It just happened.

The way Kane explained it, it was very different. There was a political class physically concentrated in the higher security areas of the major settlements, Atlantis being the largest. Everything went through them. They were essentially born into the job and, as they didn't put much effort into it, there were no dissenters from the lifetime of ease it offered. Thus, the amorphous bureaucracy brain that ruled the planet was not frighteningly intelligent. It was, however, very jealous.

The military and security arms of the FMA were charged to hunt, locate, and eliminate dissent, even if the navy in particular never quite understood that was the nature of their work. Dissent was dressed up in all manner of exciting terms like "terrorism," "piracy," "anarchism," and "rogue Terran sabotage," but often the people who ended up being quietly dumped out of airlocks or sent on one way trips to the Deeps high security facility had just made the mistake of wondering if the governance of Russalka might just possibly be done in a better way.

"The government's riding for a fall, of course," Kane had said. "They've tried to keep Secor violent but stupid, so it never becomes a threat to them. They've put so much trust into Secor now, though, they've had to step back a little, and clever people have ended up being recruited. Well, I say *clever*, but I really mean *not entirely stupid*. If they knew their Earth history, they'd know how much trouble they're heading for. Give it a year or two and, in the normal run of things, there'll be a *coup d'etat*."

"Meaning what?" Katya had asked.

"Meaning Russalka would end up being run by the military. That always works terrifically well. People just love being ordered around by soldiers. But, not to worry. The way things are, Russalka doesn't have a year or two. No pressure, Katya, but the fate of the world rests on your shoulders."

Or to be exact, Katya thought as she poured her second cup, *in the electronic box of tricks that I have in my bag.*

At least there wasn't a gun in the bag with it. Tasya had offered her a small maser, but Katya had declined. She'd used one once and never wanted to do so again. Besides, if things ended up in a fire fight, the mission was a failure anyway. Kane had run off to his cabin and returned with another piece of Terran technology that she might accept instead. It was a small black cylinder about twenty five centimetres long and two and a half in diameter, a press-and-hold button on the shaft, and a smooth metal plate at the end.

"Taser stunner," he'd explained. "Good for about four shocks. Small chance of killing your target, but it really is small. Otherwise, they're stunned or unconscious for about five minutes. Oh, and make sure there's no contact between you and them apart from the plate when you press the button, or you'll be dancing together into the arms of Morpheus." Katya and Tasya had both stared at him until he had added, "I mean, it will electrocute you too. Nobody appreciates classical allusions anymore, do they?"

The coffee was good, even now that she was getting down to the grounds. It was as good to smell as it was to drink, and as often as not she inhaled its rich, heavy scent before actually letting the liquid flow across her tongue. She'd long since realised that coffee was the only luxury she truly craved, and it was right and proper that she indulge herself in it now. But, quickly enough, the coffee in her cup was gone, the pot was empty and that was that.

She called for the bill, but when it arrived she was bemused to discover that it came to a grand total of nothing at all. "We decided to waive it," said the waiter. "We recognised you from the news when the war started. Helping the crew of the *Novgorod* escape from the Yagizban, and everything."

"Thanks," said Katya, a pit filled with concentrated embarrassment opening beneath her feet, "I appreciate the thought, but, really, I can't accept."

"Your money's no good here, Ms." The waiter smiled, aware of how awkward the situation was becoming but staying his course.

Katya thought for a moment and said, "How about this? I pay, and you give the money to the Veterans' Welfare Fund? Then we're all happy."

The waiter nodded and accepted her payment. "You're a good woman, Ms Kuriakova," he said. "I'm proud to have met you."

He returned to the counter, leaving Katya feeling wretched. The warm happiness the coffee had given her had all but burnt away. Guilt was growing within her. "I'm proud to have met you." *Not for long, you won't be.*

Out on the corridors again, Katya decided that she should just get on with her mission as soon as possible. The longer she delayed, the longer she would dwell on what she had to do and what it would result in, and the greater the guilt would grow. She doubted she would decide not to do it for practical or moral grounds, but the possibility that such guilt would make a coward of her haunted her.

She needed to harden herself somehow, to find some way to make herself as ruthless as she needed to be. Unbidden, the image of Tasya Morevna materialised in her imagination. Was this what had happened to her? She had to make a hard decision, and the only way she could go through with it was to make herself into a monster? Perhaps it was the only way Katya was going to be able to do this. She smiled to herself; she had never expected to find herself earnestly wondering, "What would the Chertovka do?" A war criminal, perhaps. A cold-blooded killer, certainly. *Oh, Katya, what wonderful inspirational figures you worship these days. The pirate and the She-Devil.*

The door was on one of the less grand shopping corridors, small permanent stalls lining it on both sides. Perhaps a third of them were locked up, the businesses within them gone, the signs removed or painted out. They had probably sold silly fripperies, at least by Russalkin standards, and the economies of war had starved them of revenue. It was sad, but convenient, as the door she was heading for was between two such abandoned stalls and thereby hidden from casual observation.

Exercising the skill of a professional criminal in giving the impression that she had every right to do such a thing, Katya walked to the door, tapped the sequence Tasya had taught her into the lock pad, and entered. The door clicked behind her, and the mission was on.

Not for the first time, Katya wondered just where Kane got all these pieces of information and, not for the first time, she thought it just as well she didn't ask. Door codes, blueprints, schedules, procedures… he had touched upon so many things in his briefing that he had no right to know, yet mysteriously did. His network of informants and fixers ranged wide and their services ran deep, but there was one thing they could not provide him with, and that one thing was why she was there.

Katya was in darkness. She had been told not to switch on the lights as there was a chance the power usage in that area might be noticed. In the moment she had the door open, however, she had seen the electric torch sitting on the floor inside the disused access corridor, just as Kane had said it would be. She felt for it now, found it, and switched it on. In its light, she took her identity card from her pocket and examined it.

It had been slightly disappointing to discover that Kane didn't really need *her* for the mission; he needed her security clearance. Beta Plus was a grade usually only entrusted to senior military and high ranking officials. Most people had Gamma ratings and might go their whole lives without even seeing a blue Beta card. In a purely practical sense, it was a greater honour than her medal, her Hero of Russalka decoration in its beautiful wooden box. That was aboard the *Vodyanoi* now, in a locked drawer of Kane's desk where he'd put it for safekeeping. It wasn't so much the medal she treasured, but – when her disgrace inevitably came – she couldn't bear to think of them taking away the box.

She started to follow the route she had memorised through the forgotten corridors. Not that it was entirely necessary to trust to her memory – whoever had prepared this part of her journey in advance had left clear tracks in the grime and dust. It was faintly disappointing that she had memorised the directions when somebody had left a trail that any fool could have followed. Out of sheer bloody-mindedness, she primarily used the directions, only glancing at the disturbed layer of dirt on the floor to corroborate them.

She was not amused when she discovered the route took her into a lift shaft, the doors braced open with a misappropriated hydraulic jack. Her instructions had merely been, "Climb three levels" at this point. That skipped the trifling fact that this would mean stepping across a void that was too deep for her torch's beam to reach the bottom, but which – judging by the echoes of lapping water beneath her – would end in a fairly considerable splash should she fall.

Muttering foul curses down on the heads of Kane, Tasya, and whichever genius had reconnoitred the route yet failed to mention it involved gymnastics, Katya shifted her bag so the weight fell on the small of her back and squared up to step across to the maintenance ladder running up the left of the shaft.

She stepped back from the edge and looked at her torch; it was too big to hold between her teeth, so she would either have to make the step with only one hand free or in pitch darkness. She ruminated for a moment, then picked up a piece of broken ceramic from the floor. It looked like it had once been part of an electrical insulator, probably something very important in the running of the lift. She doubted the thing would ever run again even if it was powered up.

She tossed the ceramic chip into the shaft and waited, counting off the seconds. The splash when it came seemed very distant. She did a couple of quick calculations in her head and made a guess that there were five levels to fall before hitting water. Even better, the fatalistic part of her mind told her, if she managed to climb the ladder and *then* slipped, she'd have eight levels to fall, and wouldn't that be fun?

Finally, she clipped the torch into one of the side-pockets of her shoulder bag so that it shone onto the wall to her right. It wasn't perfect, but at least the reflected light was better than nothing. Rallying her courage, she shuffled to the very edge of the shaft, took a deep breath in and out, and stepped out into nothingness.

The shadows played hell with her depth perception, but she had made a point of gauging the distance when the ladder had been under the full beam of her torch, and she trusted to that knowledge rather than the shifting shapes cast before her now. It worked; her leading foot came down heavily on a rung a split second before her hands found the verticals and held on firmly. It was just as well she did, because the firm blow her foot had delivered to its rung seemed to disengage something in the ladder's structure that was not supposed to disengage. Some catch or ratchet or bolt or screw had been quietly corroding away there for years, and all it took was one good thump to make it fail.

There was a metallic *plink!*, sharp and final. She hesitated, confused by the sound echoing from the concrete sides of the shaft, and then felt her lower body moving away from the wall. The ladder was constructed from two-metre lengths and while the length her hands were gripping was secure, the one her feet had landed on was anything but. The uppermost stanchion connecting the section to the wall had broken cleanly and now the length of ladder from her knees down was levering out into the shaft, pivoting at its lowest bracket.

Katya gasped and gripped the uprights even more fiercely as she felt the ladder beneath her push her legs away from the wall. She tried momentarily to keep her feet on the rung, but the free end of the ladder section was pushing painfully against her kneecaps and, a moment later, she felt her feet slide off the metal.

With surprisingly little noise, the ladder section fell away quickly enough to snap its connections to the next section down, and dropped down the shaft with the quietest sound of sheering air that ended with a small splash as it landed vertically five levels below, slicing cleanly through the dark, waiting water.

"Oh, shit," said Katya in a small voice. Her hands were starting to slide down the ladder verticals.

Making an instant decision that certainly saved her life, she released her right hand's grip and slapped it onto the first rung she could find. Her left hand followed suit, but this time she reached up to grab the next rung up. Using the panic-borne adrenalin to power her screaming muscles, her feet scrambling at the wall to find whatever footholds they could, she progressed up the ladder in a series of short, staccato pull-and-grabs until a foot found a rung and she was able to pause, relatively safe.

Now reaction set in, and she felt cold sweat prickle across her even as her muscles seemed to weaken. She had to make the most of the dwindling strength the near fall had given her, and used it to drive herself up the ladder, not thinking of anything but the next rung, and then the next rung, and then the next rung. Only when she had climbed three levels, found another door held up with a jack, and stepped smartly across did she have a chance to be afraid, only then did she allow herself to think about what the broken ladder meant for her future.

Her planned escape route was now impassable.

THIRTEEN
DANGEROUS CORRIDORS

So much for the carefully worked-out plan. Kane had been frank in explaining that her chances of getting away were no better than 50/50. Now they had just lengthened considerably.

She had a paranoid thought that perhaps the ladder had been sabotaged for exactly this reason, but that made no sense. She could just as easily have died in the lift shaft, mission incomplete, and that would have profited no one but the FMA, who would never have known about it. No, it was just one of those things. One of those silly, random things that, in this case, pretty much guaranteed a death sentence.

Katya's sense of fatalism deepened. Her future now contained only two potential outcomes – she either successfully completed the mission, or she didn't. That something bad would subsequently happen to her was a foregone conclusion, so she disregarded that. Success or failure was all she need concern herself with, and she much preferred to be a successful martyr to global peace than another of the war's faceless dead.

She made her way along the dark, damply smelling hallways, second right, first left, first right and found herself in a cul-de-sac where the old abutted the new. Here there was a locked door, using an old-style keystick lock of a type that had been deemed obsolete even before her parents had been born. Katya searched around until she found amongst the debris in the corner what looked like an abandoned toolkit box. Inside she found a keystick and a change of clothes. Kane had said she'd get filthy in the old corridors and that wasn't even taking into account the scuffs and tears her coveralls had taken during the incident in the lift shaft.

Changing clothes in an abandoned corridor was possibly not the strangest thing she'd ever done in her life, but it felt odd all the same. Once, this had been a busy place, and a ghost of that liveliness still hung around it. It seemed strange to be in her underwear there, leaning against the wall with one hand while trying to kick off her dirty coveralls, which had taken on a sudden emotional attachment to her right ankle.

After another five minutes of undignified hopping around while she tried to keep as much grime as she could off the new clothes while dressing in them, she was ready. She made sure her identity card and the keystick were in her left breast pocket, ran the route she had been given through her mind one last time, and doused the torch.

In darkness, she stood close by the door and listened. It was vitally important that she was not seen emerging from the door – even the dullest observer might wonder why somebody had been in the disused sections – and so she waited for a full minute simply to get used to the sound levels beyond.

Kane had told her that it was little more than an access corridor, well off the main byways, and few people should be walking them. She heard one pair of feet walk by and then a muffled greeting that brought the footsteps to a halt. A conversation ensued, rendered irritating by its length and boring by being muffled into meaninglessness by the door. Finally, after almost ten minutes, the conversationalists remembered they had jobs to be getting on with and they parted. Katya waited until all the footfalls had faded away before sliding the keystick into the slot in the lock. There was a very solid *clunk*, terrifying in the quiet, and the door opened easily under her hand.

She regretted not leaving the torch on until the last moment when she stepped into the brightly lit corridor and had to blink away tears as she tried to adjust to it after the darkness. It had seemed like a clever idea at the time, to take away light so she could focus entirely on sound. If anyone turned the corner now, however, they would have found a strange young woman blundering blindly about with an open door behind her which was marked with a prominent sign, "KEEP SEALED. DANGEROUS CORRIDORS BEYOND THIS POINT." Katya's cover story was not likely to survive such a spectacle.

The corridor remained obligingly empty for the minute it took her vision to clear, however. She closed and locked the door, quickly checked that she hadn't got any dirt on her fresh clothes that might mark her out as somebody who had recently been in the DANGEROUS CORRIDORS, hoped her short blonde hair didn't look like a pipe brush, and mentally retuned herself to be somebody who had every right to be in that hall.

In one sense, she did. Every person on that level had at least a Beta grade security pass. Kane had been grudgingly complimentary about the standard of the passes.

"Gammas are easy to fake, and Gamma Pluses not much more so. There's a huge jump in the standard between Gamma Plus and Beta, though. Nanoscale identifiers, unique polymer tagging, even some fancy business with quantum encipherment. What that all means is that Beta passes and upwards cannot be forged. Not by us, or even by the Yagizban and, believe me, we've tried. We can come up with something that fools the eye easily enough but, as soon as it gets scanned, the game is over. Where you're going, you can't operate a console or even open a door unless your card's in a reader. Borrowing yours or stealing one is no good, either. There is a variety of biometric tests to confirm the user is who it's supposed to be. I'm sorry, Katya – you're the only person we know who could walk those corridors and stand any chance of getting away with it."

Lucky me, thought Katya as she walked the Beta security level corridors.

From the door she walked coolly and confidently right, first left, second right, up a short set of steps leading to a section that was slightly offset to the rest of the maze, turned right, first left, all the way along to the end of the corridor where it opened out into a round chamber.

Katya knew that the lack of bulkheads meant that she was well inside the mountain into which Atlantis was built. This was fortunate, as she could guarantee that every bulkhead would require her ID before allowing her to proceed. The further she could go without using it, the better her chances.

The whole episode of the disused corridors had been to avoid her having to enter the Beta graded section by the usual routes, all of which involved an ID check. Her card was authentic, but she had no reason to be here. Attention would have been called to her and that would have been the end of that. Her Beta Plus was like her medal: an honour of no practical use.

Until now. Right at that exact moment, the entry database was disconnected from the internal usage logs. Usually, the facility computer logged people into the site when they entered, and off it when they left. If a card was used on site that had not been logged in, there would have been a security alert. Currently, however, a small piece of computer code that had begun life in a Yagizban espionage sciences facility had separated the two and would continue to do so for another twelve hours. During that time, anybody with a Beta grade or above could wander around the place whether they had been logged in at an entrance or not. The security failure would only be discovered if and when somebody decided to go through the usage logs themselves.

Katya thought it was very likely that some poor soul would end up doing exactly that when the FMA discovered what she had done. Assuming she had a chance to do it.

The chamber was in the form of a hemisphere with its floor lower than the entry corridor. In the centre was the group of computers that handled traffic control and communications. They rose high, embraced with coolant systems, and ringed with a mesh walkway. Destroying them would cause the Federal forces perhaps a day of disruption before the workload could be fully assumed by the multiple redundancy back-ups dispersed elsewhere in the mountain. Katya, however, was not there to do anything as mundane as simple sabotage.

The situation was complicated by the discovery that the room was not unmanned. This was a surprise – the computers were very low maintenance, and would be left entirely alone for days at a time. It was just her lousy luck to walk in on one of the rare occasions when somebody else was working on something there.

A technician in white coveralls, his Beta card clipped to his pocket, was checking the valves feeding the coolant system. He looked up in surprise when Katya entered. "Oh! You made me jump," he said. "I thought I was alone." He smiled awkwardly.

Katya didn't smile at all. "This is the traffic control and communications hub, yes?" she said curtly. She nodded at the open doorway. "I'm surprised there's no secure access to this room. Why is that?" She said it as if it was his idea not to bother installing a pass-locked door.

"I... don't know. I could ask?" The technician was in his twenties, possibly ten years older than Katya, but two wars had made such a mess of Russalka's demographic spread, it was unsurprising to find seniority was not necessarily attached to age.

"Don't bother," she said. "I shall include it in my report."

"Your report?" He looked her up and down, trying to decide who she might be. "Pardon me for asking, but may I see your identification?" Katya looked at him icily, trying to mimic the marrow-freezing effect that Tasya managed so well. "Please?" added the technician.

With an expression that indicated she was now sure she was talking to the facility idiot, she smoothly withdrew her pass from her breast pocket. There was no indication of job on it, but it did contain an entry for "Domicile." Hers was marked "None." On a Gamma card this wouldn't have earned it a second glance; lots of submariners lived like Katya aboard their boats with the occasional night in rented rooms or a capsule hotel. Beta card holders didn't live that sort of life, and a Beta Plus definitely wouldn't. "Domicile: None" meant a senior grade that travelled constantly, and there weren't many reasons for that.

All these thoughts had run through the technician's head so obviously that Katya felt like a mind reader. He licked his lips nervously. "May I ask what your role is, please? Ma'am?"

"You may," she conceded. "But do you *really* want to know?"

In a small psychological coup that she had not entirely understood until now, Tasya had ensured that Katya's replacement coveralls would be dark grey, a shade not formally used by any section of the Federal apparatus. The impression thus created screamed, "Secor field agent" to all.

"No, ma'am," he said meekly.

"I am merely having a look around. That, for example," she pointed at a spiral metal staircase that ascended to a sealed hatch in the ceiling. "What's up there?" Of course, she knew full well what was up there.

"Uh, nothing. Well, something, but nothing very important. Not really important. Just the data lines to the comms arrays."

"Show me."

"I can't, ma'am. It's a Beta Plus lock. But," he waved vaguely at her left breast pocket, trying to indicate her card and not the breast. "But you can."

Inwardly, she quailed. This would be the first time she had actually used the card here, and this would be the point where she discovered whether the Yagizban computer exploit had worked. If not, she would have armed company very quickly.

Showing substantially more confidence than she felt, she mounted the steps. She noticed the technician was following her and stopped.

"Where do you think you're going?" she demanded of him. "Beta Plus, remember? Go back to your work."

He nodded, embarrassed, muttered some apologetic noises and descended again. She watched until he'd returned to the computers, then continued up to the sealed hatch.

The reader was mounted against the axis shaft of the steps. "This is a Beta Plus security point," she read on its small screen. "Insert identification card to proceed." Trusting to the distant genii of the Yagizba Enclaves, she slid her card into the reader's slot.

No alarms went off. Instead the screen now read, "Retinal scan confirmation required. Please look at the red dot in the scanner with your right eye. Do not blink."

Katya had to lift herself on her toes a little to get the scanner level with her eye. She had barely got herself in position when the scan was complete. "Identity confirmed. Welcome, Katya Kuriakova." She read her name with a tight cold feeling in the pit of her stomach. Now there was incontrovertible proof that she had been here. Her last opportunity to walk away from the mission had just been destroyed before her eyes. Specifically, she corrected herself, her right eye.

Above her, with a thump of disengaging bolts and the hum of servo motors, the hatch slid back. Parsecs away on old Earth, condemned criminals had once mounted the hangman's scaffold with the same slow tread that Katya now used as she climbed the steps into the restricted area.

The room at the top of the spiral staircase was small and spectacularly cluttered. The sheer profusion of wall-mounted boxes and identical blackly insulated cables running around the place like the limbs of a cybernetically-enhanced eikosipus family – a species similar to the terrestrial octopus, but with twenty tentacles rather than eight – panicked Katya for a second; how could she possibly find the right junction in this mess?

After she swallowed down her nerves, however, and looked again, she saw that there was actually an order underlying the apparent chaos. Indeed, when she looked closer still she found that all the boxes and all the cable sockets were clearly labelled. Thirty seconds of searching found her the one she was looking for.

Working quickly, conscious of the technician below who was probably bursting with curiosity to know what she was up to, Katya took the bland metal box from her bag. It was bare metal, a coolly glinting titanium alloy, whereas the boxes already there were all finished in a silken black. Yet it didn't look too badly out of place once she had pulled out a lead from the wall box, and replaced it with one of the leads from hers. Its other lead was pushed into a power feed and that was that. She stowed it behind a mass of cables where they fed into the floor, arranging them to hide it as best as she could.

On the top edge of the box was the covered switch. She flipped back the cover, and flicked the switch. It glowed a reassuring green, although whether that meant anything truly reassuring at all, she had no idea. She closed the cover to hide the glow, took a deep breath, and then exhaled it slowly. She had done what she had come there to do. If the box was left alone for even a few minutes, it would do its job.

She turned to descend the steps and found the technician's head poking up through the hatch. He frowned suspiciously up at her. "What's going on in here?" he demanded. "I heard you messing around with things."

"If I told you," she said, her imperious descent forcing him to back away from her, "my colleagues would just have to *untell* you. Do you understand?" It was a threat she'd once heard on a drama and seemed very impressive coming from the formidable heroine.

Apparently it sounded far less impressive coming from her.

"You stay right there," he said. "I'm calling my superior."

"No, you're not," said Katya, and hit him in the side of the neck with Kane's taser.

She was glad she'd had the foresight both to have it ready, and to lift her other hand from the metal staircase's banister before using it. He had one hand on it, and she saw a couple of blue sparks leap between his knuckles and the metal. For an agonised second the technician shook and grimaced, then collapsed as the taser deactivated, falling into a heap across the steps.

Katya quickly checked his pulse, and was relieved to still find he had one. She hadn't known quite what to expect from the taser, but she'd been hoping for a quick flutter of eyelids and a collapse into a dreamless sleep. What she'd actually got was a painful looking series of spasms, and the smell of burning hair in the air. Even the screen on the security lock had wavered in the taser's electromagnetic field. That gave her an idea.

She set the hatch closing and, as soon as the locks had re-engaged, she tasered the card reader. The screen flashed on and off several times, then an ugly mass of random symbols came up and stayed there. It looked very broken to her.

She pocketed the taser and stepped over the technician. She considered dragging him down to the chamber floor and hiding him somewhere, but couldn't help thinking she'd do him more harm than she already had if she tried. Besides, he was barely visible from the chamber exit.

She resisted the urge to run from the chamber, holding it down to a determined walk. She remembered when she'd passed herself off as a minor Yagizban official; that had gone reasonably well. Yes, she'd been caught, but not because her impersonation had been poor. All she had to do was look like she belonged.

She reached the side corridor that contained the sealed off access to the old facility without seeing even a single other person on the way, and this boosted her confidence enormously. It was only as she approached the door itself that it occurred to her that this was very much at odds with her experience when going the other way. Then she had seen several people in the hallways; that they were so empty now was a cause for suspicion, not comfort.

Four figures in FMA military uniforms turned the corner ahead of her as she reached the door to the DANGEROUS CORRIDORS. She would have attempted to bluff them by walking by if they hadn't come to a concerted halt at the sight of her.

The lieutenant leading them pointed directly at her. "That's Kuriakova."

FOURTEEN
LITTLE FLAG

Katya didn't hesitate. She drew the keystick, stabbed it into the lock, and was through the door before the startled marine troopers could even reach for their sidearms. She slammed the door behind her and was rewarded by the solid clicks of bolts being inserted into all four sides of the frame. There were heavy footfalls on the other side of the door, and the handle was wrenched up and down in frustrated fury from the other side.

On an impulse Katya placed the contact plate of the taser on the metal of the handle and triggered a charge. There was a cry of pain, and the sound of a fall. She moved away from the door just as she heard the cracks of maser bolts hitting the door. They didn't penetrate, but it had been ridiculous using them against the metal of the door in the first place – the whole point of using masers was that they were as bad at penetrating metal as they were good at punching through flesh. This way a missed shot wouldn't result in letting in the whole ocean.

Katya had the torch on and was running back the way she had come. At the same time, she was trying to think of a way out of Atlantis. The escape route she had been given was broken, and somehow the Feds had found out who she was.

Her first thought was that the Yagizban computer hack had failed, but then she realised that this could not be so. If it had failed, then the reader on the communications room would have interrogated the entry system, found she wasn't supposed to be there, and refused to open.

Had somebody found the technician? Had he woken up within seconds of her leaving rather than minutes, and raised the alarm himself? But the empty corridors, if not a coincidence, suggested a quiet evacuation of the area had been taking place even while she'd been installing the Yagizban electronics unit.

None of it made sense. She was missing something.

Any further thoughts on the matter were interrupted by finding herself at the lift shaft. Three levels down was a gap in the ladder that she wouldn't have tried to negotiate in full light and a drop of three metres onto a foam mattress. That she would be trying it in the deep shadows cast by a torch pointing almost everywhere except where it would do some good, and that the drop was five levels and finished in water that had, at the very least, a jagged section of ladder waiting beneath the surface, put her right off the idea.

Should she stay on the same level, then, or try her luck on one of the others she could reach from the lift shaft? She would have to prise the doors open, but doubted that would be too difficult. In a nearby office she found a chair, its seat broken, lying on its side. A minute's work with her multi-tool's screwdriver had a leg off. She slipped it into her bag and went back to the shaft.

Trusting to obtuse light and ageing architectural fittings with all the enthusiasm she had displayed last time, Katya stepped into the void and found the ladder with her hands and leading foot. The ladder creaked alarmingly under her weight, but obliged her by not coming away from the wall and dropping her eight levels into the inky waters that waited below. She paused; from somewhere she heard a loud bang that echoed around the walls of the abandoned level. They were through the door, and would be following the trail through the dirt soon enough right to the lift shaft. Fear spurring her, she started to climb.

One level didn't seem to be enough, so she pushed on to the next. Here she climbed up far enough that she could step across to the concrete lintel below the door edge with one foot, her other still on the ladder. Bracing herself against the cool metal of the doors, she drew the chair leg from her bag and jammed it into the crack that separated them and heaved. The door slid over a centimetre or so, then stopped dead with solid certainty.

Katya glared at it as if it had personally insulted her, and leaned hard against the chair leg. She could see it bowing slightly under the force, but the lift door remained solid. Below her she could hear boots running, echoing, growing closer. The fear grew in her; they were almost there. In a moment they would be at the lift shaft, they would look up, and it would all be over. In desperation she put her body weight into it, pushing as hard as she humanly could in such a position. Something gave inside the door, the chair leg slid free, and she found herself thrown against the inner side of the left hand door. Her hands scrabbled hopelessly at the sheet steel for a moment, and then she fell, the chair leg falling down the shaft, ricocheting off the sides as it went, announcing her presence to all.

She cried out and grabbed at anything she could find. Nothing for a moment, then she crashed heavily against the concrete lintel, knocking the breath from her. Her hand found a structural stanchion beneath the lintel and she held on for her life.

A torch beam shone up at her from the open door two levels below her. "She's here!" a male voice called. "I found her!"

The lift shaft was illuminated by another torch. Looking up, she could see the shaft in better detail than ever before. The door she had bounced off stood open perhaps thirty centimetres. It looked like whatever had been holding it shut had finally given way. She could see the ladder not far away. If she swung her right foot into it, she could be on it in a couple of seconds, another three or so to climb up to where she'd been a moment ago, step across, grab the door edges, open it, dive through. In fifteen seconds she could be running again.

"Shoot her," said the lieutenant.

Katya realised she was never going to run again, because in fifteen seconds her corpse would be in the water, ten levels down.

There was nothing she could do. A half-formed thought that perhaps it would be better to fall than be shot and fall. At least she would be the one who made the final decision of her life.

"Belay that order!" A new voice, confident, authoritative, and angry. "Do not fire!"

"Sir!" she heard the lieutenant say, then they stepped away from the mouth of the shaft and she couldn't make out anymore.

Then there was a distinct, "Yes, sir!" and the lieutenant was leaning out to look at her.

"Can you reach the ladder?"

"I think so," she called back.

"Then do so. You have my gun at your back. If you attempt to escape, I will kill you without hesitation, Kuriakova. Do you understand?"

She understood very well. Moving slowly, she got her foot onto the ladder and slid her hands along the stanchion until she could reach the rungs. Here she rearranged her shoulder bag so that the strap was no longer across her chest, but only hung on one shoulder.

"What are you doing?"

"The strap's caught on the rung," she called back. "It's alright. It's free now." She climbed down at half the speed she had ascended, giving the lieutenant no excuse to fire. When she reached the level where he waited, she stepped across and stumbled very deliberately. Her bag slid from her shoulder and fell down the shaft. "My torch!" she cried as she grabbed the doorframe, trying to give the impression that was all she was concerned about, and not that she was trying to get rid of any evidence that it might contain. A taser of Grubber manufacture would be hard enough to explain by itself.

Her upper arms were grabbed painfully hard and she was half lifted, half dragged out of the lift shaft, before being dumped on the filthy floor of the corridor.

She looked up and found herself ringed by the four Federal troops she had seen in the corridor. Then she saw the fifth man and her heart sank. He was one of the Secor agents who had interrogated her after Shurygin was shot. She'd always had a feeling that she might cross paths with Secor again sooner or later, but had been very much hoping for "later."

"You owe me your life, Ms Kuriakova," said the agent.

Ringed in harsh torch light, she squinted up at him. "I'd rather they'd killed me."

Her arms were dragged behind her and she felt restraint strips being wound around her wrists. She started to struggle, but they were too strong. A fabric bag was pulled down over her head and secured around her neck.

"Yes," admitted the agent. "You'll find yourself thinking that often over the next few days."

They led her back to the door into the Beta grade section. When they reached the door, they had her lift her feet high and she thought it must be because they had blown down or cut through the door, and there was still a bit of it in the bottom of the frame. She never knew for sure.

After that, she had no idea where they took her. The corridors were silent and she guessed they were still evacuated. They took her to another level in a lift, along more corridors, and nobody spoke. It was only when they took her through another door and the sound ambience seemed to change that she realised that she was now in a room, and not a large one. She was put in a chair and she felt straps being secured around her upper arms even though her wrists were still restrained. They double checked her wrists, then she heard the door close.

Katya listened for a minute or two but couldn't hear anything at all; no breathing, no sound of somebody shifting their weight from one foot to another. Experimentally, she tried pushing down with her feet, but the chair wouldn't move at all. It seemed to be bolted to the floor.

In a strange way, it was a relief to be caught. She had no idea what Secor had planned for her, but they weren't there for the moment, so she found it hard to care. She'd worry about it when they came back. Right then, however, she could just feel the tension fading from her to be replaced by an exhaustion that seemed to soak through her flesh down to her bones. She leaned forward as far as the straps would let her and her head sagged until her chin touched her chest. They would probably use sleep deprivation against her soon, she thought. She'd better grab any sleep she could now.

She was asleep when they came for her. She had no idea how long she'd slept, but it didn't feel nearly long enough. She was roused by the arm straps being released and was still drowsy and only half aware when she was dragged to her feet. She guessed they were taking her somewhere new, so she stood straight and waited to be guided from the room.

The punch to her stomach was completely unexpected. She grunted and doubled up, but somebody grabbed the back of the bag over her head and pulled her upright again, the cloth stretching tautly across her face. Then she was punched in the stomach again. This time she was allowed to fall, her head banging smartly against the edge of something – The chair? A table? – as she did.

"Careful," she heard someone say, but they said it as if a cup was at risk and not a fellow human's skull.

The blow to her head stunned her, and she felt disorientated, her sense of which way was up wavering badly. She could offer no resistance when she was pulled back to her feet and held while somebody punched her once, twice, in the face. She tasted blood in her mouth and could feel that a tooth was loose. Every blow disconnected her further from reality. It was becoming harder to believe she had ever woken up.

Her feet were kicked out from beneath her and, unable to use her hands to break her fall, she went down heavily, her head banging on the floor. Somewhere away from the pain, she distractedly thought, *They're going to beat me to death.*

A boot caught her in the pit of her stomach, a new agony borne upon her. She vomited violently, bringing up little but water that reminded her vaguely of expensive coffee. It soaked into the fabric of the hood, the stomach acid stinging her skin.

"Don't let her choke," said the voice again, offhand with a mild air of disgust. "Secor want her."

So she wasn't going to be beaten to death here and now after all. She had no idea whether to be relieved or disappointed.

The hood was untied and pulled off. While she screwed her eyes shut against the brilliant light of the interrogation room they gagged her mouth open with the end of a baton. One of them cleared her mouth with a gloved finger and made sure her tongue was clear of her airway.

"She's fine. Pass me the water." The officer washed the vomit from his hand and threw the rest of the beaker's contents in her face. "The bag will need rinsing," he added offhandedly.

There were voices elsewhere. Orders given and accepted. Still groggy, Katya was pulled back to her feet. She grimaced, tensing her stomach for another blow, but they only put her back in the chair and strapped her upper arms to it once again. There *was* a table, she saw, and another chair opposite to her. That one didn't have restraints. The FMA officers left her then, leaving the door open.

A moment later the Secor agent entered. The door closed unbidden behind him as he walked over to the table and sat in the free chair, placing a metal briefcase by his chair.

He looked at her, and then at the discarded bag and pool of watery vomit streaked with blood on the floor.

"This isn't how it works in the dramas," said Katya, her speech slurred. "The hero on your side of the table asks questions, the fellow on my side lies, gets caught in a lie. 'Curses, you caught me out. I'll tell you everything.' Maybe I missed where the hero beats the crap out of the fellow."

"Oh, that wasn't part of the interrogation, Katya," he said. "That was just some patriotic citizens expressing contempt for a traitor. This," he waved a hand back and forth to indicate the both of them, "*this* is the interrogation. The first of many, I'm sure."

He lifted the briefcase onto the table and opened it, the lid blocking Katya's view of the contents. "We don't get many traitors, Katya," he said conversationally as he took out a memo pad and placed it on the table beside the case. "Not proper ones. Federal citizens are very loyal to their fellow citizens." A recorder joined the memo pad. "You're really something of a rarity." He took out one last item and held it in one hand while he closed the case and returned it to the floor with the other. Katya's felt cold; it was the Yagizban device she had planted.

He placed the device on the area of empty table between them, rested his hands on the table edge, steepled his fingers, and looked at her expectantly. Katya returned the look defiantly, although she was having trouble keeping one eye open. One of the punches to her face had caught the cheek bone, and the flesh was swelling. If she had seen him on the halls, she would have thought he possibly worked in engineering, he had that air of practicality about him. Dark, close cut hair, somewhere in his mid-thirties. Otherwise, it was difficult to get a grip on what sort of person he was. His clothes were the sort of thing an engineer might wear, too, right down to the sleeveless jacket. People who worked in the docks often wore them because it could get cold there, and the jackets provided extra pockets for gear.

He tapped the box. "What is it?"

Katya shrugged.

He watched her keenly for a moment, and then made a note on the pad. Then he asked again, "What is it?"

Katya shrugged again.

The Secor agent pursed his lips, thinking. Then he reached inside his jacket and produced a maser. He placed it carefully on the table and gestured at it.

"You're a traitor, Katya. You will never be interrogated to find out if you are or not, because we know you are. It's an empirical fact." He smiled warmly, and laughed. "We don't even care why. Maybe later, but not right now. Our concern at this immediate moment is what were you doing in the traffic control centre? What were you doing with this?" Again, the light tap of a fingertip on the box's metal casing.

She looked at the gun, then at him, but still didn't reply.

He looked at the gun with the mildest mannered surprise, as if he'd forgotten he put it there. "What's this for? That's what you're wondering, isn't it? Well, I'll tell you. It's your ticket out of this. I've seen your file, Katya. You're no idiot. You know what happens to traitors, and you know what's going to happen to you. There are still choices you can make, however. A maser bolt to the head, in the right place, will kill instantly.

You're not even aware of it." He snapped his fingers, a life going out. "Or, you can live. Day in, day out. Week in, week out. Months, and years. The men who beat you, look at the mess they made. No training. We can make your every day a hell, Katya. Your every living day." He laughed again, leaning back in his chair and shaking his finger at her. "I know what you're thinking! You're thinking, 'Where there's life, there's hope,' aren't you?"

His smile slowly faded. He leaned forward again. "Life is *pain*, Katya Kuriakova. You can guess how much pain. Now, answer my questions, and I can save you living a life that is ten shades worse than death. The box. What was its function?"

Katya looked at the box. Then slowly, she turned her head to one side and spat blood on the table.

"I can see cut marks on it," she said. "You've already had it open. You know what it is." She could also see a band of discolouration across the bare metal where it seemed to have oxidised. She hoped it meant what she thought it did.

The Secor agent sighed. He peeled a few tabs of tape from the box's edges and lifted off the top.

The box had indeed been opened, and its contents had told the FMA technicians precisely nothing. Inside was a mess of burnt wiring and components, the partially melted remains dusted with white powder and globs of metal.

Katya smiled, though her lip was split and the smile made it bleed again. "Oh, dear."

"Oh, dear," agreed the agent. "Yagizban design, of course. They're very ingenious like this. It did its job, and

Jonathan L Howard   209

then a thermite charge melted the processor and memory core. However, not to worry." His eyes narrowed. "We still have *you*."

Katya looked at him coldly. Then she giggled. "Do you always talk like that? 'I'm with Secor. We're so threatening'?" She couldn't help but laugh. She shook her head, grinning at him. "You idiot. Thanks for that, by the way." She nodded at the box. "Until you showed me that, I didn't know if I'd succeeded or not. Now I do."

The agent wasn't smiling. "You don't seem to appreciate exactly what is going to happen to you."

"No," she said. "No, *you* don't seem to appreciate exactly what is going to happen to *you*. You joined Secor because it looked like a nice, safe berth, didn't you? You get respect, decent money I would think, and you get to feel important. You're probably a bit of a failure as a human being, aren't you? Oh, and you get to work out those sadistic impulses you feel now and then, torturing prisoners."

Now he smiled, but it was just a pattern of tightened muscles and stretched skin across his face. His eyes said something different. "This isn't about me, Kuriakova..."

"It is exactly about you." She couldn't tell if she was being brave or just reckless. Either way she was as good as sunk, so she decided to just let herself go with the delightful flow of hatred that was running through her now. "The FMA is finished. Everything you have hung your little flag on is finished. It might take a while, but this war is as good as over. And when it is, and Secor is closed down, what's going to keep you safe then, Mr Above-The-Law?"

The Secor agent's eye twitched. Abruptly, he leapt to his feet, snatching up his pistol. He clamped the muzzle against Katya's forehead, released the safety catch, and she would not, could not stop laughing.

"Go on!" she snarled at him through bloodied teeth. "Fire! Something else for the judges when they try you for war crimes! Fire, you bloody coward!"

FIFTEEN
TRAITOR'S GATE

The next Secor interrogator Katya had was interesting in that he barely asked any questions.

He came in and chatted at her. Not with her, because Katya had decided to maintain a stony silence when asked about anything to do with her immediate situation. If he asked her what she would like for lunch, she would tell him. If he asked her what had been the function of the Yagizban device, she would just look at him with her arms crossed.

It was nice to be able to cross her arms. The new interrogator didn't seem to believe in restraints and had neither had her strapped to her chair or had her wrists taped. He just sat there and talked about what was going on beyond the walls of the interrogation room.

He kept this up for two days. Finally, she interrupted a story he was telling her about an uncomfortable trip he'd once had aboard a shuttle when he was eight, by asking, "When do you start torturing me?"

"Soon," he said, and then went back to describing the funny smell he remembered from the shuttle.

He had been very solicitous about her injuries and had called in a medic almost the minute he first saw her. The swelling to her eye had almost gone and the bruising was fading, the cut to her scalp where she'd fallen against the table was cleaned and sealed, and she'd been declared free of internal injuries from her beating.

With all his talking, reminiscing, gossiping, and reading out news stories from his memo pad, Katya found it easy to ignore him, and to think about her situation. She didn't need her stereotypical Russalkin fatalistic streak to know that this was only a small diversion on the road to Hell. When he said she would be tortured soon, it was no idle threat. The only thing that she couldn't guess was why they hadn't started yet.

Other things she had managed to guess, though. The mystery of how Federal security had started looking for her so quickly, for one. It was an ugly conclusion at which she did not wish to arrive, and she tried a dozen others of increasing ridiculousness to try to avoid it. The most obvious conclusion is almost invariably the correct one, however, and that it saddened her so deeply did not alter the grim logic.

Sergei had betrayed her. It was the only thing that made any sense at all. He'd sat at Dunwich racked between his patriotism and his loyalty to her, and to the memory of Lukyan, his friend, her uncle. Finally, something had given way inside him, and he'd decided he needed to warn the Feds.

She could guess all the self-justifications – that she'd been led astray by Kane and Tasya, lied to, conned into doing some job for them. She could also guess that he would have begged the Feds he told his story to at Dunwich to go easy on Katya, that she was just a kid; that she didn't know what she was doing. In her mind's eye, she could see them giving him assurances that they never intended to keep, and poor, gullible Sergei walking away, believing them.

He wouldn't have been able to tell them much, but it would have been enough. The search for her must have begun when she was already in the old corridors. She imagined Secor agents turning up at the coffee salon, asking questions. If she hadn't stopped for coffee, she might have got away, or at least further. She might just have made it back into the water.

Then, of course, the base defences would have sunk her in seconds. No, she didn't regret stopping for the coffee.

It must have been a shock when an internal reader reported her card being used; not one at an entrance to the Beta halls. So they'd called around everywhere in the vicinity but for the communications hub chamber where the card was in use, ordered everyone off the corridors, and been on their way to arrest her when she almost walked into them.

Poor Sergei. Lukyan would never have forgiven him for such a betrayal, and that meant he would never forgive himself.

On the morning of the third day, everything changed. She was taken from her cell and escorted to a sick bay, where she was given a cursory examination that seemed primarily concerned with her head injuries. They took some pictures, and a dour woman who stood silently in the corner throughout said, "Good enough" at the end of it.

The man with the camera went out into the corridor, and two tall and strikingly handsome Federal officers entered.

Katya looked at them suspiciously. "What's this? What's going on?"

"You're leaving Atlantis soon," said the Secor agent. "This is all part of the preliminaries. Don't let them trouble you."

"Preliminaries? What do you mean, 'preliminaries'? What kind of preliminaries?"

"Don't let them trouble you," he repeated, and smiled blandly.

The officers took her out into the corridor, where the cameraman was already waiting, the small unit held at chest level. Katya didn't care to be the subject of any more pictures and kept her head down as she was walked past him. She was surprised when she heard him say, "Perfect!"

She turned back to find the dour woman and the Secor agent looking at the camera as the cameraman replayed the scene of a moment before. The woman nodded. "It will do."

"What's going on?" demanded Katya, but nobody would answer her. She was led back to her cell and left there.

••••

On the morning of the fourth day, they came for her while she was sleeping. She was dragged from her bunk, and a set of fresh underwear and some yellow coveralls were thrown at her as she blinked up in bewilderment from the floor.

"Clean clothes for you," said the Secor officer, leaning against the doorframe. The officers were women, and forced her to change despite the male Secor officer never leaving his place by the door.

"Enjoying yourself?" she sneered at him, but he just smiled that infuriatingly bland smile of his, and nodded.

When she was dressed, they put her into an armlock while they placed restraint tapes on her wrists and hooded her. Then she was led out of her cell. They walked her for a long way until they reached a lift. From the subdued voices that stilled as she approached, she received the impression that her bodyguard was about to become an entourage. From the sounds of footfall, she guessed there were perhaps six or seven, perhaps even eight people with her in the lift when they entered.

They descended in silence for twenty seconds, which meant they must now be well outside the Beta levels. Katya was trying to deduce where they might be heading for when the lift slowed to a halt, and the door slid open.

Instantly, a wave of sound swept in, leaving her shaken by its violence. There were screams and shouts and catcalls. So many voices, so much hatred, and it was all directed at her.

"Traitor!"

"Kill her!"

"I hope you die, you bitch!"

Inside the hood, Katya's eyes opened wide. She had a sudden terrible premonition that they were just going to throw her to the mob and stand by watching while she was torn apart.

"Back!" she heard an authoritative voice command – the dour woman. "Make way! You're interfering in Federal business."

"Make a hole!" demanded one of the Federal troops. "Coming through."

Katya was taken forward, held by her upper arms on both sides by the troops.

"Traitor!" somebody shouted nearby. "Traitor to Russalka!"

There was the sound of scuffling to her left, and somebody hit her through the bag. It was a quick blow, its hastiness rendering it light, but the surprise of it made her cry out.

"Hey!" she heard the trooper to the left shout. "Try that again, friend, and I will break your arm in two places. You get me?"

"Enough of that!" said somebody else in her group. Katya wondered what they were talking about. Then she felt something pat against the cloth, and she knew they were spitting on her.

She was taken forward, an agonisingly small step at a time. She could only guess how many people were there, how large the crowd was. They'd come there to hate her, to curse and spit on her, and to kill her if they got the briefest chance.

"Give me that!" she heard the woman behind her say, and was then momentarily deafened by the woman's amplified shouting through a public address override. "This prisoner is of use to the war effort. If any attempt is made to harm her from this moment onwards, it constitutes a schedule two felony under the Wartime Powers Acts. Lay so much as a finger on her and you can join her in the Deeps!"

Katya realised at the same moment as the crowd that the dour woman had to be an Alpha Plus – nobody else would or could invoke the Acts like that, or use the Deeps as a threat in public without the authority to back it up. They were in the presence of a senior member of the government; that fabled species. The knowledge cowed the crowd, and soon enough it would start Katya thinking about what was really happening to her. That would be later, though. Currently, her whole attention was focused on a single thing.

The Deeps. They were sending her to the Deeps.

She wished the first interrogator had executed her while he had the chance.

There were another five minutes of shouting and spitting, death threats and insults. One man shouted that he would find her family and kill them. Katya smiled humourlessly inside her hood at that. Then, with the abruptness of the door that slid shut behind them, the sound of the crowd was instantly cut off.

She heard somebody ahead approach and recognised the voice of her second Secor interrogator. "Well, that went rather well, I thought," he said, as if talking about the first rehearsal of an infant school play.

"I have *saliva* on me," replied the Alpha Plus with brittle resentment.

"There's a restroom just over there, ma'am. In the meantime, we'll get the prisoner into some clean clothes and get her packed off."

They had more clean clothes waiting? Katya was beginning to appreciate the degree of stage management in all this. She was led off by the female officers again, released from her restraints and the hood, and told to change her coveralls. The previous set was slimy with spit, and some stains that suggested food or worse had been thrown at her. She ignored it; it didn't matter what people thought. All they knew is what the FMA had told them. She couldn't blame them; she'd spent most of her sixteen years believing that what the FMA said and the truth, were plainly the same thing.

When she had changed, they cuffed her again but didn't bother with the bag. Another walk, this time with just the Secor agent and the two female officers. The Alpha Plus had disappeared, presumably off to lie down in a dark room after having to share a corridor with Gammas, thought Katya, a thought that was neither charitable nor essentially inaccurate.

They took her down narrow access corridors, lined with cables, pipes, and conduits on both sides and across the arched ceiling. At the end, another pair of troopers, not nearly as handsome as the ones who'd accompanied her through the screaming gauntlet earlier, waited.

Beyond the corridor was a military boat dock, a moon pool design with a small lake within an artificial cavern. There were several small vessels around, and another she recognised instantly. The hulking black form of the *Novgorod* seemed to overwhelm all the other boats there. The last time Katya had seen her, she'd been lying half-beached up a ramp in another moon pool, her skin torn by weapons fire, her heart stilled. It was strange seeing her alive and imposing like this. Her hatches were up, and torpedoes were currently being lowered in through the massive forward accesses into her weapons rooms. Many Novgorods were on deck or by the dockside, directing operations. On her conning tower, Katya saw a group of senior offices watching the loading. One of them stood noticeably taller than the others, and as she realised she recognised him, he looked over at her. The loading operations ceased to be of great interest to him and he walked to the tower's rail to watch her.

The Secor officer noticed the attention and asked, "Who's your admirer, Katya?" He laughed when she shot him a filthy look.

She knew it was stupid to feel ashamed. She knew she had done the right thing. The ones who should be ashamed were the ones up in the Alpha Plus corridors, not that she thought they were capable of it anymore. Yet for all that, she still couldn't bring herself to look up and meet the gaze of Lieutenant Anatoly Petrov, a man she respected and who, until this minute, she thought might still respect her. Now he just watched her go by from on high, looking down upon her in all senses.

Still feeling Petrov's gaze upon her, she was actually glad to reach the military boat that would be taking her to the Deeps, perhaps the first time anyone wearing a convict's yellow uniform had been eager to get under way as soon as possible. She was heading for the patrol boat at the end of the quay when one of her escort stopped her and gestured at the boat they were passing. "In there, prisoner."

She looked at her guards as if they were idiots. They had stopped by a military shuttle; a small vessel not so much larger than her own boat. More comfortable, a little bit faster, but less flexible in its mission capabilities than the *Lukyan*, the shuttle sat at full buoyancy by the quay with an ineffable air of smugness about it, as if to say it had a proper toilet aboard it and didn't care who knew. Katya's newfound self-image as a major war criminal was taking a little bit of a knock. All they could be bothered sparing for her was a shuttle?

"It's going to take almost three days to reach the Deeps in this thing," she said to the Secor agent.

"Perhaps you'll be rendezvousing with a larger vessel, Katya," said the agent.

"Will I?"

"Perhaps. Well, here's where I say goodbye for the moment. I may be called in later for some follow-up work on your debriefing…"

"Debriefing?" Katya tried to reconcile "debriefing" with blood and pain.

"…but that's only a 'maybe'. Otherwise, this is goodbye, Katya."

Katya thought that if he was expecting her to wish him a fond farewell, he would be waiting for a good while. Instead she said, "One question. What happened to the other Secor agent? The one before you?"

"Him? Oh, he was reassigned. You upset him, Katya. He's a sensitive soul."

Without another word, the Secor agent turned on his heel and walked away. Katya watched him go with disbelief before her escort grew impatient and hustled her across the gangplank and onto the shuttle's small deck. As she descended the ladder, she could see Petrov atop the *Novgorod*'s conning tower turning away from her. Petrov was a sensible, intelligent man, she consoled herself. One day he would understand why she had done what she had done.

She had never been aboard a shuttle before. Her uncle had always been hugely dismissive of them as "boats for corridor rats" and she had absorbed much of his disdain. It was pleasantly appointed within, with comfortable seating, plenty of space, a small galley, and, of course, a proper toilet. The boat's air of smugness, distinct enough outside, was overpowering within. Katya hated it.

"So how long are we in this scow before transferring to a real boat?" she asked.

Her escort ignored her question, and instead busied themselves removing her wrist tapes so that she would fit more easily into the restraints of her seat. Katya guessed that these straps were a recent addition, unless – just possibly – this was actually an admiral's personal launch, in which case they were probably a standard feature. The private hobbies of FMA admirals were a running joke amongst all submariners. Absolutely any sin or eccentricity could be put at their doors whether it was true or not; not all the prizes of rank are looked for.

The other feature of the shuttle that she wasn't used to was that the pilots' positions were behind a bulkhead. It felt strange not to able to look forward and see them sitting there. Instead there was just a beige bulkhead with a screen on it that cycled a vastly simplified status screen, then an active navigational chart, then a view ahead with some navigational data overlayed upon it, and then back around again. Since the passenger chairs all faced a central aisle, she had to look to her left to look at the screen, and she knew watching it for any length of time would give her neck pain.

The view opposite was hardly fascinating, either; the male troopers had returned to the quay after making sure everything was in readiness and this left Katya with the two female officers sitting directly across the aisle from her. Katya was very hopeful that they would be meeting another boat to take her onwards; the prospect of staring at them while they stared at her for three days was a depressing one, probably for all of them.

The hatch lowered on powered hydraulics, sealing with a muffled clump and hiss, both of which Katya decided sounded unforgivably self-satisfied. There was a sound of grating metal as the gangway disengaged, and Katya felt the slight wallow of an untethered boat. A moment later, a gentle hum told her that the drives were engaged and that they were underway. The shuttle pulled away from the quay and headed for the tunnel cut through the mountain connecting the moon pool with the ocean. Almost immediately the pilot began flooding the ballast tanks; the tunnel was flooded along its full length from its mouth in the moon pool, down a shallow descent, and then exiting into open sea.

"So," said Katya. "You girls do a lot of this sort of thing?" She'd seen how they watched the hatch close like a death sentence, and seemed disconcerted by the boat's wallowing when they'd been on the surface. The logical deduction was that they'd been seconded from base security, and were not frequent travellers.

One of them got up and went to the toilet unit. The other sat there, pallid as they listened to her colleague being sick very audibly because of the imperfectly closed door. Throughout, Katya smiled pleasantly at the seated trooper.

She'd apparently broken the first Secor interrogator, after all; perhaps she could break a few more Feds before she reached the Deeps. She balled her hands into fists and felt the restraints around her wrists. Yes, she decided, it was good to have a hobby.

SIXTEEN
ADMIRAL'S LAUNCH

For the first couple of hours, the names of her escort were "None of your business, traitor."

Then, for about the next five hours, they were called "Officers Volkova and Shepitko to you, prisoner."

And finally they were Oksana and Alina, and Katya was now just "Katya."

Neither of the officers seemed greatly motivated by their current mission and settled easily into scuttlebutt and scurrilous tales about their fellow officers, their watch commander, and one of their husbands, who was very dreamy by all accounts.

Katya tried to explain to them why she'd done what she'd done, about the drowned colony ship, slaughter at the evacuation site, the lies that threaded through every part of FMA operations, but Oksana just shushed her and said they'd been specifically ordered not to discuss the details of Katya's case so, if it was all the same to her, wouldn't she rather hear about the brilliant practical joke Oleg played on Grigory with a length of flexible piping, a quantity of liquid laxative, and a fire extinguisher? Katya had to admit that sounded pretty interesting, so they talked about it for a while. It turned out that Grigory stills hated Oleg because of the incident, and Katya said she couldn't blame him, because Oleg had gone too far.

As the chronometer showed the standard "day" turning to standard "night," Katya said, "Those pilots must have steel bladders. Do they have their own head up front or something?"

Oksana and Alina looked blankly at her, until she remembered that they'd probably never been on any submarine journey worth the name. "Head," she explained. "It's just the name for a boat's toilet."

"There aren't any pilots," said Alina. "Everything's automatic."

Katya looked at her in astonishment. "No pilots? What if anything goes wrong? Can you get to the pilot positions?"

"Nothing's going to go wrong," said Oksana, whose confidence in the competence of her superiors tended towards complacency.

"Maybe it won't," said Katya.

There was no point talking to her guards for anything other than information and amusement. Recruits for Base Security were not renowned for their native intelligence, just their loyalty and a modicum of common sense. Okasana and Alina were not much older than her, and she was sure they'd signed up for Security out of a sense of patriotism and a desire to help their fellow citizens.

They were goodhearted, but they were not very bright. There was no possibility that they would realise what was going on, and that was exactly why they had been chosen for the job.

"Listen to me," said Katya, "there's nothing we can do about it, but I'm going to tell you what your superior didn't when he gave you this mission. We will not be rendezvousing with another boat. A piece of junk like this..."

"It's an admiral's launch!" said Alina, scandalised.

"Maybe twenty years ago it was an admiral's launch. These seats are new to this boat. If you look under yours, you can see new mountings have been drilled for them. Same thing with the display on the forward bulkhead. You can see the outline of the original one, which was a little bit wider. You can still smell the gel filling agent they used to neaten things up a bit. Believe me, two days ago this scow was sitting in storage."

Alina fell quiet and Katya continued, "A piece of junk like this will not be able to carry out an automatic docking at sea. It will be going all the way to the Deeps. I guarantee I will need the head before then. Now, back that way," she nodded towards the rear of the boat, "no closer than five thousand metres and no farther than ten, there is at least one boat following us. I'd make a guess at the *Novgorod*. She was preparing to leave when we boarded. She knows the exact route we'll be taking because we're on automatic pilot and you can bet our shadows have the exact waypoint and timings list for the whole journey."

Oksana looked at her suspiciously. "How do you know all this?"

"I don't know it. Not for a fact. But I've lived my whole life in submarines and there are ways of doing things, and when those ways are changed you have to ask yourself, why?"

Oksana shrugged. "Well, even if you're right, having a warboat like the *Novgorod* is a good thing. I feel safer," she added, speaking to Alina.

Oksana's unquestioning belief in the nobility of her masters had irked Katya in their earlier conversations, but now it was beginning to look like wilful ignorance.

"You shouldn't. Think about it – if a warboat is shadowing us all the way to the Deeps for our protection, why didn't they just ship us there in the warboat?" She let that sink in before adding, "We're bait."

"Bait? What are you talking about?" demanded Alina. Katya had already come to the conclusion that Alina was less impressed by her superiors than Oksana.

"Well, I'm the bait, obviously. You're... bait minders, I suppose." She could see Oksana was about to express her resentment at the term, so she quickly said, "You see, somewhere *that* way," she nodded her head forward, "they're hoping the *Vodyanoi* is waiting, or maybe some Yagizban boats. They try to rescue me, and our shadows jump in for the kill."

Oksana's eyes had grown large. "That's exciting!"

Alina looked at her as if she was insane. "Oksana! It's not exciting! It's terrifying!"

Oksana snorted dismissively. "They won't shoot at us."

"They won't have to," said Katya. "Torpedoes are pretty smart, but once they're off guidance, if they've lost target lock, they'll search to re-acquire it. This scow must be as noisy as hell. We might as well have a target painted on our tail. If we could control her, the smart thing would be to kill the drives and just dive quietly trying to find an isotherm to hide under. But we can't. Alina's right to be worried, Oksana. If we end up with, say, the *Novgorod* on one side and the *Vodyanoi* on the other exchanging torpedo fire, we're as good as dead."

"But," Oksana was trying to find a flaw in the logic, "but you're a high value prisoner. They wouldn't dare!"

"Maybe, but I'm not as big a prize as the *Vodyanoi*. She's been weed in the FMA's fans since the war. They'd sacrifice me in a second if it meant sinking the *Vodyanoi*. Sacrifice *us*." Oksana's face fell; this was an argument she could understand. Alina already looked sick with fear. Katya smiled sympathetically. "Not that I want to worry you or anything."

After that, an air of doom-laden pessimism set in with her guards and they became far less strict with Katya. First they freed her hands, the theory being that she couldn't reach them across the aisle while her ankles were still restrained. It was a reasonable theory and she had no desire to provoke them any further by trying anything suspicious. She did consider for a while pointing out that their main threat was far more likely to be boredom rather than torpedoes, since she had neglected to point out that Kane would never be stupid enough to fall for such an obvious trap. But frightened people tend to cling together, and she preferred the comradeship the phantom threat had created aboard the little shuttle.

Then they let her use the head unsupervised, and – without prompting – let her walk up and down the aisle for a few minutes every couple of hours to keep her circulation up. One or other of them would sit with their gun in hand as a matter of form, but without enthusiasm. Katya considered ways of taking control of the shuttle, but every plan foundered on the necessity of shooting one or both of her guards once she'd taken one of the poorly protected pistols, and then the certainty that the shadowing submarine would never allow her to get away even if she somehow managed to gain entrance to the control section.

Katya was pleased that the former reason influenced her decision not to attempt an escape more than the latter. Despite everything, she hadn't turned into the Chertovka yet.

At least the little boat's supplies included changes of clothing for Katya. Oksana and Alina's kitbags had already been loaded when they'd come aboard and, when they had realised that they would be in the small vessel for almost three days, they had changed from duty uniforms to much more comfortable fatigues.

By halfway through the second day, they were no longer bothering to restrain Katya at all. This change in affairs had been caused when, during one of her exercise walks up and down the aisle, she noticed Oksana's gun lying by her folded uniform on one of the seats while Oksana was in the head using the shower unit. Katya coughed and, when Alina looked up from reading a book on her memo pad, pointed at the unattended maser. "You might want to put that somewhere where I can't get it so easily," advised Katya.

The knowledge that their prisoner could have killed the pair of them – yet didn't – convinced them that Katya was not at all violent, which made her status as a traitor all the more baffling to them. After Alina had finished shouting at Oksana about the pistol, she said to Katya, "So, just what did you do?"

"Alina!" Oksana was scandalised at the flouting of their orders like this, but Alina just fobbed her off with an impatient flap of her hand.

So Katya told them. She told them of how she'd been involved with the beginning of the war, and of how she discovered the Yagizban treason, although she did not tell them of the *Leviathan* because her story was complicated enough as it was. She described how she had become a darling of the news services for a day or two, of her decoration as a *Hero of Russalka* and of how much she loved the medal's wooden box. Then she told them of the axis of enemies, of Havilland "Killer" Kane (who wasn't the monster he was made out to be) and Tasya "Chertovka" Morevna (who pretty much was). Then she told them of how her boat was hijacked by the *Vodyanoi*, her voyage into Red Water, and what she found there – the massacre of Yagizban civilians, the grave of the Terran colonists.

"The war has to stop," she finished. "FMA versus Yagizban doesn't matter anymore. The survival of the Russalkin is all that matters. That's why I did what I did."

There was a silence. Then Oksana said, "The Yagizban base. It must have been a set-up. The Yags conned you, Katya."

"And they built a full scale replica of a Terran colony ship and sank it in the middle of the Peklo Volume? I know what I saw. I always thought the FMA was there for all of us. It never crossed my mind to ask what was going on in the governmental corridors."

She thought of something Kane had once said. He'd been right, damn him.

"People are people," she said. "Our ancestors put power into the hands of a small council with insufficient checks and balances as to how they used that power. Corruption had set in long before the Terrans returned, but that was a perfect opportunity to declare martial law. Since then it's been endless wars. War against the Grubbers, or war against the pirates, and now war against the Yagizban. We're so busy trying to be patriotic heroes we never even question if the wars were ever necessary."

Oksana wasn't having it. She shook her head defiantly. "The Federal government would never do any of these things you've said they have."

Alina looked sideways at her. "That's a pretty nice thing to say considering they've staked us out here like kraken bait."

"I'm sure they thought it was necessary." Katya saw the light of desperation in Oksana's eye, the fear of change. She'd seen it in Sergei's, too. "They know what they're doing."

"Yeah," agreed Alina, "they know exactly what they're doing. What they're not doing is caring a bucket of fish guts what happens to us. Think about it, Oks. They could have programmed this shuttle to wait in the moon pool exit tunnel while an empty one went out instead on full automatic. Then the *Novgorod* or whatever followed us out could have picked us up in its salvage maw. We'd be nice and safe in a big warboat, and who cares what happens to the shuttle? Let Kane and the She-Devil go after it, good riddance to it."

It was a good idea, Katya admitted to herself, and must surely have occurred to the people behind their current situation. It would, of course, have required substantial extra organisation. However much trouble it would have taken, apparently the three women weren't worth it in the eyes of the Federal Government. And, of course, if Katya died out there, it would be claimed the Yagizban had murdered her to keep her silent, no matter whose torpedo actually made the kill. Alina and Oksana's deaths would be entirely acceptable collateral damage.

Katya didn't think either of them really believed her about what she'd seen in the Red Water. Oksana clung to the notion that the Yagizban had somehow fooled Katya into doing their dirty work for them, while Alina somehow heard what Katya had said, accepted it, and then partially forgot about it. It was as if Katya's experiences ran contrary to the universe Alina thought she had grown up within, the resulting cognitive dissonance weakening the newer and less established thoughts. Katya couldn't really blame her; for all her apparent cynicism, the FMA was a godlike entity to Alina, and it would take more than some hearsay to break her faith.

The one thing that did stick with both her guards was that they would not be intercepted by pirates or Yagizban, so they relaxed, played games, and told one another anecdotes. Here, at least, they had no problems of belief or comprehension when Katya told them about Killer Kane and the Chertovka. Oksana was disappointed and Alina unsurprised that Kane was polite and thoughtful, and was not very keen on killing people as a rule. "Where's the return in being a mass murderer?" Alina pointed out. "Piracy is a business. Kane's a businessman." She nodded sagely at this wisdom.

They were far more intrigued by Tasya Morevna. "Is it true she collects the heads of those she kills in battle?" asked Alina with an artlessness Katya expected more from Oksana.

"No," said Katya. "She a real warrior, but she's not a sadist or a lunatic; not most of the time, anyway."

"Is it true she wears Terran armour?" asked Oksana.

"Yes, she does. She's painted it up a bit, and it's not a complete suit – the torso section mainly – but, yes, it's definitely not Russalkin."

"How does she look in it?"

"I bet she looks *awesome*!" said Alina, and they all laughed. It seemed, Katya thought, that Tasya's fan club extended even beyond the Yagizban, who certainly held her in awe.

Yet, slow as the journey was, it still had to come to an end. Katya found the shadow of her uncertain future deepening around her again, and her guards were sorry too, for they had come to like one another. They spent the last six hours of the approach tidying up the inside of the shuttle, which had begun to look like a dormitory, chatting about almost anything but their destination. Alina said at least they'd been going about as fast as the shuttle could manage; the shadowing warboat or boats would only have been making a fraction of their usual cruising speed. She mimed the helmsman pushing forward an imaginary throttle control a tiny bit and then slowly tapping his fingers while wearing an expression of slack-jawed boredom. She snapped back to herself, announced "Three days later!" and instantly returned to the same expression and finger tapping. Oksana and Katya laughed and Alina joined in.

Katya decided not to mention how glad she was that she hadn't murdered the pair of them earlier, no matter how kindly meant the comment was.

With an hour to go, the shuttle was in pristine order. Officers Volkova and Shepitko were in their duty uniforms, masers holstered. The prisoner, Katya Kuriakova, was in her yellow convict uniform sitting in restraints opposite to them. While the scene was very similar to that of three days earlier, the tone was very different. Officer Alina Shepitko had apologised when one of Prisoner Kuriakova's wrists was nipped by its restraining strap as it was tightened. Where once they had glared at her, now they cast her sympathetic glances.

"It'll be OK," Officer Oksana Volkova told the prisoner. "Just keep your head down. Don't piss off the guards. We'll give you a great report when we're debriefed. Model prisoner. They'll go easy on you."

Katya smiled. It was a weak, unconvincing smile, for she was touched by the kindness of her escorts, but she also knew what was waiting for her, and she was afraid. "Thanks, Oksa... Officer Volkova. I appreciate that. They're not bringing me to the Deeps just to lock me away, though." Her smile dissolved away altogether. "They're taking me there because it has the main Secor interrogation facility. They're going to torture me, and then they're going to kill me." She made a half sob sound in her throat and looked at them without hope. "I'm really scared."

"No," said Alina. "No, they won't do that."

"Two Secor agents have told me that is exactly what they're going to do." She tried to smile to reassure them that it was alright, none of this was their fault, but the muscles in her face twisted it into a grimace.

The shuttle carried out the approach to the Deeps perfectly, handing over to the prison station's drone control for the final docking. The screen on the forward bulkhead flickered from the status display to an image from the shuttle's nose-camera, enhanced and augmented with sonar, transponder, and positional data to summon the great bulk of the notorious prison out of its submarine gloom.

It was vast. She knew it would be, but seeing the scale metrics define it, brought it home to her. The only other thing she'd ever seen that huge had been the Yagizban floating settlement *FP-1*. The Deeps was not quite as big as that artificial island, but at a little over half a kilometre in diameter and eighty metres or so high, it was big enough. It was also, in a small irony, of Yagizban design, an artefact from the days when the FMA fondly believed that the Yagizban were happy with Federal rule.

The Deeps was unique, a tethered station; essentially a great submarine without impellers, its ballast tanks adjusted to be just on the positive side of neutral buoyancy. They could plainly see the metre-thick cables running from the boom-mounted ballast tanks down to huge pitons driven into the narrow plateau over which it hung, holding the prison in place.

"It was supposed to be a mobile originally, but they couldn't get it to move fast enough," said Alina, unable to keep the awe from her voice.

"Why would they want a mobile prison?" asked Oksana.

Alina grimaced at her. "It wasn't *supposed* to be a prison, stupid. It was supposed to be a military base. Rather than scrap it, they made it into the Deeps." She turned her attention back to the screen. "Nobody's *ever* escaped from it."

"Good to know," said Katya in a small voice.

Alina blushed.

The airlock cycled out the water, the doors opened and Prisoner Kuriakova stepped through, her hands in restraining tapes behind her back, followed a few paces behind by her guards. Four prison guards were waiting, along with a man in the uniform of a colonel of the marines, and a woman who looked so commonplace, inoffensive and every-day, that she might as well have had "Secor" tattooed across her forehead.

Officer Shepitko saluted the colonel and offered him her memo pad. "Prisoner Katya Kuriakova, sir. Please sign."

The colonel took the pad, signed it with the stylus and placed his thumb on the pad's reader to confirm receipt of the prisoner. As he did so, his gaze never left Katya.

Shepitko took the pad back and stowed it in her jerkin pocket. "Thank you, sir. You'll have our reports on the journey within the hour." Katya knew what was going to be in the reports; she'd helped the officers write much of them.

"There's no hurry," said the colonel. Katya didn't like his voice at all. She'd been expecting something gruff and military, but instead he spoke quietly with an undercurrent of subtle menace.

She'd once seen a domovoi, a type of Russalkin eel with short horns jutting out on either side of its jaws. Its body was as thick as a man's, and its teeth could penetrate a light ADS. Something about the cast of its face, however, gave it an undeserved air of intelligence. Domovoi lay in small caves, their heads at the entrance, watching the world go by with an expression of mild interest. When anything edible made the mistake of coming too close, however, it generally didn't last long enough to realise the error.

There was something of the domovoi about the colonel, and Katya decided it would be wise not to antagonise him unless absolutely necessary.

"No hurry at all," he continued. "You'll be shown to your quarters and you can finish your reports once you've settled in."

"Settled in, sir?" Officer Shepitko shot an uncertain glance back at Officer Volkova. "Our orders were to return to Atlantis as soon as possible."

"We're with Atlantis Base Security," said Volkova, a little unnecessarily.

"You've been seconded," said the colonel.

Shepitko started to say something, but a look from the colonel made her response die in her throat. "Yes, sir," she said, saluted, and stepped back.

Behind her, Katya could hear Volkova whisper urgently, "But we *can't* stay here! My mother and father are expecting me back before the end of the week!" Shepitko shushed her, and they fell silent.

The colonel was unconcerned by the domestic worries of a couple of junior officers. He walked up to Katya and stopped a half step away, looking down on her like a biologist with an interesting new specimen to dissect.

"I am Colonel Radomir Senyavin, governor of the Deeps. We are used to dealing with the worst of the worst here, prisoner. You are not even close to that. You will never escape. You will never leave. Put those thoughts from your mind now. If you are a good prisoner, you will grow old and die here. If not," something like a smile flickered momentarily around his lips, and Katya realised that this was a man who enjoyed fulfilling threats, "if not, then you will be denied the opportunity to grow old first."

SEVENTEEN
HARD TIME

They called it "induction." Katya had taken this as meaning much the same as it might if she were being introduced into a new workplace – where the toilets were, what time lunch was, perhaps a "safety in the workplace" lecture. The Deeps' induction programme was very different.

First they shaved her hair down to stubble. Then, under the emotionless supervision of two female guards, she was stripped, searched, and "showered" with a high pressure hose. The whole ritual was intended to dehumanise and humiliate her, and succeeded magnificently in the latter.

They made a show of bagging her old clothes "for incineration," watched while she dried herself with a towel that did its job about as well as a piece of plastic sacking, and then gave her a new uniform with her name already stencilled on the left breast. Beneath *Kuriakova, K* was the word *TRAITOR*.

She pointed at it. "You must be joking! The other prisoners will kill me if they see this!"

One of the guards shrugged. "Shouldn't have committed treason then, should you?"

"I've not been charged, never mind convicted!"

"I don't care."

The other guard had suddenly taken an interest in proceedings. She walked up to where Katya stood naked with the bundle of clothes in her arms. The guard's baton swept out of its belt loop and into Katya's ribs in a practiced arc. She fell heavily to the tiled floor, dropping her clothes and gasping.

"When you speak to any officer or official in this station, prisoner," said the guard standing over Katya, "every sentence you say finishes with *sir* if you're talking to a male, *ma'am* if it's a female. Failure to comply is subject to punishment. Do you understand?"

Katya could only clutch her side and sob with pain. The guard raised her baton. "*Do you understand?*"

"Yes," Katya whispered. Then quickly added, "Ma'am. Yes, ma'am."

The guard lowered her baton and smirked at her colleague. "You're going to be a good prisoner," she said to Katya. "Aren't you?"

Katya spent the next couple of days trying her very best to be a "good prisoner." Not because she had submitted to the Deeps' regime, she told herself, but simply because she didn't want to draw any more attention to herself than the word *TRAITOR* already attracted, and because she didn't want to spend all her time aching from the bruises the guards handed out for the slightest infringement of the rules. There were a lot of rules. She told herself that was why she was trying to be a model prisoner, but sometimes after lights out when she lay in her bunk, she wondered if she was just fooling herself. Perhaps the Deeps was slowly beating her into a compliant inmate, after all.

Her cell was much like those in a cell hotel – a dormitory wing consisted of a hallway with two layers of cells laid into each wall. Each evening the women in her wing sounded off like troops as they filed in, climbing into their individual cells, the transparent doors sliding shut and locking behind them. If they had to use the toilet in the night, they used a call buzzer mounted into their cell's wall. They were then escorted to the end of the hall where they would be let into the "surveillance head," a toilet with a security camera watching the inmate. After her first experience of it, Katya tried to be sure never to have to use it again.

Two things surprised her about the first few days of her incarceration. Firstly, she was not the only one with *TRAITOR* on her uniform. They weren't as common as *THIEF* or even *MURDERER*, but there were five or six just in her wing. She managed to talk with a couple of them, and told them what a relief it was that she wasn't the only one. She had never even heard of anybody being convicted of treason, yet here they were. One of them was an angular woman called Dominika Netrebko. She could seem washed out and waiting for death one second, then vibrant and angry, burning with life the next.

"The FMA has a broad definition of treason. I used to produce news programmes. One day I put forward an idea for a thread about how long martial law had been in place and maybe we could step down from it. Next day I get a visit from Secor. I've been here for four years now."

"I don't understand why your trial wasn't in the news," said Katya.

"Trial? What a quaint idea. 'Traitor' on your uniform means you've never had a trial."

"How is that legal?"

"It's martial law, they have military fiat. Do you know what that means? It means they can do anything they like. The Alpha Pluses, they may swan around in expensive clothes and look like senior administrators. But there isn't a single one of them that doesn't carry a rank and have a fancy military uniform hanging in the closet."

One thing she didn't expect to trouble her, yet it did, was the construction of the Deeps. The vast majority of ocean habitations were hollowed out from the rocky sides of Russalka's innumerable drowned mountains. It wasn't easy work, but it was straightforward enough to melt out a cave using plasma or fusion bores, seal it off, drain it, and then continue the work in relative comfort.

The Deeps was not like that at all. Alina had been right about its origins as an experimental mobile station. When that didn't work out, the project was cancelled when the hull was almost finished. The need for a prison had been growing for some time, however, and it seemed a shame to scrap such a nice construction when instead it could have its drive rooms given new functions, be filled with serious criminals, sunk into the black waters, and tethered below the test depths of most civilian boats.

The Deeps became a terror to those who broke the law, and a nightmare to those who might.

To Katya it was both of these things, but also a minor niggling irritation. She had grown up living in excavated settlements and travelling around in submarines. The Deeps behaved like a settlement, but felt like a submarine. Sometimes she was sure she could feel the deck moving beneath her feet as the ocean flow drew the facility more strongly against one set of tethers than the others. It bothered her subconsciously, as if some small part of her was expecting the Deeps to one day arrive at some unknown destination.

That sense of something always on the very edge of happening haunted Katya's days. She waited for the inevitable day when she would be escorted off to the Secor interrogation centre, to be tortured and killed, but now they had her safe and secure in the Deeps they seemed in no hurry at all to get on with it. For the first few days she was on a knife's edge of terror, every guard walking her way seeming to be the angel of death come to collect her.

Then she decided that this was all part of their plan, to keep her nervous and disorientated, to weaken her defences for when the blow finally fell. She felt angry that they could play such games, and the fear abated as she adjusted her view of her future. She imagined herself having some fatal disease that had shortened her life to days or weeks, yet had no symptoms until the final one. It was a grim prognosis to give herself, but a sensible one under the circumstances and, most importantly, it allowed her to function. Indeed, it made every day precious.

The Deeps looked roughly circular from the outside, but internally was based upon a regular pentagon, the only external expression of this being the five outrider ballast tanks on their dual pylon mounts. One of the five sectors comprised the docking areas, the guards' barracks, and the administration sections arranged over four decks. Another three sectors contained the male prisoners, and the last was the female sector. Each of the four decks in the prisoner sectors was called a "wing," although it was nothing of the sort. Dominika told Katya that at least once a year there was a "shakeup," when all inmates were randomly assigned new cells. The official explanation was that it was to disrupt any long-term escape plans, but nobody believed that. It was believed the shakeup procedure was purely to break up any friendships that may have formed and to keep the inmates feeling stateless and with no control over their destinies.

Once a month, however, the wings within a sector were allowed common time, a brief hour to spend with friends split up by the spiteful churning of the shakeups. Katya had been in the Deeps for just under three weeks when she experienced the first of these. Immediately after lunch had been completed in the communal hall of her wing, the guards withdrew, leaving them under the watchful eyes of the security cameras with their coaxial masers, ready to burn down any troublemakers.

Then the access doors at the outer end of the wing opened automatically, sliding up into the walls. Several women who had gathered by the doors ran through as soon as they opened, while others hung back, waiting. Moments later, women from the wing below were running in to be greeted with cries of delight. Katya watched them embrace and wondered if their number would include her one day. She saw Dominika waving at a short woman with her cropped hair grey at the temples, and their joyful reunion. Feeling that she was intruding, she picked up one of the media pads that gave the inmates something to do, and went off to a bench to read.

She had been reading for perhaps ten minutes when a woman came to sit by her. Katya felt awkward, and looked fixedly at her screen in the hope the woman would take the hint.

"Don't worry, Kuriakova," the woman said. "I'm not here to make a woman of you. I doubt either of us are that desperate for human contact yet."

Katya looked up sharply. Tasya Morevna, hair cropped and in prison uniform, sat by her side.

"They captured you?" said Katya, whispering in shock. "You? I always thought..." She dithered to a halt.

"You thought right. They'd kill me on sight. That's why I'm..." she turned to Katya so she could show the

name printed on her uniform, *LITVYAK, T. THIEF*
"The T stands for 'Tasya', still," she explained. "I
wanted to be a murderer, but Havilland thought that
might draw too much attention. I wasn't very keen on
his counterproposal either, so we compromised on me
being a thief."

Katya was still having problems with the entire
situation that extended far beyond which particular
crime Tasya had decided to have on her uniform. "What
are you doing here?" she whispered.

For once Tasya looked uncomfortable. "I'm here to
help rescue you."

"From the Deeps? How? It's impossible! Tasya, it's
suicide! Kane's crazy for sending you in here."

Tasya looked at Katya for a long moment, wrestling
with what she was to say next. "Kane didn't send me,
Katya. This is my plan."

Katya could only gawp at her.

Tasya hurried on. "I screwed up. You should never have
been left without support at Atlantis. Kane's got this idea
that you're blessed, or lucky or something, and that you'd
exfiltrate the Beta levels without any trouble. It went
against my instincts, but I agreed. I shouldn't have. Even if
we couldn't have gone onto the Beta corridors ourselves, I
could have led a team to cover you going up to them and
coming back. I *should* have led a team to cover you."

"We'd never have got out. The lock defences…"

"There wouldn't have been any lock defences by the
time I'd finished with them. There's no excuse. I failed
you, Kuriakova."

Tasya was apologising. To her. The She-Devil, the terror of the World Ocean, was apologising to her. And she'd broken into the most secure location in the world to do it.

Katya had sworn not to let the Deeps make her cry, ever, for any reason, but she had to swallow now. "You could just have said sorry," she managed to say.

Tasya grinned wolfishly and lightly backhanded Katya's arm. "This *is* my way of saying sorry."

"How did you get in here?"

"There's a lot of detail you don't need to know right now. It's best if you don't hear it at all. From your point of view, you don't have to do anything. There will come a time when I come and get you. When I do, you do as I tell you without questions or hesitation. Understand?"

Katya nodded, and said, "They were expecting you to try and rescue me on the way here. They set a trap."

Tasya raised an eyebrow. "What? They told you that?"

"I worked it out."

Tasya laughed. "I keep forgetting what a clever one you are. Yes, the *Novgorod* no less, and a couple of patrol boats in wide flanking positions a couple of isotherms above. We shadowed the *Novgorod* right from the minute it passed beyond the range of the picket sensors. We could have killed it easily." She pulled a disgusted face. "That was a really boring three days."

"So, why didn't you?"

"The volume would have filled up with torpedoes. Ours, theirs, the patrol boats weighing in. Sooner or later one would have lost its lock, gone onto a search pattern and perhaps locked up your shuttle. It was too dangerous to risk."

"I'm glad you didn't, and not just for me. Petrov's still an officer aboard her."

"Petrov?" Tasya nodded appreciatively. "A worthy foe."

"Maybe he made captain? The FMA fawned over everybody else who had anything to do with the *Leviathan* and *FP-1*. Medals and promotions for everyone."

"Maybe so. If he is the master and commander of the *Novgorod* these days, I'm glad we stayed well back."

Before Katya could ask any more questions, Dominika walked over with the woman she'd greeted earlier. "Katya!" she said smiling. "This is my friend, Naida."

"Pleased to meet you," said Naida. She seemed like a very nice person at first impression, but her uniform carried the word *MURDERER*.

"Good to see you're meeting people, too," said Dominika, looking at Tasya. Tasya said nothing, but rose to her feet, smiling slightly. Dominika looked up at her and frowned slightly, as if victim to a nagging half memory. "Have we met before?" she asked.

Then the skin on her face grew taut and her eyes widened as she finally located the memory.

"I don't know who you are," Dominika said tonelessly.

"That's right," said Tasya. The slight smile was still there, and Katya recognised it as the contemplative one she wore when discussing favourite acts of violence. "You don't know who I am."

Dominika glanced at Katya, and Katya thought she saw fear and pity in her eyes. Dominika made some mumbled farewells and almost dragged the confused Naida away with her.

Tasya watched her go. "What sort of treason is she in here for?"

"She worked in a news service. Wrote something the FMA didn't like. What was all that about, Tasya?"

"News. That makes sense. She recognised me."

"She what? How can you be so calm about it? What if she..."

"She won't say a thing. She's scared of me. That friend of hers, though, that Naida, she might be trouble. She's in my wing. I know her sort. She'll be sniffing around trying to find some sort of advantage." Tasya fell into a thoughtful silence.

Katya noticed the slight smile had reappeared. "Don't you dare kill her!" she whispered.

"Can't promise that, Kuriakova," said Tasya with an easy complacency that frightened and sickened Katya. "Only as a last resort, though." She smiled a little mockingly as she sketched a cross over her heart. "Promise."

Katya knew Tasya's list of alternatives to killing people who might present problems was very short, so it wasn't much of a promise. It was, however, the best she was going to get.

"I'd better go and wander around. It's not a good idea for us to be seen too much together," said Tasya. "Keep watching for anything unusual and, unless things move ahead quickly, I'll see you next time."

"I can't believe you're fine with staying in this cess silo for as long as that," said Katya.

Tasya shrugged. "Do you know if the unit activated properly?"

"Yes. They actually showed it to me. The inside was molten slag."

"Good job, Kuriakova. Then the war's as good as over. Might take a few months, though, and here's as good a place to wait that out as anywhere. Take care, stay out of trouble, and I'll see you in a month."

"If Secor haven't got around to interrogating and killing me before then."

"They won't. You worry too much, Katya. Be cool." And so saying, Tasya wandered off amongst the chattering groups.

Katya didn't know how Tasya could be so confident, but events proved her right. The days after the so-called "Freedom Day" mounted up and still Secor couldn't seem to develop any sense of urgency.

Dominika had wanted to talk to Katya immediately after the inmates returned to their respective wings ("All inmates have five minutes to return to their correct wings. Any inmate found in the wrong wing or on the stairwells after that time will receive a Level Two demerit and associated punishments"), but the governor called a general appel – the name used for a head count in the Deeps – and there was no time.

After the evening meal, however, Dominika managed to take Katya to one side. "That woman you were talking to, she's dangerous, Katya. Just a piece of advice, but you should stay away from her, as far as you can get."

"She's just a thief. Misallocated food supplies for the black market or something. I'll be fine. Don't worry."

Dominika shook her head emphatically. "Katya, you have no idea…"

Katya took Dominika's hands in hers and looked her in the eyes. "She's just a thief. She's nobody special. I wouldn't give her another thought if I were you."

Finally Dominika understood. "I hope you know what you're doing, Katya." The evening tidy up was called at that point. Dominika squeezed Katya's hands and let them go. "Be safe."

Then, ten days after Tasya had assured her that Secor had lost interest in her, guards came to escort Katya to the interrogation section.

EIGHTEEN
WHITE DEATH

The guards turned up midmorning during a citizenship lecture. That most of those present would never again be a free citizen was not an irony that escaped them, and the presentation did not go without a commentary from the inmates. They grew quiet when the guards entered, identified Katya, and took her away with them. Katya had believed Tasya, and was so shocked she had trouble standing when they called her name. They led her off and the lecture continued more soberly than before.

It didn't help that one of the guards was Oksana Volkova, because the other was not Alina Shepitko, and so they could not talk openly. The only comfort to be had from Oksana's presence was a sympathetic glance from her when the other guard was looking away for a moment. Otherwise, the group walked in silence to the Deeps hub to take a lift down to the lowest level of the administration wing.

Down there the corridors were grey-walled and contained only utility lighting, apparently a legacy of their original intended function as drive rooms. The bleakness of the echoing walls may have been as much a reason for their retention as economy; it was impossible to walk them without sensing something terrible waiting around every corner.

They took her to a room much like the room in which she had been beaten in Atlantis. Two seats, one of them bolted to the floor, a table also bolted down, restraints straps on the secure chair, and a steel hasp on the table surface to hold a manacle's cable. Sitting in the interrogator's chair was the pale, fragile-looking woman Katya remembered from her welcoming committee over a month before. The woman looked up briefly when Katya was brought in, but promptly lost interest, studying her memo pad and drinking water from a plastic cup as the guards shackled Katya and then restrained her in the chair, locking her manacles' cable down, her ankles and waist held in the chair.

When they were done, Oksana and the other female guard stood by the door. The Secor agent looked at them with faint surprise. "You're dismissed. You'll be called when I want you to remove the prisoner."

Oksana looked uneasy at the phrase "remove the prisoner," an uneasiness Katya shared. It sounded like an order to remove something inanimate. The other guard said, "Are you sure, ma'am? We could wait here in case you need us."

"I don't require an audience," said the interrogator. "Besides, these are early days. Ms Kuriakova and I will just be getting to know one another." To punctuate the thought, she lifted a medical case from the floor and laid it on the table.

Katya remembered something Kane had once said about Secor interrogation techniques, "Sensory deprivation, psychotomimetic drugs, RNA stripping, the usual. They're quite old fashioned in their ways, bless them." Now some of the tools of torture were sitting before her, she couldn't find it in herself to be as flippant as Kane.

Nor was she the only one affected by the case's appearance. Oksana flinched and the second guard took an involuntary step back.

"There's a guard room by the lift," said the interrogator. "Get yourself some food. I shall be a little while here. I shall call you when we're done."

The guard Katya didn't know didn't need any further encouragement and was out into the corridor in a second. Oksana lingered a moment, her anxiety evident, but then she was gone too.

Katya looked back to find the interrogator looking keenly at her. There seemed something disarranged about the woman, as if great passions surged behind that placid face. Her skin was pale, her cheekbones pronounced, her red hair pulled back into a bun that was just short of perfect, the few stray strands adding to the impression that all was not well within her.

"That guard seems very concerned about you, Kuriakova. Why do you suppose that is?"

Katya had made her mind up that she wasn't going to give anything up to Secor, not even the time of day. She would make them drag each syllable out of her with iron pincers if need be. Thus, she sat there in hostile silence, and glared at her tormentor.

The interrogator found this amusing. "Oh, I know why, of course. Three young women shut up in a shuttle for that length of time, naturally you talked."

She reached inside her jerkin and produced a recorder that she set down on the table between them. She watched Katya's face as she pressed the "Play" stud.

It took a moment for Katya to realise what she was listening to, to place the disembodied voices. She remembered the conversation before she realised one of the voices was her own. It was Oksana, Alina, and herself aboard the shuttle. Katya recognised the tail-end of Alina's anger with Oksana for leaving her pistol out where Katya could have taken it, and with a sudden sick feeling remembered what they had spoken of next.

"So," she heard Alina's recorded voice say, "just what did you do?"

The interrogator reached out and clicked the recorder off. "And you told her, didn't you? You told both those poor innocents just what an ugly world they actually live in, and what a foul, evil little empire the Federal Maritime Authority truly is, didn't you?" Her face hardened. "You've doomed them, you realise. The FMA cannot tolerate that sort of information in the hands of a couple of stupid girls like Shepitko and Volkova."

She glared at Katya's pallid face. Katya was starting to sweat as shock gave way to fear. The interrogator continued, ruthlessly driving home what was going to happen and that it was all Katya's fault.

"Secor won't allow them to return to Atlantis when there is the slightest chance they might tell anyone what you told them. Nor can they stay here. They'll talk sooner or later, Kuriakova. They'll hint, to try and seem clever. Somebody will ask them what they mean by that, and they'll talk just like you did. Some thoughts and ideas are as deadly as any disease. The one you've contaminated those women with will kill them just as surely."

She leaned back and regarded Katya with unconcealed disgust. "What did you hope to accomplish by telling them?"

Katya glared at her, shaking with hatred. "Don't you dare. Don't you lay a finger on them, you parasite."

"Oh," said the interrogator in very understated mock fear. "Threats now?"

"You've got the upper hand for the moment, but that won't last long. You'd better start making some friends because the day is going to come when you will need them."

"And it will come soon." The interrogator had become serious. "I know."

Katya shut her mouth before she said anything else that might reveal too much. The Secor interrogator didn't seem to care. She gestured at the cameras mounted in opposite corners of the room.

"They're switched off. I'm allowed to do that. I pulled a couple of leads to make absolutely sure. They're all scared of me anyway. They know the kind of things I've done to prisoners in here." She smiled to herself, as if torture and executions were lovable whims. "Apart from the governor. I don't think he's scared of anything. He's a strange man. Fancies himself as a marine biologist, you know. Almost every day he has drones out going down into the valley below to seek out new creatures, some of which he then has cooked and eats. As I say, a strange man."

Katya could only stare at the interrogator, and strain quietly and uselessly at her restraints. If the interrogator decided to draw a knife and cut Katya's wrists, there wasn't a thing she could do to stop her.

"You're frightened, aren't you? Me, too. Seven years I've been a member of Secor. Before that, I was in Base Security in Lemuria. Ten years... almost eleven now, I suppose... eleven years ago, we fought Terran troopers – commandoes, they were – when they attacked Lemuria. Corridor fighting. We outnumbered them, but they were so well equipped, so well trained. It was a victory every time we managed to bring down even one of them. I thought we were going to lose, then. Not just that battle. The whole war. I was terrified." She blinked, bringing herself back from the past. "Then the war just faded away. We were default victors, but we pretended we'd earned it. Oh, the celebrations.

"We're losing this one, too, and so are the Yagizban. I have Alpha clearance. I see the reports. I've had Yagizban agents sitting exactly where you're sitting, and when I've peeled away all the training, the lies, all the defences and

I'm left with the pure naked truth within, I see the same thing that I see within myself."

She took Katya's hands in her own, just as Dominika had. "You shouldn't say anything. It's wiser if you don't. There are two people that you can trust on this station and two only. The Chertovka and me."

Katya tried not to react, but apparently did a poor job of it as the interrogator laughed.

"You're not very good at this game, are you? I could have opened you like a clam inside twenty-four hours. Well inside. Don't trust me until you've spoken to her. You would be a fool to believe anything I say before then. Until then, you might want to consider how a war criminal like her managed to get through the Deeps' induction checks without being identified."

There was a small amount of pain involved in the interrogation after all. Most of the subsequent hour ("The guards will wonder what's going on if an interview takes less than an hour.") was spent with Katya reading a patriotic novel on a memo pad while the interrogator rested her head on the table top and listened to a selection of Poliakov concertos, humming along quietly to them. Then, when the closing chords of his Fifth had died away, she roused herself, looked through her case, and located a small pressure syringe. Before Katya could react, the interrogator injected her through the skin of her wrist.

"It's nothing much," she told Katya. "Just a mild debilitant. If you're not exhibiting any signs of interr-ogation, it would look odd."

"I could have pretended!" said Katya, tugging uselessly at the hasp holding down her manacles.

The interrogator grimaced and shook her head. "Not you. You're a terrible actor."

By the time Oksana and the other guard arrived a few minutes later at the interrogator's summons, Katya could barely stand.

"You can put her back into the general population," the interrogator told them. "I'm done with her for the time being."

The guards had to half carry Katya back to the lift. "What did they do to you?" asked Oksana.

"Don't!" snapped the other guard. "Don't ask. *Never* ask about Secor business."

The guards took Katya to the sickbay, where they seemed to be expecting her. An orderly put her on a bed fully clothed and told her to sleep it off. Katya tried to say, "Thank you," but her tongue just lolled uselessly around in her mouth. The orderly shook his head, rolled her into the recovery position, and left her there.

Prisons breed gangs, factions, and cliques. For her first month, Katya had steered around the edge of them with some help from Dominika. There was always a strong feeling however, that sooner or later, she would run into one or another group. On her return from interrogation, this feeling utterly evaporated. That Secor had its attention on Katya was more than enough reason to give her plenty of space.

It didn't mean people weren't curious, though. When Katya was having her first evening meal after her "interrogation," she was joined at her table by a couple of inmates to whom she'd never spoken before. One had *TRAITOR* on her uniform and the other had *MURDERER*. Katya found herself just thinking of them by their crimes. Neither of them looked at all extraordinary; if it wasn't for the cropped hair and the uniforms, she wouldn't have looked at them twice had she seen them in a station corridor.

"Been a guest of Maya, have you?" said the Traitor.

Katya looked up from her broth and regarded them suspiciously. "Who?"

"Maya. Maya Durova, the 'White Death.'"

It was clear from Katya's expression that none of this meant much to her. While the Traitor slouched with irritation, the Murderer said, "The Secor woman. The redhead. Does the tortures."

Katya wondered why they were interested. She remembered the interrogator – Maya Durova, apparently – telling her only she and Tasya were trustworthy, and that Katya should check with Tasya before even believing that. Since then, she'd avoided talking to anybody about what had happened during her interrogation. She might say something she shouldn't, some subtle point that she didn't even realise was fatal until it was too late. Now here she was, confronted by a couple of utter strangers who seemed far too concerned with her business.

"If you mean, was I taken to see her, yes. I was told not to say anything to anyone." She returned her attention to her broth.

"She just sometimes pulls people out of general population to practise on," said the Traitor. "Is that what she did with you? You looked pretty ill when they brought you back."

Katya paused, her spoon almost at her mouth. She was getting irritated with these two, and showed it by emptying her spoon back into her bowl. "How would you know?"

The Traitor grinned and tapped her arm, where she wore a red band with "TRUSTEE" printed upon it. "I help out there. In the sickbay. I saw you."

Katya looked at the pair of them and said, "You want to know what happened? Fine, I'll tell you. They took me down, she played some music, she pumped me full of drugs, I don't remember much else." It was a true account as far as it went; the patriotic novel had been so blandly predictable that Katya had already forgotten almost everything about it. She returned to shovelling the reconstituted protein shapes in stock that it pleased the kitchen to call "broth" into her mouth.

"You didn't tell her nothing, though, did you?"

Katya had had enough. She put her spoon down and said, "There's nothing else to tell. They had it all from me in Atlantis. She didn't ask me anything. Not a single question. She just said she hated traitors and she was going to shred the minds of every single traitor in the Deeps to pieces using sensory deprivation, psychotomimetic drugs, RNA stripping, the usual. And when she'd destroyed them, the drooling mess that was left would be going out of the airlock." She picked up her spoon again and used it to point at the conviction flash on the Traitor's uniform. "*Every* traitor." She went back to eating her broth.

They left her alone after that.

Katya was called for further "interrogation" five more times over the next sixteen days. Neither Oksana nor Alina accompanied her on any of these occasions, which was just as well. Katya had felt guilty at Oksana's concern for her after the first session; it felt like lying when she couldn't reassure her that it was all just a charade. Not that she could have, not with the White Death's parting gift of a dose of debilitating drug washing around in her bloodstream. She was always pale and nervous when she was taken down, and this was an honest reaction. Katya hated that drug.

On her third visit she made the mistake of telling Durova that.

"You should have told me earlier," Durova said, sorting amongst the phials in her case. "I'll use something different this time." And she did; a drug used as part of a sensory deprivation torture cocktail. The syringe was hardly away from her skin before Katya went blind. "There," said Durova, "that's better, isn't it?"

It wore off after four hours, but next time Katya said she appreciated the thought and all, but could she go back to the previous debilitating drug? Please?

Tasya found all this very amusing when they talked again at the next "Freedom Day."

"Yes, Durova is one of ours. She enacted Secor protocols to get me in and to arrange it so I wasn't identified."

"Do you trust her?"

"Not really, but I can read her instincts. Those are all going our way. She's intelligent, and she can see this war isn't a winning proposition for anyone. She isn't very loyal to the FMA, either. May have been once, but after what they've had her doing, I don't think she's got much idealism left in her. Where's your friend Netrebko today?"

"Dominika? She went to visit her friend in her wing this time around." Katya looked at Tasya. "She definitely knows who you are."

"Oh, yes. But she's smart enough to keep that to herself. Informers don't do very well in places like this. So, anyway, what's the escape plan?"

Katya looked at her with astonishment. "What? You don't have one?"

"Of course I don't," said Tasya, unabashed. Finally understanding Katya's concern, she added, "And I don't expect you to come up with one, either. The good Dr Durova is supposed to be doing that. She's the one who's been here for years and has all the pass codes. Hasn't she told you what she's come up with?"

"No. She told me I shouldn't trust her until you'd confirmed I should."

"That's wise, I suppose. What have you been talking about in your interrogation sessions, then?"

"Nothing. I read a bad book, she listens to music. Usually Poliakov, although she listened to some Kapitsa last time. Then she doses me with something to make it look I've been undergoing chemical questioning and calls the guards. If I'm lucky, I don't throw up in the lift."

"You have all the fun."

"Want to swap?"

Tasya smiled wryly, and shook her head. "Sorry about that. I wasn't expecting her to use interrogations as a way of communicating with you. It makes sense, but I thought she'd use intermediates. I can see why she didn't. Her way's far more secure. Anyway, next time you're in with her, find out what the plan is. The sooner we're out of here, the better. The *Vodyanoi*'s waiting in the Enclaves for word. She'll need at least three days' notice if she's going to be here to pick us up."

"How are we going to tell them?"

"We've got a senior Secor agent aboard this dump on our side and you're wondering how we can get a message out? Come on, Kuriakova. Use your imagination."

Katya accepted the logic of that, but something else was bothering her. "If the White Death is supposed to be planning all this, why are you here, Tasya?"

"Two reasons. One, because you'd never have accepted a Secor interrogator's word without some assurance that she was telling the truth."

"I might have."

"No, you wouldn't. Two, I'm here to expedite things once the plan gets under way."

Katya knew Tasya too well to see "expedite" as anything other than a euphemism for "kill anyone who gets in the way."

"I really hope you don't have to do any of that."

"Expediting?"

"You know what I mean."

Tasya looked at her, all levity gone. "That very much depends on how good Durova's plan is."

Katya nodded. Then she asked, "Is she really a doctor?"

Tasya's grim smile returned. "With specialities in psychology and pharmacology. Kane tells me that on Earth, doctors have to make an oath. Starts with, 'First, do no harm.' Maybe we should have something like that on Russalka, too."

NINETEEN
EXTRAORDINARY FREEDOM

The next interrogation session involved the reading of no further adventures of firm-chinned heroes of the FMA seeing off enemies of the state, and not nearly so much music either. Once she had confirmed that Tasya had spoken to Katya about her, Dr Durova said, "Good, because I've already sent the message to bring the *Vodyanoi* on station." Then she set her recorder to play some keyboard pieces by Poliakov.

"You've done what?" said Katya. Tasya had said it would only take the *Vodyanoi* three days to reach them. Surely the escape couldn't be happening so soon?

"We need to move ahead as soon as possible. The governor is behaving oddly. I think he is suffering from stress." She steepled her fingers, every centimetre the psychiatrist. "I offered to talk to him. He declined."

Katya couldn't help but look at the medical case, full of things specifically intended to make the patient feel a great deal worse. She could sympathise with the governor's decision.

"I detect growing paranoia in Governor Senyavin. He has become withdrawn, stays in his office throughout the day, and rarely speaks to his subordinates, just handing down increasingly petty edicts. At the least, I would expect him to impose changes on the prison's routine. At worst, he may decide he does not trust his senior staff and change them. It would be difficult for him to displace me – he has no direct authority with Secor – but it isn't impossible."

"Yes, I see what you mean, then. It would…" An ugly thought occurred to Katya. "*Paranoid*, you said?"

"Yes. It's come on quite quickly, which leads me to conclude that either the FMA is putting him under pressure of which I am unaware, or there are problems in his personal life that are creating stress in his professional one."

"Or something else. There have been some odd things happening in the stations, doctor. Secor is keeping them quiet, but they're happening all the same."

Durova raised an eyebrow and took up her memo pad. "Perhaps I've been lax in reading the general Secor alerts. So little of its business directly affects the Deeps, except what walks in through the airlock." She touched the pad's screen a few times, and cocked her head to one side in evident interest. "You're right. Marked increases in psychotic fugues experienced. They've put it down to a stress disorder. I find that hard to believe. There was nothing like this in the war against Earth." She scrolled through the reports, tapped in a couple of search parameters, and read in silence for a couple of minutes.

"Some nonsense about the possibility of it being due to some sort of Yagizban biological or chemical weapon. Delivered how, exactly? Besides, in confined environments like ours, the chance of them biting their creators is too great. The FMA has considered and dropped any number of viral and chemical projects down the years for exactly that reason. No. There's something else going on. If Secor command could concentrate its faculties on finding a common thread between these occurrences instead of just covering them up, we might have some idea of what's causing them."

Abruptly she shook her head and put the pad down. "This is a discussion for some other time. You need to be briefed on the escape. The secret of any successful operation is simplicity; therefore my plan is very simple. I bring in the Chertovka for questioning... yes?"

Katya raised a hand. "She doesn't really *like* being called the Chertovka. At least, not to her face. You might want to get into the habit of thinking of her as Colonel Morevna."

The doctor considered this for a second. "Very well, I bring in Colonel Morevna for questioning and have her put in the holding cell next to this one. Then while she 'stews,' I have you brought in for your interrogation. I call an emergency lockdown, release Morevna, and the three of us make our way to the escape pod at the end of the corridor. We leave in it, and are picked up by the *Vodyanoi*, which should reach its surveillance position in the next few hours."

"Next few..? It takes three days to get here."

Dr Durova looked at Katya as if she were slightly stupid. "I sent the message to come three days ago."

"What?" Katya would have liked to raise her hands in an expression of surprise, but the manacles held by the staple on the table-top prevented it. "But I hadn't even seen Tasya about you then!"

"I knew she would confirm my story, Katya. Why wait?"

Which left Katya at an impasse. Indeed, why wait?

Keen to not look like a complete idiot, Katya turned her attention to finding problems with the plan. "What about the guards?"

"Both Morevna and I shall be armed. The guard room is in the opposite direction to the pod access, and it is unlikely we will even see the guards. If they attempt to intervene, we will kill them."

Katya did not like the way she said it so easily. *First, do no harm.* "Let's hope it doesn't come to that. You can get a couple of guns in here?"

"I could get an entire armoury in here. I am a senior ranking officer of the Security Organisation directorate. It will not be a problem." Durova looked at her, and Katya was very aware of the analytical processes going on inside the interrogator's head. "I won't get one for you," she said finally. "You show too much compassion to be reliable in a gunfight."

Katya felt slightly stung by that, although she had a feeling it was almost a compliment. "I don't like guns," she said, and moved on quickly. "How will the *Vodyanoi* know the pod's been released? Oh, wait. I can answer that myself. The pod'll be transmitting a distress signal and a sonar pulse to aid detection, won't it? That's automatic."

"Any other questions? Really, Katya, all you have to do is as you're told."

Katya was beginning to think this was less a "rescue," and more a "recovery." Fine – if they were so sure all she had to do was follow them around and keep her mouth shut then that was what she would do. "Tasya said the same thing."

"Tasya is right. All done then?"

It was a simple plan, and it would probably have worked. They would never know.

The first hint that all was not well was when the next day was declared an "Extraordinary Freedom Day." Not only would it actually last all day and not just an hour, but the doors were opened between the prisoners' sectors. For the first time, the male prisoners would mix with the females. The guards withdrew from the wings on the governor's command, but they were clearly unhappy about what such an event might do to discipline.

Katya found herself a quiet corner and prepared to wait the day out. Male inmates started appearing in the wing within minutes, and she didn't like the look of them at all. It seemed the culture in the male wings was very different from the female; whereas the women generally just accepted their incarceration philosophically and continued to act much as they had in their free lives, the men had adopted behaviours that would have been entirely unacceptable in the corridors of a settlement. Tattooing was unknown on Russalka, but the men seemed to have re-adopted it as some sort of tribal ritual. Katya couldn't even guess what they were using for ink, and in many cases it seemed ink hadn't been used at all, resulting in scarification. She thought it looked hideous and alien, and the men scared her. She was very relieved when Tasya found her.

"What is *wrong* with the men?" said Katya. "Why have they done that to themselves?"

"Fear," said Tasya, her disgust plain. "They pretend all this machismo and then tattoo themselves to fit in and to show loyalty to one gang or another. If they weren't scared, they wouldn't do it. If they actually had any guts, they wouldn't need to. But they're animals, and animals need a pack."

They looked around the wing with disquiet. The atmosphere was becoming tenser by the second. Most of the women were in for non-violent crimes, and even the murderers had used non-violent methods more often than not – a dash of poison here, a sabotaged life support unit there. The men, it seemed, liked to use their hands, and almost every uniform bore the word *MURDERER*.

"One of the old timers in my wing says she's never heard of an 'Extraordinary Freedom Day,'" said Tasya. "And she's been here for fifteen years. This is insane, Katya. They'll have a riot before the end of the day."

"What about the plan?" asked Katya in a half-whisper. It was hardly necessary to whisper at all – the sound of chatter was becoming deafening.

"The plan... That, I am worried about. I don't like this, and I really don't like the timing. Maybe it's a coincidence, but I'm not fond of 'maybe.' I can't decide if this will help us or hinder us. I'm tending towards the latter. We should postpone the escape."

"But the *Vodyanoi*'s waiting for us!"

"It can wait a bit longer. Just a day. Kane will hang around for up to a week, depending on how hot the surrounding water gets with Fed boats."

Across from them, one of the male inmates who had been talking to a couple of the more impressionable girls from Katya's wing was pushed aside by another man. There was some terse language, and a punch was thrown. "Fifteen minutes. That's all it took." Tasya looked up at the security cameras that were swivelling to lock onto the fight. The inmates called them "cameras" to try to make them seem less threatening – the camera was actually only a tiny part of the device. Most of it was a maser. "Come on, then. A warning shot. At least use the directional speaker to break it up."

But the camera/gun did neither. It just watched the fight as it developed, now drawing in more men from the original antagonists' respective gangs.

Katya noticed a lot of the women looking up at the cameras with confused expressions. It had always been explained in terrifying detail what would happen if any prisoner laid hands upon another and, now that maser bolts were not raining down into the rapidly developing brawl, it was as if righteous believers in a wrathful god had just discovered that the atheists had been right all along.

Then, God spoke. Or, at least, the public address system hummed into life with its usual introductory three notes to gain the attention of the inmates. At the same time the main display screens changed from their usual image of the Federal Penal Office logotype to show Governor Senyavin at his desk. He was flanked to his right by the head of security, a man whose name Katya had never heard but who wore a major's uniform, and to his right by Dr Durova. The major was looking red in the face, like a man who'd just been overruled in an argument. The doctor looked even paler and more drawn than usual. Only the governor seemed relaxed, even pleased.

"Inmates," he said, and his voice boomed into every corner and crevice of the facility, bringing an end to fights that the notice announcement chimes had not.

Senyavin paused, and smiled beatifically out of the screen.

"Inmates. Today is a truly extraordinary day, a propitious day, a day that may well live in history. I want to share with you, with all of you, a few deep truths about our existence here on Russalka, a few revelations that I have recently been blessed by, and that will light all our paths in what must follow." He clasped his hands together and continued. "I would like you all to ask yourselves a very important question: why are we here?"

"Because we got caught!" shouted one of the men who'd only recently been fighting. Those around him laughed, even those from the opposing gang.

"Why are we here on this world? Russalka got along perfectly well for untold millions of years all by itself.

What did we bring? We brought ourselves. We brought filth. We brought evil. We have taken from this world, and we have given... nothing. Nothing but pollution and corruption and the cancer we call *humanity*. Oh, we speak of high aims and morality and such, but really, look at us. We are just a virus that spreads across planets. But, and here is the vital point, at least we are a virus that may recognise ourselves as such. I have a dream, a recurring dream. In it, I see us for what we are, a pestilence, and I see you, the inmates of this foul, pus-filled abscess it pleases us to call a correctional facility, as a particularly malignant strain."

"Insane," said Tasya.

Katya was watching Dr Durova. She was looking at the back of the governor's head as if she could see within, to where twisting worms of madness were eating the governor's mind. Katya knew the doctor was thinking of the Sécor reports of clinical paranoia. Durova looked sideways at the security chief, but he was looking straight ahead, his astonishment at his senior officer's speech apparent in his eyes.

"You corrupt others." The governor seemed to be talking to every one of the inmates. "Did you know that? Your sins have put you not only beyond correction, but you are causing others – good, decent people – to become monsters too. I know, I know. I couldn't believe it at first, either, but then I started to look, to *really* look, and what I found horrified me.

"It humbled me, too. I am only human, and I know I am no stronger than those around me. I am contaminated by your evil. I am corrupted by your sin. There is no hope for me, but by my actions, perhaps there is still hope for Russalka."

"Oh, no," breathed Katya. "Oh, no!" She could almost sense Senyavin's madness, and worse yet, she knew how it would find expression. "Tasya! He means…"

Senyavin rose from his chair, and all the inmates and the guards saw the heavy maser pistol in his hand. The doctor and the major were the only people in the Deeps who, standing behind the governor, could not.

Senyavin turned to the major. "Thief," he said simply, and shot the man in the head before he could react.

Doctor Durova cried out in surprise and backed away. Senyavin brought the gun to bear on her calmly, almost leisurely. "Traitor," he said, and shot her.

There were shouts and gasps of disbelief from the inmates. On the screens, Senyavin sat down again, placed the pistol on the desk top, and looked into the camera. "Two good, reliable, honest people, turned to scum by contact with you. As for the guards, they are in contact with you every day. They are all compromised. We all are. We are all inmates. We are all beyond redemption." He turned to his desk console and tapped in a few commands.

"Warning. All secure bulkheads are opening," said the automated voice of the central computer in the slightly testy tone computers the planet over always took when issuing a warning. The bulkhead doors that had closed off the areas the guards had withdrawn to less than half an hour earlier started to slide back.

"The inmates outnumber the guards five to one," said Tasya. "This is going to turn into a massacre."

"But the guards are armed," said Katya, watching in growing anxiety as the two formerly opposed gangs started to move together towards an opened door. By it a sign read "No Inmates Beyond This Point."

"I'm not saying it's the guards who'll be massacred. Some of these scum are wily, though. If there's a way to get their hands on guns, they'll find it. This is going to get messy really quickly." Tasya took Katya's wrist. "We're going to have to get moving."

"Where to?"

"We'll find an escape pod and a guard or somebody else with clearance to open it for us."

"What? Why do we need clearance?"

"In case you haven't noticed, this is a prison. You can't have the escape pods being easy to get into. The late Dr Durova was supposed to be doing the honours for us, but I think we can say that whole plan is in ashes now. We're just going to have to make this up as we go along."

Tasya pulled Katya along, heading for the door the gang of men had just gone through. As she was dragged along in the Chertovka's wake, Katya was muttering balefully.

"It's a simple plan. Nothing can possibly go wrong."

By the time they reached the door, there was shouting beyond it. The male inmates were challenging and swearing at the guards, invisible beyond the wall of yellow convicts' uniforms. The guards were telling the inmates to return to the hall immediately or suffer the consequences. The guards sounded young and frightened. Katya recognised them.

"That's Oksana and Alina!" she said. Tasya looked at her questioningly. "The guards who brought me from Atlantis."

"The guards who...? And you're on first name terms? You really do know how to make friends and influence people, don't you, Kuriakova?"

Through the crowded corridor, Katya caught a glimpse of them and realised that Oksana and Alina were alone, backing away from the advancing inmates, masers drawn and levelled, but looking terrified all the same.

"Those are the sorts of friends we could do with at the moment," said Tasya, a calculating look in her eye. "Stay right behind me. Don't stop for anything."

Without waiting for Katya to say anything Tasya strode forward. When she reached the men, she started shoving them aside. "Stand aside. Coming through. Make a hole there."

The men parted, the conditioned reflex of any Russalkin to step aside at the sound of the magical phrase "Make a hole" too deeply ingrained to be resisted. Tasya cleared the front rank of the men and walked steadily towards Oksana and Alina. Both of them swung their guns to aim at her.

"No! Don't shoot!" said Katya, running to catch up. "It's OK, Tasya's OK!"

The young guards saw her and wavered. In that moment, Tasya reached them. "Do as I tell you and we will live through this," she said to Alina while simultaneously and in a single smooth motion putting Oksana's gun arm into a lock hold and taking the maser from her momentarily paralysed hand. Tasya released Oksana, who sank to her knees, clutching her wrist.

The men shouted their approval at seeing a gun in the hands of a fellow inmate and started to surge forward. They got less than two steps before the leaders realised that the fellow inmate in question was pointing the maser at them. In the sudden quiet, the sound of Tasya thumbing the maser's safety catch to the "off" position seemed very loud. Alina started to point her gun at Tasya but Katya quickly stepped between them, shaking her head and mouthing "No!" urgently.

"What these girls wanted you to do still stands. Back the way you came, and don't come back through here if you value your lives."

One of the men's leaders was a massively built specimen, whose uniform predictably bore the crime *MURDERER*. The sleeves of his coveralls were rolled up to reveal densely muscled forearms, covered in gang scars. He laughed at Tasya. "Is that so, bitch?" he said, took a mocking step forward, grinning malevolently as he did so.

He died instantly, a maser wound appearing exactly at the top of his nose, between his eyes.

The men shuffled a horrified half step backwards as they looked at the dead man and then at Tasya.

"I am Colonel Tasya Morevna of the Yagizban Special Forces Executive," she said in loud, clear tones.

"Sometimes called the Chertovka. I have killed many, many times. If I kill every one of you, it won't even come close to doubling the number of lives I have taken." The group of about thirty men stood indecisive. "I will start shooting at the count of three. I rarely miss. One..."

The men ran.

Tasya watched them go with evident distaste. "*Such* children. Playing in gangs at their age."

Oksana had climbed back to her feet and was looking at Tasya with wide eyes. "You're... not *really* the She-Devil... are you?"

"I am Tasya Morevna. I'm not much concerned with what people choose to call me. Keep rubbing your wrist. The sensation will return soon." She nodded at the corridor through to the wing, now populated only by the corpse of an over-confident man. "Can you seal that door?"

"No," said Alina, her gun now down by her side. "The governor's overridden all the lock codes. We can't do a thing with them. We were trying when the inmates came through."

"Never mind," said Tasya. "Where's the nearest escape pod?"

"What?"

"We're escaping. There are pods for that. Where's the nearest one?"

"We can't..."

"We're coming with you," said Oksana. They all looked at her, Alina with her jaw dropping open. "The Deeps is screwed, Alina. If we can't keep the inmates back, we're worse than dead."

"We've got the guns!"

"Alina! Don't you get it? The governor has unlocked *all* the doors. All of them!"

Alina suddenly understood. "Oh, gods. The weapon lockers."

"Weapon lockers?" said Tasya. "We have to get moving right away."

"The nearest escape pod is this way," said Oksana. She ran off up the corridor.

It was close, no more than fifty metres away, but even before they reached it, the red lights on the status board next to the pod's entrance hatch did not bode well.

"Has somebody already taken it?" said Katya.

Alina looked at the board while Oksana ran her identity card through the hatch control reader to no effect. "It's locked," Alina said. "The governor's ahead of us. He's locked down all the escape pods."

"Then I shall just have to persuade him to unlock them. The security systems, I see they use retinal scanners. Do they check whether the eye is in a living body?"

Oksana looked sick. Alina said, "Yes, they check whether there's a pulse in the eye's blood vessels."

Tasya was disgruntled. "Damn," she said. "There goes my first plan. OK, lead us to the governor's office. We'll have to take him alive."

TWENTY
RETINAL IDENTIFICATION

All of the lifts had been immobilised, so the party took to the stairwell to get to the command level of the administration sector.

As a submariner, Katya had already thought of the alternative escape route of taking any boat that happened to be in dock, but Oksana said the docking ports were all unoccupied. Even the shuttle that had brought them had long since departed on other Federal business. There was no alternative but to force the governor into enabling the escape pods. Katya wasn't looking forward to seeing what sort of force Tasya would bring to bear.

The stairwell was imposing in itself; a great spiral in a steel tube running up the full height of the Deeps. Between every level a horizontal bulkhead ran across the shaft, a wide arced opening in it allowing personnel to climb and descend through it. If the bulkheads were to be closed, a heavy hatch slid across to cover the opening, its leading edge engaging with a step's riser and then the whole thing locking and sealing. Russalkin tended not to dither in the openings of bulkheads equipped with automated doors – the spectre of being crushed by an emergency closure haunted their nightmares. A doorway can be stepped through in a moment, though; it took several to climb the steps through one of these horizontal guillotines. Even Tasya noticeably sped up as she passed through them, the quicker to be clear.

They reached the door leading out onto the topmost corridor and paused to listen.

"Can I have my gun back?" whispered Oksana.

"No," said Tasya, and that was that.

Satisfied that there was no sound ahead, Tasya signalled that they should follow and moved forward. The group of them breasted the curve of the corridor together to discover several frustrated looking guards standing outside the governor's office.

There was an astonished pause, and then Katya and Tasya found themselves looking down the barrels of six pistols, one of them – judging from his uniform – held by a sector leader. Katya froze from fear, Tasya from tactical common sense. She could see the guards were confused rather than aggressive – perhaps they could talk their way out of this. She just needed to come up with a convincing lie...

"Lower your guns, you idiots!" said Oksana. "They're Secor!" She stepped past Tasya to speak to the guards. "They're agents!"

The sector leader had a black eye and a bloody nose, apparently having already run into prisoners out of bounds. "What are you talking about?" he demanded, "they're prisoners!"

"No, the White Death had them in here to spy on the inmates. Why did you think they had her," she nodded sideways at Katya, "in for interrogation so many times? She was making her reports."

The other guards looked confused enough to accept anything at this point, but the sector leader wasn't going to be convinced so easily. "She's got a gun," he said, levelling his own at Tasya's. "How do I know you haven't been threatened into saying this?"

Oksana let her shoulders droop with visible exasperation. "I *gave* her my gun," she said. "She's a better shot than I am, to be honest. We're not being held at gunpoint. Look..." She turned to Tasya and held her hand out. Without hesitation Tasya reversed the pistol and placed it in Oksana's hand grip first. Oksana took it, held it up to show the sector leader that she was in full control of it, then returned it to Tasya in the same way. "She's Secor. And an amazing shot. She put down Bubnov when he and his gang tried to get us."

This news did more to convince the sector leader than even the demonstration with the gun. He lowered his own and said, "Bubnov? You killed Bubnov?"

"He was a threat," said Tasya without emotion.

The sector leader smiled. "Oh, madam, you're an angel among us all. You killed Bubnov. That's the first piece of good news I've heard today."

Tasya went to join the group of guards. Katya followed a pace behind, reapplying the mindset she had adopted while pretending to be a Secor operative in Atlantis. She found it in herself quite easily – mild arrogance, some impatience, and a limited sense of humour, all of it acid.

"He's locked us out of his office," said the sector head, "as well as the entire security system. There's only one fully operational console in the whole facility, and it's on the other side of this door."

Katya weighed the door up, then looked at the group of guards. She pointed at the maser carbine that hung at the shoulder of one of them. "I'll take that," she said, fighting down the urge to say "please."

With the reluctance of a child giving up a favourite toy, the guard handed the gun over. "OK," said Katya, feeling very professional as she put the carbine's shoulder sling over her head and let the weapon hang by her side. "We're going to need a perimeter to protect this location while we work. If you could place a fire team one bulkhead down on the stairs, and then station some sentries to keep the other approaches covered, then that would do the job. Can you organise that for us, sir?" She said "sir" in the tone beloved of officials who mean "I am saying this as a courtesy, but we both know I am the more important one here." Then she looked the sector leader in the eye.

"Yes, ma'am," he said immediately. "Team 2! On the stairs, one bulkhead down. The rest of you, with me!" Four guards headed for the stairs while the rest ran off around the curve of the corridor until they were lost from sight. Katya waited until even the thumping of their boots had faded before sagging with relief.

"Good work, Kuriakova," said Tasya. She looked at the door. "Now, our next problem. How do…"

She was interrupted by Katya raising her carbine and firing at the wall beside the door at about head height. She aimed down at knee height and fired again. "My mother worked in maintenance," she explained. She shouldered the carbine again, put the flats of her hands against the metal of the door and started to drag her hands horizontally across it. Remarkably, it started to slide under her grip. "She once showed me that these internal doors are much less secure than they look. Two little metal catches holds them shut. That's all." The door was a few centimetres over in its frame by now, almost starting to show an open crack at the frame. "When the lock jams, they drill these catches out. Maser's faster."

The edge of the door was far enough clear of the frame to get fingers through. Alina grabbed it and pulled. Inside, Katya saw the large desk so familiar from the weekly "Words from the Governor" broadcasts, Radomir Senyavin himself sitting at it, regarding them with tranquil equanimity. But on the floor behind him, Katya could see the bodies of the security chief and of Dr Durova.

The governor rose from his chair as if to welcome them, and Katya thought this might go easier than she'd been anticipating. Then she saw his right hand rising, the heavy maser gripped in it.

The crack of a maser discharge was shockingly loud, but then, it wasn't the governor's that was firing. Tasya's gun had gone off only a few centimetres from Katya's ear. It wasn't a very loud noise, but it was sharp, and would be ringing in her hearing for a few minutes.

The governor's gun fell to the floor, and for a moment Katya feared Tasya had killed him. Then she noticed the governor's middle and ring fingers were lying beside the dropped gun.

Senyavin looked down to examine his maimed hand with utter detachment, as if he had just noticed a hang nail. They were barely bleeding, the maser having cauterised the wounds as it made them. "You blew off my fingers," he observed. "You're a very good shot."

Tasya walked quickly to him, kicked one of his legs out from beneath him and, moving behind him, applied a foot to the back of the other knee to bring him to his knees. "Thank you," she said. "And just think, you have another six fingers and a couple of thumbs for me to amputate if you don't do exactly as you're told. Katya, get his identity card."

As Katya went through the governor's jerkin, giving him an apologetic smile as she patted his pockets, he said to Tasya, "So, you're the Chertovka."

"I am. How long have you known?"

"I knew they were contaminated," he said, looking back at the bodies. "I planted surveillance bugs in the interrogation rooms and in the chief's office. I listened to him making deals, misappropriating supplies. I listened to her making deals too. I knew it was too late for all of us then." He nodded at Oksana and Alina, standing nervously by the door. "Even the newest guards have been corrupted by this sink of filth. Criminals, and deviants, and perverts. All of you."

He looked at Katya then, and his eyes narrowed as if seeing something new. "But, what are you? The light burns... I can smell the truth in you..."

Katya had found the card and held it in her fingers. Governor Senyavin's unblinking stare froze her, though. Froze her with a fear she hadn't felt for a long time. A squirming in her mind that hinted that somehow she knew exactly what he was talking about.

Then Tasya impatiently snatched the card from her, and the moment was gone. Senyavin was just a raving maniac again, not the holder of some secret reality that Katya could almost, *almost* see.

Tasya swiped the card through the desk console's reader. An eye scanner mounted by the display activated, its red targeting beams spiralling across the governor's face as Tasya pulled him toward it. She noticed he had clamped his eyes tightly shut, a small act of defiance that did nothing for her temper.

"Open your eyes right now, you worthless bucket of vomit, or I will cut out your eyelids," she hissed in his ear.

The threat apparently did little to frighten him, despite its undoubted sincerity. Instead, he smiled slowly and, just as slowly, opened his eyes. The red beam found his right eye, locked onto it and in a moment the screen displayed the Deeps' top level system administration protocols.

Tasya shoved the governor to one side, sending him sprawling on the floor. He lay there watching her as she started to sort through the operations menus, seeking out the one that she wanted. The whole time, his smile did not waver.

Katya spared the display a sideways look, but she found she couldn't look away from Senyavin. She had a feeling something was coming, something that was burning inside his head, that flooded him with a religious ecstasy, something she could almost perceive.

"Tasya..." she said. The sense of menace growing by the moment made her voice waver.

"In a moment," said Tasya. "There! That's what we want." She tapped on the board display and was rewarded by a perky little upbeat bleep. "Escape pods are enabled. Now let's get the hell out of here before the guards steal them all."

"I embrace my destiny," said Senyavin.

The console's screen suddenly changed to a display of a complex waveform. "What the hell...?" said Tasya under her breath.

"By my sacrifice, I absolve us all," said Governor Senyavin, and closed his eyes. His smile grew rapturous.

Too late, Tasya recognised a speech analysis program accepting a verbal trigger. She reached for the board, but the display had already changed to read, "Project: REVELATION active," and then went blank. Tasya snatched up the governor's identity card from where it lay on the desk and swiped it through. The console remained inactive, with not even a tone to indicate a failed card reading.

Furious, Tasya turned to Senyavin. "What did you do?" she demanded. He said nothing, but only smiled. It was not a wilful smile, nor was it one of triumph. It was a smile of pure joy. Tasya drew her pistol from her belt and placed the muzzle against his forehead. "*What did you do?*" she snarled.

"Tasya, leave him," said Katya. "We have to get out of here, right now!"

"What? Why?"

"He's committing suicide, and he wants to take us all with him."

Tasya looked at the governor, sitting on the floor, Durova's corpse behind him. Then she looked suspiciously at Katya. "How do you know?"

Katya couldn't say. She couldn't explain how she could see the glow of an unearthly fire within Senyavin's mind, how she could smell his sanity ablaze. So instead she said, "I saw it in his eyes."

Tasya looked straight into Katya's eyes and, remarkably, broke her gaze first. She seemed slightly rattled. She reached down, flicked away the stubs of the governor's fingers, and recovered his dropped gun. "Come on," she said, re-establishing control. As she reached the door, she gave the governor's gun to Oksana. "The grip's a little melted at the front, but it's still serviceable," she said, and walked out into the corridor. Oksana and Alina followed her, Oksana complaining that there appeared to be some skin still sticking to the melted polymer.

Katya tarried a moment in the doorway. The governor had made no move. He just sat there, smiling as if he had just seen the most beautiful thing in all creation or beyond it. Tears rolled down his cheeks. He looked at Katya, and he spoke, but too quietly for her to hear him. She wasn't sure if she read his lips, or if she heard his voice in her mind, but she knew what he said.

"You understand."

Tasya's shout of "Come *on*, Kuriakova!" brought her back to the moment, but the half realisation fluttered at the edge of her consciousness, and scared her so badly she pushed it away to where she didn't have to think about it.

She did. She *did* understand.

She ran after the others.

As they approached the straight length of corridor that would take them to the observation blister and its attached pod, Katya said, "What happened to the guards?"

In the corridor was a barricade of desks, chairs, and even a daybed that had all apparently been pulled out of nearby offices. Behind it crouched the sector leader and three of his men. Further down the corridor there was a flash of yellow coveralls visible in one of the doorways.

"Down!" barked Tasya, grabbing Katya and Alina by the sleeves and dragging them down. There was a sharp crack and Oksana cried out.

Katya grabbed her belt and pulled her down with them. "I'm hit!" said Oksana, looking in disbelief at the burn hole in her upper sleeve.

"Maybe next time I tell you to get down, you'll do it."

"But I'm hit!"

"And still talking, so it can't be that bad." Tasya turned her back on the aggrieved woman and said to the sector leader, "What's the situation?"

"They must have found an unsecured arms locker. There's a bunch of six or seven with carbines and pistols.

The only good news is that they're not good shots, and they didn't take any of the riot gas grenades or they'd have used them by now. What happened with Governor Senyavin, ma'am?"

"His mind's gone. I disarmed him and left him there."

"The computers…?"

"He's locked everyone out, even himself. We're stuck here until the next boat arrives."

"That's not the procedure. If security is totally compromised, we're to lock down the computers, grab as many weapons as we can, and take the escape pods. There's one at the end of here, past these scum. The plan is to kill them, take their weapons, and abandon the base."

"How many people can a pod take?"

"Ten."

Katya saw the real reason behind Tasya's question – whether she would have to kill the guards or not once the inmates had been dealt with. Ten places meant they might live yet. Tasya might have been on Katya's side – at least for the moment – but there was barely a thing Tasya did or a thought she expressed that didn't frighten or sicken her.

An inmate ducked out of a side door about twenty metres away and fired a burst from his carbine. All the bolts went high, burning away the corridor's already utilitarian wall covering and melting long score marks in the plastic laminate beneath. Tasya watched him with evident disdain over the top of the overturned day bed, lifted her pistol, and shot him dead.

"Did you see that? Out of cover and he fired from the hip. They've got their training from watching dramas. No professionalism at all."

Another convict stepped out from a doorway on the other side of the corridor, shouting something incoherent about how he was going to get the Feds because they shot his friend. He held his pistol on its side with the back of his hand uppermost and fired indiscriminately, bolts hissing down the corridor over their heads or splashing ineffectually against the metal of the office furniture barricade.

"Oh, for heaven's sake," said Tasya peevishly, and killed him too.

She either didn't notice or didn't deign to notice how perturbed she had made the Federal guards. "Yes," Katya said to them. "She scares me, too."

"The only way those idiots are going to represent a threat is if you get careless and do something stupid," said Tasya, adding insult to Oksana's injury. "Are any of these offices connected?"

"No. They're all discrete rooms."

"So much for flanking. We'll just have to do this the hard way. Clear and secure. Volkova's hit in her main arm, so she's out of this. That leaves you, your team, Shepitko, and myself. We'll split into two teams of three, I'll take..." she cast an eye over the sector leader's men, "Glazov," she read from one of the guard's name patches. "The teams alternate, cover/clear, all the way down to the pod."

She noticed the leader, Sevnik, looking at her oddly. "What's wrong?" she said. Shielded by her body from

Sevnik, but visible to Katya, Tasya's hand tightened on her pistol. Was it possible that he'd recognised her?

"I've... I'm sorry, ma'am, it's just all the Secor I've ever met have been... well..."

"Useless in a fight, expecting others to go at the front and they tidy up afterwards? No offence taken. But I was recruited from anti-piracy operations. I'm used to combat."

The explanation seemed to convince and, indeed, impress him. "Anti-piracy? I envy you. I put in for that, and ended up here. Glazov, you're with... I don't even know your rank."

"Colonel, but you have command here, captain."

"Thank you, ma'am. Glazov, you're with Colonel Litvyak." He nodded at Katya. "What about you, ma'am?" he asked Katya.

She was momentarily at a loss what to say, but Tasya had an almost-lie ready and waiting. "Ms Kuriakova is a civilian volunteer for this mission. She's not a combatant."

Captain Sevnik grinned. "I knew all that stuff about you being a traitor had to be rubbish," he said to Katya. "You won the Hero of Russalka. They don't just hand those out to anybody."

"I've always tried to do what was right," Katya replied, and managed a wan smile. She shrugged the carbine's strap over her head, feeling like a fraud.

"Could we get on, please?" said Tasya, taking the weapon. "These inmates aren't going to just shoot themselves, you know."

TWENTY-ONE
FALLING FORWARD

Naturally, Tasya insisted on clearing the first room, much to the consternation of Glazov and Shepitko. While Sevnik's team provided covering fire, she moved up, Glazov and Shepitko stacking up on her position as she reached the door. Katya heard Tasya say to her team, "You *have* done this before, haven't you?" and Shepitko say, "Uh…"

"You're in third, in that case. Glazov, whichever way I go, you go the other way and clear the door so Shepitko can come in and engage ahead and above. Move fast and don't pause in the doorway unless you like being repeatedly shot. Got it?"

Whether they got it or not, she wasn't waiting. She reached the door, tapped its control, and led through, swinging right, Glazov was through immediately behind her sweeping left, and Shepitko came through on their tails, looking worried. They vanished out of sight. There was a pause of a few seconds before Tasya reappeared, using the doorframe as cover. "Clear," she said with obvious disappointment. "Your turn, captain."

Sevnik nodded, girding himself for danger. Just as he and his team were about to break cover, however, an inmate leaned out of one of the doors further down the corridor. There was a hollow "pop" sound, and something sailed through the air towards them, trailing a thin streamer of smoke.

"Gas!" shouted Sevnik, ducking back behind cover.

When things happen together, it is in the nature of humans to first assume that the events must be related, no matter how unlikely. When the gas grenade bounced off the Feds' barricade, it landed on the floor, rolled back a metre, and then coughed gently as the fuse initiated the payload and riot gas started to flow out from it in thick, opaque waves. At the same moment, the Deeps shook with a sudden violence that was enough to knock Katya over. In a moment it had gone, but no dweller in the Russalkin depths ever feels a corridor floor vibrate and then dismisses it as nothing.

There was a horrified silence after the vibration, and they remained in tableaux, waiting for an aftershock. Then Sevnik said, "The gas grenade." At first Katya thought he was suggesting the grenade was responsible, but then she heard the tinny rumble over the hiss of the gas. Holding her breath and squinting, she looked quickly over the barricade.

The grenade was rolling away from them, back towards the prisoners' positions.

On the one hand, it should have made her happy. The grenade had barely started to produce gas, and although there was enough of it in the air to make her eyes sting and water a little, there wasn't nearly enough of it to be debilitating. On the other hand, *it was rolling.* All floors in stations and facilities were level to several decimal places. Any slopes within them were deliberate with black and yellow danger stripes at both ends and plentiful signage. Nowhere else could you drop a ball and expect it to roll away from you.

The speakers clicked into life. "On ancient Earth, we came from the sea," spoke the governor's voice, "and now, we are consigned to it; to wipe away our sins, to expunge us from a universe that will do better without us."

Sevnik turned to Katya. "I thought you said the governor was no longer a threat?"

"He isn't. It's a recording. He had this planned all along." The tilt in the corridor floors was becoming obvious. "What's he done?"

Sevnik swallowed hard. His complexion was grey. "He's blown the ballast tanks."

"He's blown the tanks?" That didn't seem so bad to Katya. To a submariner, "blowing the tanks" just meant driving out all the water with compressed air to give them maximum positive buoyancy. "So we're rising?"

Sevnik shook his head urgently. "No, I don't mean he's blown the tanks empty. I mean he's blown them *clear off.*"

One of the desks making up the barricade fell over.

Katya saw sweat starting to appear on Sevnik's brow. Being shot at had not bothered him unduly, but now he was afraid. "There's an emergency protocol in case the prisoners ever took control of the facility. It detonates charges on the tanks' pylons. We're sinking like a rock."

"Tasya!" shouted Katya. "The governor's scuttled the whole station!"

"I was beginning to work that out myself," she shouted back. "Better to kill the prisoners and the surviving guards than allow a mass escape. Wish I could meet the genius who came up with that and bang his head off the wall a few times. Captain! No time for subtlety. We have minutes to live unless we reach that pod."

All caution gone, the captain hurdled the barricade. "Come on!" he shouted to those still sheltering behind him. "Follow me! If it moves, shoot it!"

Tasya and her team were out of the office door in a second following him and, as soon as they could get over the barricade, so was the remainder of the captain's team, Oksana, and Katya.

The inmate who'd thrown the grenade watched it roll back past his doorway. "Hey!" he shouted to anyone who might reply. "Hey, what's...?" As he spoke, he leaned out of cover and was shot by Captain Sevnik.

As they ran, Katya's mind was working quickly. Why was the Deeps tilting like this? Why didn't it just sink?

Because it was roughly saucer shaped and one edge of it was slightly heavier, she told herself. Out of the five sectors, the administration sector contained the main boat docks. That was why it was heavier, and that was why, without the ballast tanks in place to keep the station trimmed, it was sinking a little faster.

Above them there was nothing but the corridor ceiling, some service utilities, and the inner hull. Through it, she could hear a slowly growing roar. The Deeps may once have been intended to be mobile, but that scheme had been dropped early. Now its outer skin was festooned with sensors and other equipment that rendered it well short of perfectly hydrodynamic. The roaring was the sound of the sea moving more and more quickly over the station's skin as it sank.

Katya recalled what she could remember of the Deeps and its location; she'd once had to plot a course to it what seemed like a lifetime ago, but which wasn't even a year. The first time she'd ever met Kane, that accursed day.

The Deeps was held in place by cables running from the ballast tanks; with the tanks gone, so had the tethers. The station was anchored over a small plateau, the shoulder of an extinct submarine volcano. The approach was from open water, heading towards the mountain. At this sort of angle, that meant...

"Wait!" Katya shouted. "We're going to crash!"

She grabbed Oksana's wrist and the back of Tasya's coveralls. Tasya whirled, her natural assumption being that anything unexpected was potentially dangerous. The rest of the party slowed to a confused halt, except Captain Sevnik.

The impact was a moment later. They all fell and rolled along the corridor floor. Sevnik, however, had been running too fast. He couldn't stop and, to his horror, felt the deck sloping even more rapidly now. With a cry of impotent anger, he was airborne.

"The offices! Quickly!" cried Katya. "The whole place is turning over!"

Tasya was on her feet in a second, bodily throwing Alina through an office doorway next to them. There was a male shout from inside, and the crack of a maser going off. It seemed that Tasya had found an armed inmate to take her wrath out on after all.

Quickly they streamed through the door, Katya and Oksana last, but as Oksana reached the doorway, an office chair from the barricade rolled by and clipped her, knocking her off balance.

The tilt of the corridor was too great for her to climb the flooring and, terrified, she started to slide away from them.

Tasya had stayed on the door. She saw Katya look back and started to say, "Leave her."

"Grab my feet," said Katya, and dived after Oksana.

Oksana had, naturally, been reaching out with her injured arm, and naturally, that was the one Katya grabbed at. She locked both hands around Oksana's wrist and felt Tasya's hands clasp around her own ankle just as the corridor became less like a corridor and started to remind Katya of the lift shaft she'd enjoyed so much in Atlantis.

"Oh, gods, Katya! Please! Don't let go!" Oksana begged as gravity swung her off the floor.

Beyond her, Katya had an impression of a body spread-eagled a hundred metres away against a bulkhead surround. She tried to ignore it, although she knew it must be Captain Sevnik.

Everything was in chaos, the crash of the furniture as it left the office floors and fell against the walls, cries from all around, and Tasya swearing in grunts as she held onto Katya's ankle, bearing the weight of both her and Oksana.

Behind them, a rumbling was growing louder. Katya saw Oksana's eyes look past her and widen. The barricade that so recently had sheltered them from harm was coming to kill them.

Katya risked a look over her shoulder. Tasya, always sensitive to danger was already looking into an "up" that was recently a "back." Above them on the slope, the desk was barely in contact with the floor anymore, accelerating rapidly towards them.

It was impossible for Tasya to pull both Katya and Oksana back in time and, if she stayed where she was, she would be hit too.

Tasya looked down and her eyes met Katya's.

"Let go," said Katya.

Without hesitation, Tasya did.

Oksana screamed as they fell. Katya didn't have time for such a luxury. She drew up her legs and kicked against the wall, pulling Oksana closer as she did. The desk, heavy and already travelling at speed, clipped her hard enough to hurt but not to disable. She ignored the pain and grabbed the edge of it with her left hand. As she wrestled herself and Oksana across its underside, its corners kept scraping the floor and wall, threatening to flip it.

Suddenly, they hit the bulkhead surround she'd seen from above. The impact drove the breath from her, and she felt something break inside. Through the wave of pain, she had a momentary vision of Sevnik's body on the other side of the surround, his eyes open, the left of his skull crushed. Then the desk flipped over the edge of the support and they were falling again.

Oksana was no longer screaming. *Perhaps she's dead and all this was for nothing*, thought Katya. But she'd had to try.

But now "down" wasn't neatly along the corridor anymore. Katya kicked against the floor with her failing strength and the desk moved towards the ceiling. As it slowly became the floor, she hoped that it wasn't just made of cosmetic tiling, or they would be falling through it in a moment. The surface of the desk touched down tentatively, then solidly, and Katya found herself sledging along the ceiling. As the angle grew less, the desk started to slow. Behind her she could hear shouting, and she looked back to see the guards and Tasya running down the ridiculously steep slope of the ceiling. She knew they had no choice; the fact that there had been no further impacts beneath their feet meant that the Deeps had rolled off the edge of the plateau and was falling. Below them was a drop of two thousand metres ending in a lake of the Soup. If the water pressure didn't crush the prison, the massive pressures within the heavy metal cocktail of the Soup definitely would.

Katya was trying to drag Oksana to the escape pod door when the others reached them. The corridor was flat by then, but already starting to pitch over again as the Deeps toppled towards destruction. Tasya was with her in a moment, pulling Oksana's arm over her neck and pulling her along.

"Get that hatch open!" she barked at the guards. They needed no second telling.

"Is she still alive?" asked Katya gripping her side. The pain was blossoming, blazing through her ribs every time she took a breath.

"Don't know," replied Tasya, and they carried the limp body to the opening hatch.

Whatever formalities about boarding an escape pod the guards may have learned during training was largely ignored in the rush to get clear of the doomed prison. Two guards took positions on either side of the entry into the circular pod, and more or less threw the others inside as they reached the doorway. The pod's circumference was occupied by ten inset seats, albeit seats currently over the heads of the escapers, and they moved under the seat they planned to take, possibly the only bit of the escape drill that had survived the chaos.

Alina was one of the guards and helped Tasya and Katya get Oksana inside. As soon as they were all in, she hit the door closure control.

"Don't eject until we're more or less upright," warned Tasya. "It was never built to work upside down." Then to the others, "Grab hold of anything solid."

The pod, and the Deeps around it, slowly performed another one hundred and eighty degree flip. Long before it had completed it, the seats were at an angle they could all climb into and pull on the safety harnesses. Katya stayed with Oksana to lock her into her seat. Before she ran to her own, she quickly checked Oksana's throat for a pulse. It was there; not strong, but at least she still lived.

For a brief moment, the escape pod was perfectly the right way up. Alina needed no prompting to arm and trigger the release mechanism.

For a moment nothing happened, and despair sparked in more than one heart. Then there was a dull thud beneath their feet and a sense of movement. No longer the slow tumble of the sinking prison, but a slight rocking as the escape pod – a convex underside and a conical upper, connected by a metre and a half high cylindrical section – rose towards the surface.

"Evacuation unit Alpha-4 has successfully disengaged and is operating normally," announced the pod's computer in the soothing tones somebody had decided would be most beneficial to those in an emergency. "A distress signal is already being transmitted. Help is on its way."

"Does it know that, or is it just saying it?" asked one of the guards.

Katya knew a signal wouldn't reach anyone until they got to the surface, but she didn't want to speak because that meant taking a breath, and breathing really hurt.

"You've cracked some ribs, Kuriakova," said Tasya. She nodded at Oksana. "She probably has, too. That was quite an impact you took." Suddenly she grinned. "I loved it when you said 'Let go.' I could just see the calculations going on inside your head. You're like me. You figure out the odds and take the crazy risk, even if it's not quite as crazy as it looks."

"I didn't take a risk," said Katya and winced. Cracked ribs. Yes, that would explain a lot. "You were going to let me go anyway."

Tasya looked like she might deny it, then shrugged. "So why did you tell me to let you go?"

"So, if it was the last thing that ever happened to me, it was because I asked for it. It was my choice."

Tasya looked at Katya with appraising eyes. "Is that pride I hear, Kuriakova?"

Katya said nothing. It hurt too much to say.

The pod broke the surface to find fourteen others already there and, while they watched, another surfaced about a kilometre away.

Russalka's weather system was having close to the best weather it seemed capable of – a stiff breeze and a fine rain. Above them some of the dense cloud cover was distinctly thinner than others areas, allowing moderate amounts of light in. In Russalkin terms, this was balmy weather. It was more than calm enough for them to have opened the evacuation hatches on the pod's upper surface to look around.

"Well, that's sixteen transmitters squawking," said Glazov, the guard. "That should draw something."

As if answering him, the water boiled some two hundred metres away. Rising slowly from the depths, they saw a rakish conning tower break the surface, followed by the lean and lethal form of an attack boat.

"Is that the *Vengeance*?" said Glazov a little nervously. It certainly wasn't a standard Federal design. The only boat on the Federal lists that looked like that was the *Vengeance*, stolen from the Yagizban. "If it isn't, then it's Yag."

"It's neither," said Tasya airily, "it's the *Vodyanoi*," and launched a flare to attract the boat's attention.

"What are you doing?" shouted Glazov. He dropped back inside the pod to remonstrate, but found Tasya was already back inside and had her gun drawn.

"You're not Secor," he said. He turned on Oksana, but she was still unconscious, so he turned on Alina instead. "You lied!"

"To save your lives," said Katya wearily. "Feds," she pointed at Tasya, "the Chertovka. The Chertovka," she wafted her finger around to take in the increasingly worried Federal guards, "Feds. There, now you're properly introduced and perhaps you're beginning to understand why Oksana and Alina lied. Put down your weapons and don't do anything stupid, and there's no reason you shouldn't live through this." The pod began to bob violently in the water as the *Vodyanoi* came alongside. "And here's our ride."

The pod was cleared with less urgency than it had been filled. None of the guards seemed very keen to throw themselves upon the mercy of a notorious pirate and his crew of cut-throats. When the notorious pirate turned out to be a mild-looking man of perhaps forty years who insisted on shaking their hands and welcoming them aboard, and when the cut-throats just looked like a regular crew, they calmed down a little.

The guards were taken below to be checked over and placed in the brig, with the exception of Oksana who was taken to the sickbay, and Alina because Katya feared the other guards might turn on her for her deception. Despite her ribs, Katya stayed topside with Kane. He was looking ruefully at the pods bobbing in the waves.

"Awful. Even if every one of those pods is full, that still means close on a thousand lives lost. Another psychotic break, you say?"

"Governor Senyavin went mad," said Katya. Only now did she have time to think of all those who'd died. She thought of Dominika and the others. More deaths to haunt her.

"Mad. Mad is such a simple term for something so complicated. As for *went* mad, I have my doubts about that. He may have been driven to it."

Abruptly the ocean erupted with a great rushing gout of air and debris some three kilometres away. Kane's binoculars were at his eyes in a moment, and he watched it grimly. Neither needed to say what it meant; that the Deeps was crushed.

Katya turned away, unable to look. Kane lowered the binoculars and looked at her; she was crying silently, misery in her every fibre.

"It would have happened whether you were there or not, Katya," he said gently. "This was Senyavin's doing."

"Can't I just weep for the dead, Kane? There were a lot of scum in there, but there were good people, too. Political prisoners, dissidents. People whose faces just didn't fit." She looked at him, furious. "Tell me they died for something, Kane. Tell me they'll be the last."

Kane looked at her, rocked his head from side to side as if considering. "Let's go for a cruise," he said finally. He pulled a communicator from his pocket and said, "Ms Ocello, make for the rendezvous, would you, please?"

Katya heard the first officer reply. "Aye, captain. If you'll come below, we'll secure for diving."

"No," said Kane, drawling the word out. "It's such a nice day. Let's stay on the surface."

"Captain?"

"Seriously, Genevra. We're staying on the surface. *Que será, será* as they say." To Katya he said, "On Earth. Somewhere. I forget where. Oh, and, Genevra, start transmitting a truce signal." He put away the communicator. He smiled at Katya, but she could see the nervousness under the surface. "*Que será, será*. It means 'Whatever will be, will be.' We've done all we can. You, far more than most."

"Did it work?"

"I hope so."

TWENTY-TWO

DESPERATE TIMES

The *Vodyanoi* moved away from the group of escape pods at surface cruise speed, which was only two thirds of the maximum. Slowly the pods dwindled into the distance. With Katya on the conning tower, Kane watched them go through his binoculars, impatience making him fractious.

"Oh, come on. Where are you? There's a whole high security facility been destroyed and you can't…"

Sudden rapid boot falls on the ladder made him pause. A moment later, Tasya emerged from the hatch. She'd changed into her trademark Terran trooper's partial armour, Yagizban combat fatigues visible beneath it. "It's the Feds."

"Oh, super," said Kane with unfeigned pleasure. "I was getting worried."

"It's the *Novgorod*. They're in our baffles, communicating through the hydrophones."

Kane produced his communicator again. "Hello, Number One," he said into it. "Could you relay comms through my handset, please? Thanks. Thanks ever so."

There was a pause and then, loud enough for them to all hear, "...*ovgorod* to hostile vessel. You are to surrender immediately. Failure to comply will result in..."

"Hello!" said Kane brightly. "Hello, is Petrov there? Captain Petrov, that is? This is Havilland Kane. Hello?" He waited, but there was near silence, only moderated by the artefacts of normal oceanic sounds that were being filtered out by the communications system. The two submarines were talking using the sea itself as the connecting medium, transmitting sound through their sonar grids and receiving it through their hydrophones.

"You've gone all quiet," persisted Kane. "Hello? Anyone there?"

"This is Petrov. Surrender the *Vodyanoi* immediately, Kane, and prepare for boarding."

"Yes, and lovely to hear from you, too. How are things?"

"I'm not playing games, Kane. Heave to, or we will launch torpedoes."

"That would be rude of you. I'm transmitting a truce signal and everything."

"You're asking for a truce?"

"Mmhm. As is every Yagizban vessel and floating facility. In fact..." Kane looked ahead through his binoculars, "in fact, I can see *FP-1* ahead. I know you didn't have a very good experience there last time, but if you listen, you'll find they're transmitting for a truce, too."

"What are you playing at, Kane?"

"Captain, I have a great deal of respect for you. You are an honourable and intelligent man. I will not lie to you. We have done a very desperate thing. If it comes off, the war will be over and there will still be Russalkin alive at the end of it. If it doesn't, the two sides will just keep on hitting one another until there's no one left. The truce is entirely sincere. Our tubes are closed and loaded only with noisemakers. You are in our baffles. We are at your mercy. Please, surface. We will not engage. You can keep your tubes open and blow us out of the water if we try anything."

"Your reputation for cunning makes me distrust you."

Katya gestured to Kane to hand her the communicator. He nodded and gave it to her without hesitation. "Petrov? Captain Petrov?"

"Who is this?"

"Katya, sir. Katya Kuriakova. Please, Kane's telling the truth. If you don't trust him, maybe you can trust me."

"Ms Kuriakova." Petrov seemed unsettled. "I thought you must have died in the Deeps."

"I nearly did. But even if I had, it wouldn't have mattered, not to Russalka. Please, this is bigger than the war. This is about everything." She tried to think of something to convince him, something she would never offer up under duress. When she thought of it, she had to take a second to steel herself to say it in an even voice. "I swear it on my love for my uncle, Lukyan Pushkin."

"I see." Petrov was silent for a moment, then said, "Kane? Are you there?"

"Yes, captain."

"If I get even the ghost of a bad feeling about this, I will engage you without a second thought. Do you understand?"

"The truce is genuine, captain."

"If you've made a liar of Ms Kuriakova," said Petrov evenly, "I will kill you myself. Petrov out."

Kane pulled a face. "He sounded quite impassioned there, didn't he? By his standards, anyway." He lifted the communicator to his mouth. "Ms Ocello. The *Novgorod* will be surfacing off our stern in a moment. Please don't do anything to make them more excited than they already are. They're on a bit of a hair-trigger."

"Aye, captain."

Two minutes later, the waters three hundred metres aft of the *Vodyanoi* heaved and split, cascading from the *Novgorod*'s conning tower as she rose, huge and ominous. Almost twice the length of the *Vodyanoi*, she was as capable and as deadly as she looked. Formerly she'd been called a "shipping protection vessel," but that had just been a polite name for a warboat built in peacetime. Her bow torpedo tubes were open, their threat explicit.

Kane gave them enough time for the water to clear her hull cameras, and for the forward facing lenses to find him. Then he smiled and waved.

"Provocative as always," said Tasya.

"Just being friendly," said Kane. "You can't launch torpedoes at someone who's waving at you. It'd be inhuman." He noticed Katya wince. "Just trying to lighten the mood," he apologised. "I... oh. It's your ribs, isn't it?"

The *Vodyanoi*'s medic had checked Katya over and told her that she'd cracked three ribs and would be in "some discomfort" for the month or so it would take for the bones to set. She'd been given some pain medication and told to come back the next day. Oksana's breaks were far more severe, one rib threatening to puncture a lung. The medic assured Katya that he'd dealt with much worse, and shooed her out of the sickbay so that he could get on with his job.

"Yes, it's my ribs." She felt very tired, and the thought of having trouble lying on her left side whilst trying to sleep didn't appeal to her at all. Yes, she had sedatives to help with that, but she didn't enjoy the prospect of swallowing so many drugs. The Russalkin distrust of drugs ran deep, even medicinal ones. "There's somebody over there!"

Indeed there was. Petrov had appeared on the *Novgorod*'s conning tower along with another officer and two marines. Both the latter took firing positions on the rail, and levelled maser carbines at Kane, Tasya, and Katya.

"You know, I don't think he trusts us," said Kane.

"No," corrected Katya. "He doesn't trust *you*."

"Hurtful," said Kane philosophically.

A shortwave signal came in and the captains spoke. "Very well, Kane. What is the purpose of this truce?"

"Well, probably easier to show than tell, Captain Petrov. Let me just check my chronometer." He looked up, lips pursed. "Does anyone know why we don't just call chronometers *watches*? Sorry. Random thought. Can you see *FP-1*, captain?"

It was a somewhat patronising comment; Petrov would have had to have his eyes shut or be facing the other way not to see the massive floating military airfield. It was close enough now to be filling a good section of the visible horizon. Vast, grey, and imposing.

"Of course I can see it."

"Then I think this is as good a place as any to stop. Warn your helm we're going to go all engines stop in a minute."

They saw Petrov speak to his officer and the *Novgorod* immediately started to slow. With its great inertia, it couldn't hope to come to a full halt quite as quickly as *Vodyanoi*, it began the manoeuvre early.

By the time both boats were no longer cutting bow waves, they had finished less than a hundred metres apart. The *Novgorod* had turned slightly to starboard while slowing to avoid any possibility of collision.

Kane's communicator blipped and he changed to another channel, listened for a moment, and closed the call. "Captain Petrov," he said after re-establishing the link to the *Novgorod*, "the war is over. Don't get yourself and your crew killed at the last minute by doing something silly."

"What are you talking about, Kane? The Yagizban have surrendered?"

Thunder rolled, a ripping, tearing peal of thunder that seemed to stun the waves. Petrov scanned the horizon looking for lightning, but there was none.

Kane passed the communicator to Katya. "He'll take this better from you."

Katya looked at him and tilted her head. "You think so?" she said, a little sardonically.

"Fractionally. Just tell him."

Reluctantly Katya lifted the communicator and spoke. "Hello? Anatoly? It's Katya again."

"Ms Kuriakova," said Petrov cautiously. "Just what is Kane talking about?"

It was hard to sum it all up. To take all the reasons and the need and the desperation of it, and put it into words, especially when she'd spent her time in the Deeps doing her best to force it from her mind.

"The Terrans didn't start the war, Anatoly. We did. The FMA high command might have given the orders, but we all just stood around like idiots and believed them. The last eleven, twelve years have been a big lie, but the Alpha Pluses were lying to us long before then."

"That's dissident talk, Ms Kuriak…"

"No! You haven't seen the bodies. You haven't seen just what's lying in the middle of the Peklo Volume. I'm not guessing at the truth – I've *seen* it. The FMA is as good as dead. You should start thinking about what's coming next."

"And what precisely is coming next?" He sounded impatient, a man talking to a fanatic. Katya realised that he'd put her into a nicely stereotyped category in his mind so that he didn't have to think very hard about what she said. She couldn't blame him. How many times had she heard similarly dark muttering from others, usually put down by a friend's concerned whisper of, "Careful. Don't let Secor hear you talking like that."

"I'll tell you what I wouldn't tell Secor. I'll tell you what I did in Atlantis, what made me a traitor. I placed a transmitter box in a disused relay station."

"A microwave relay. I know. I saw the report. To communicate with all the surface Yagizban elements. To what end?"

"Is that what the report said? It's wrong. Atlantis is the oldest settlement, with equipment not found at any other station. Equipment we've lost the ability to replicate elsewhere. The microwave relay I plugged that box into was the old satellite communications link."

"There are no satellites left. The Terrans destroyed them."

Petrov was sounding angrier than she'd ever heard him. Was he beginning to suspect? If so, it didn't surprise her. He was a clever man.

"The Terrans destroyed all of our satellites, that's true. Then they deployed their own."

Across the water between the two boats, Katya saw Petrov lower his communicator as he understood exactly what Katya had done. She continued to speak. Perhaps he could still hear her.

"The Yagizban collaborated with the Terrans and were given the satellite network's access codes. Anatoly… one of them is a long range faster-than-light communications array."

In the clouds above *FP-1*, the lightning flashed long after the thunder had died away. Blue, unnatural lightning. As they watched the flickering blue grew stronger and brighter, illuminating the whole cloud bank above the waiting platform. Then the clouds rolled aside.

It was beautiful. It was terrifying. Katya thought of how the *Novgorod* had looked as she broke the surface. This seemed so similar, as if the clouds were the surface of an angry sea and they were looking down upon it.

Petrov's voice came through the communicator, taut, angry, fearful. "Katya. What have you done?"

She turned it off. There was no point talking now. She had either helped save a world on the edge of destruction, or pushed it over the precipice. She had called across the stars, and her call had been heard.

The Terrans were here.

EXPERIMENTING WITH YOUR IMAGINATION

Meet Meda. She eats people.

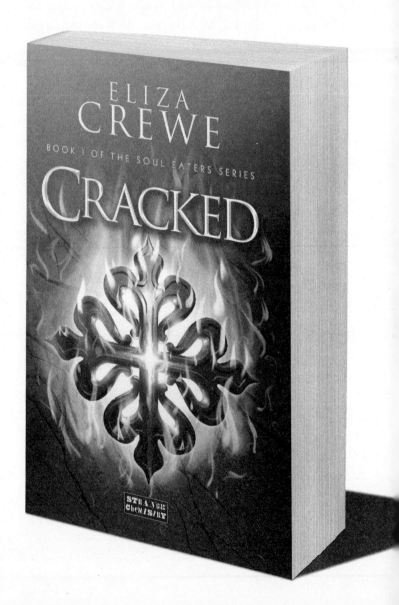

EXPERIMENTING WITH YOUR IMAGINATION

Run free through the dark streets of London...

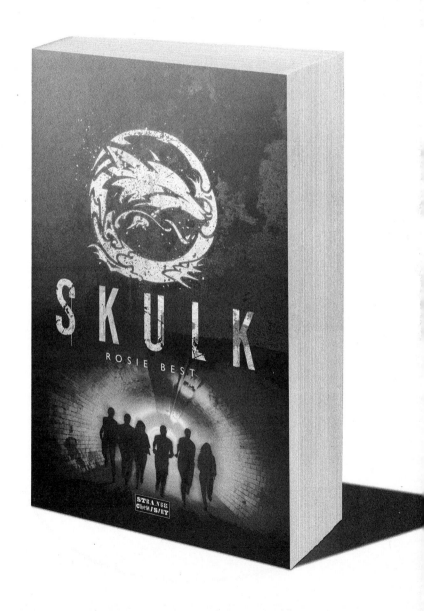